Everything You
Ever Wanted

Everything You
Ever Wanted

Rosalind Wyllie

To Eve
Hope you enjoy
Rosalind Wyllie
x.

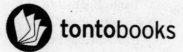 tontobooks

www.tontobooks.com

Published in 2008 by Tonto Books Limited
Copyright © Rosalind Wyllie 2008
All rights reserved
The moral rights of the author have been asserted

ISBN-13:
9780955632631

British Library Cataloguing in Publication Data:
A catalogue record for this book is available from
the British Library

Printed & bound in Great Britain by
CPI Cox & Wyman, Reading, RG1 8EX

Tonto Books Ltd
Newcastle upon Tyne
United Kingdom

www.tontobooks.com

For my unconditional parents.

Chapter One
Tiggy

I love what I do. There's nowhere else I would rather be. Under the lights, inhaling other people's smoke and their fantasies. I'm every woman they have ever dreamt of. I'll do anything. I'll do things they didn't even know they wanted.

Back-lit, with smoke rising, and my silhouette curving in all the right places, sometimes I enjoy it so much I want to do it again. Straight away. I'd do it for free if they'd let me. Or at least that's what I need to make them believe.

I'm late for work again.

I'm running along Regent Street. It's mid July. A few minutes ago the sky was clear blue. Now it starts to rain. Not the normal soft city drizzle, instead clouds off-load in reckless monsoon proportions. I pull up the hood of my sweatshirt, and start to run, huddling my blue canvas holdall to my chest and leaping over puddles. The moment it rains in London every drain refuses to work, and the pavements are filled with instant pools.

I pass a group of large-stomached men in black suits and bow ties holding newspapers over their heads, searching the streets for a black cab, knowing already that all the taxis will have vanished. A red car steers towards me, too close to the curb. I hold my breath and make ready for the slow motion curve of gutter water that surfs into a crescendo over my body.

Inside Valerios my hair hangs in rat-tails around

my neck. I am dripping onto the dense red carpet. I have a doglike urge to shake myself dry.

Valerios is a hostess club just off Berkeley Square. The small neon sign outside shows a naked woman of fantasy proportions, her back arched and her mouth ecstatically open. There's not a woman inside the club who looks anything like her.

Men at reception are slurring some complaint about the price. Mario is handling it with easy Italian charm, all 'Well, what can I say eh? You want the best, we have the best. Our ladies are beautiful. I will personally guarantee you one hundred per cent satisfaction. Come on we're all men here.' He pushes his hand through his thick, overly-oiled hair and gives me a toothy smile. Mario Valerios would fleece you for every last penny and you'd still feel like he was doing you the favour.

I smile back because he's the boss and I need the money.

I take off my sodden sweat top and pull open the doors. A disco beat pumps over the empty dance floor, lights rotating candy colours over the walls. The warm air is shaded with cigarette smoke and expensive perfumes.

I wave to Dan, holding up my fingers to show I need ten minutes. Then I grab a booth and a hand towel and try to dry off. I'm enveloped in a muggy film of steam as my clothes adapt to their new environment.

The disco track ends. Dan taps on the end of the microphone.

He coughs and then says with a suggestion of a smile, 'Gentlemen and Ladies, we have just ten more minutes before the lovely Viola Viola will no doubt fly you to the Moon.' He winks again, taking his seat behind the piano, rolling inevitably into a rock jazz version of *Fly me to the Moon*.

The club is lit to give the illusion of intimacy. Red velvet booths with pink rococo candles as their centrepiece line the dance floor, facing the stage, creating private spaces. The waitresses dress like celluloid vamps, black fishnet stockings, leotards and silver high heels. Their trays are filled with champagne and cartons of cigarettes. They hang languidly near the booths, making boredom into an art form.

The hostesses are all dressed in something tight, in red or gold, the unambiguous fantasy whore ensemble. Most of them are already partnered up in the booths, laughing and smiling. Georgia and Lola are chatting together at the bar, drinking tap water from champagne flutes.

I don't know the names of all the girls, some come and go within weeks. Georgia and Lola were here long before me. Lola's mid 30s, bottle blonde and has calamitous dress taste, deliberately dressing against her figure. Her clothes accentuate her thick stomach and flatten her chest. Georgia is Russian or Eastern European or something, spiky faced and nervous. She has this scared, haunted look in her heavily made up eyes, as though she's half expecting a knock at the door and the KGB to drag her off to some snow laden forest and interrogate her.

Georgia and Lola don't get booked much.

Scarlett, one of the younger hostesses, is giggling coyly as a fat Chinese man strokes her thigh. She leans forward and places her arm over his shoulder, champagne flute in hand. She is whispering to him, her lips are brushing his ear. Behind his back her red fingernails clutch the glass and with practised and cynical expertise, she disposes its contents into the ice bucket. The man's eyes are gazing at her cleavage, with

9

unashamed hunger. She positions a cigarette between her red lips and waits for him to light it, then raises her glass, feigning surprise at its sudden emptiness and her prey obediently orders another bottle.

I wonder what her real name is. Scarlett suits her though. Blood red. She's almost faultless in proportion. Inscrutable, beautiful and blank. When she smiles or laughs or frowns those expressions slip across her face like afterthoughts, like impressions of emotions.

Some of the hostesses, like Lola, show their experiences on their skin. By the make up creased into their wrinkles or their nicotine stained fingers. Superficially Scarlett looks as though she is one of them, but on closer inspection, it's not a good fit. It's as though she has trawled second-hand markets for the jaded, bored façade and underneath there might be something else.

She looks over, aware that I am staring. I quickly look away and feign concentration on towel drying my hair.

Backstage I take off my jeans and top, tugging a small red baby doll dress over my sequinned underwear. My hair is still a little damp so I quickly twist it up and clip it into a chignon. Slipping my feet into patent red stilettos. I apply glossy red lipstick and a thick line of blusher using a small hand mirror. I knock back a quick shot of vodka, and then add an extra layer of eyeliner.

I am a comedy caricature of myself.

Dan takes my cassette and I wait for him to give me my cue. 'Ladies and gentleman, as promised, I present the wonderful, the beautiful, the exquisite... Viola Viola.'

There's a drum roll and I step out onto the stage to a few half-hearted claps. The music begins. The spotlight hits me. Viola Viola grinds and gyrates like the little tart that she is.

Not for the last time, I wonder what the hell I'm doing here.

Chapter Two
Tiggy

A t 3.30am Dan drives me home in his battered blue
Fiesta. The streets are blank and grey, uninhibi-
ted by the urgent daytime traffic. We sweep along the
Westway not speaking, enjoying the silence after the
smoke and noise of the club.

'Do you want to come in?' Sometimes he does, sometimes he can't.

He looks at his watch, 'Well I suppose an hour
wouldn't hurt.'

Three high-rise buildings tower over Shepherd's
Bush roundabout. I live in the second block, Daffodil
House. The yellow one. The foyers of each building
have their own colour coding; red, yellow and green.
The heavy front doors of Daffodil House are painted
sunshine yellow. The façade is a mosaic depicting multi
coloured children playing together happily. Or it was.
Most of the mosaic is a now a smudge of graffiti and
scrawled obscenities. Two of the mosaic, hand holding,
children have the tender phrase FUDGE PACKERS
written above them.

My flat is on the 14th floor.

Neither Dan nor I mention the stink of fresh urine
or the shattered green glass and crushed lager cans as
we stand in the lift.

The first week here, I disinfected the whole thing.
Figured that maybe people used it as a toilet because it
stank like one. That if I made it smell like Forest
Meadows then they would stop using it as a urinal. It
took four hours and repeated sluicing to get it smelling

like a tree had been anywhere near it. The following day it smelled like a forest of piss. I gave up.

My sitting room is strewn with clothes and magazines. The curtains still drawn. I should try to make something of the place, but it's not as though it's permanent. I'm lucky to have so much space. Two bedrooms, sitting room, kitchen and bathroom. All mine for £115 per week, thanks to the Evening Standard and a probably illegal subletting deal with the owner. But this is renting in London and you don't ask a gift-horse to show you his teeth.

I liked the flat the moment I saw it, in spite of the lift or the noise from the neighbours. The telltale creaks from the ceiling that give me more information than I need about the people upstairs. There's something weightless about being so high above the city. From this height the screeching brakes, sirens and engines below are of another world.

I light the candles on the coffee table then move a few piles of books to one side. Pretending not to notice the red light from the answerphone flashing insistently.

'Hey come on Tiggy. Sit down, leave all that.'

Dan pours us both large vodkas, adding tonic to his. He takes a silver tin from his pocket and heats a chunk of resin with his lighter. I sit on the sofa next to him, removing my make up with cotton wool pads as he pulls small specks onto the tobacco. He has perfect pianist fingers, long and dexterous. I wonder how many women have enjoyed them. How they would feel on me.

'You're quiet tonight. You okay?' He pushes his dark fringe back away from his eyes. Dan is impossibly handsome, like a movie star with a hint of cockney rough. I love the sound of his voice. The dropped notes of his South London accent. He's the opposite of anyone I've ever met. The sort of man my father would euphemistically and patronisingly call 'salt of the earth'.

Just looking at Dan is an anti-depressant. I have a sort of half-crush on him. I can't quite understand why we're friends. He's gorgeous and funny, and I'm this total disaster.

'Tiggy? Are you in the room?'

'I'm fine... I'm just...'

What am I?

I sip the cool, sharp vodka. It's straight from the freezer and I feel it solidify somewhere down my oesophagus. Like an icicle. Shit I'm going to die. 'Death by Vodka.' Now that's a headline my father would be proud of.

The vodka melts. I don't die.

'I'm seeing my father tomorrow,' I gesture towards the answerphone. 'That'll be him leaving my instructions.'

'Ah, the monthly meeting.'

Dan inserts a folded cardboard roach into the end of a Rizzla.

'Indeed.' I scrunch up my face. 'The monthly meeting from hell.'

'So, don't go.' He makes it sound simple

'I have to go.'

'Well then don't take any shit from him.'

I don't take shit from my Dad. He doesn't give me that much shit to take. It's just he's not, well, the way that other people's Dads seem to be. As a girl I had this fantasy: Dad would sit on the end of my bed and we'd have this big heart to heart and he'd tell me how proud he was of me. Then we'd hug. But we've never even got close to that.

There's a picture on my sideboard. The standard

black and white studio portrait. The first official picture of us as a family, six weeks after my birth. My mother is looking away from me, avoiding the camera. Her eyes shooting disappointment into the distance. My father stands apologetic, tall and dark behind me. I'm lying wide-eyed and vacant. Trussed in white lace. On a cushion between them. Neither of them touching me.

It's uncomfortable to look at. I can sense their desire to flee the room. As though even being in the same frame was too much intimacy.

I finish my drink. Dan pours me another.

'He treats you like a business acquaintance.'

'Dan, he's okay, he means well... he just... oh I don't know... he's okay underneath.'

I think my father loves me. I do. He just doesn't know how to show it. And I think I love him. It's just that it's complicated.

'Last time you met him you said he was a prejudiced fucker.' Dan laughs.

'Did I?' It certainly sounds like something I might say.

'Yes, you said he was a misogynist, and a Daily Mail-reading hypocrite.'

'Well maybe it's just a phase he's going through.'

'He's missing out on so much. I mean his only daughter... he only lives ten minutes away.'

'Dan, leave it, please.'

I talk to Dan about all kinds of things, because at 4am there's not much conversation that can't be had. I do complain about my father. I know. After a few vodkas I can get into a rant about how he's never taken any notice of me. And sometimes I embellish a little. Then a few weeks later Dan reminds me of what a shit he is and I wonder where that came from. Except, of course it comes from me. And my revised version of events. Where the mean horrible Daddy ignores the sweet perfect Tiggy. A version that Dan seems to believe now, which can sometimes make me uncomfortable.

'Tiggy, what I don't get is why you put yourself through it?' The concern in Dan's voice makes me ache. Maybe that's why I do it.

'He's my father.'

I take the joint from his hands and tug a deep breath from the damp filter. I should go for some damage limitation.

'You know Dan, my Dad's... well... he's okay really.'

'Ok. Whatever you say.' He has his hands in the air in mock surrender; he looks kind of sweet like that. Though men hate being called sweet don't they? I think about kissing him, then I think about Tony and I feel guilty.

'I need the toilet,' I say.

My face in the mirror is molten. The girl staring back at me has irises like pools of black ink and tomato coloured skin, with two smears of eyeliner along one side. Very attractive.

It's best if we just stay friends.

Dan has a girlfriend. I have Tony. Besides we work together and he's my only friend.

I don't want to ruin things.

I do have a tendency to ruin things.

There was a boy I liked when I was 11. A boy called Sam. We used to play together sometimes. Then I got it into my head that I loved him. I wrote him a letter. I said that I thought he was *perfect* and that I wanted him to be my boyfriend. I stuck it in a red envelope, spraying it with Charlie or Tweed. Something mock grown up. I wrote S.W.A.L.K. on the back and posted it. I was so excited when his letter came back to me. But he said no. *'It's not because you are fat or ugly. I just don't like you that much.'*

I stared at the letter for ages, you could have strapped me to a Catherine Wheel and I'd have not known a thing about it.

'I just don't like you that much.'

Harsh enough to deal with the rejection, but what really got me was the other bit.

'It's not because you are fat or ugly.'

It had never occurred to me that I might be fat or ugly. After that, it was the only way I could see myself.

I wash my face free of its tribal stripes and go back through to the sitting room.

We smoke the rest of the joint. Then Dan rolls another and smokes it alone. I'm a lightweight on pot. More than a few puffs and I can get morbidly gloomy.

He looks at his watch. 'Well, I'd better get going.'

'Okay.' I move away.

'What the hell, I've got a few minutes.'

He pours me another drink and then fills his own glass with water from the fridge. He doesn't mention the piles of unwashed plates and cutlery. I make a mental note to have a spring clean in the morning.

I'm reassuringly drunk by the time Dan picks up his leather jacket from the sitting room floor. I wonder what would happen if I asked him to stay.

'See you tomorrow?' His jacket is on. Too late.

'Go on then, you'd best get going.'

He looks at his watch and winces. 'Shit, it's gone five already.' He kisses me quickly on the cheek and then he is gone.

I triple lock the door behind him then step back into

the scrap heap of my flat, collecting up the cotton pads and the glasses. Then changing my mind, I leave them on the coffee table to sort in the morning.

I ignore the petulant flicker from the answerphone. My father can wait. In my bedroom I light the end of Dan's joint and smoke the few last puffs, thinking of him driving home. Through the suburban streets and parking in his driveway. I turn on the radio and wonder whether I am the only person in the world who listens to the graveyard slot and knows who Adrian John is. He sounds tired. I like that. That he doesn't pretend that this is the best time in the world to start your day. Or to finish it.

Pulling back the curtains I look out over the city. The office windows are bright against the dark sky where cleaners are setting up the world for the morning. Lights in the opposite tower block occasionally come on and off. I think about the sleepless people pacing their floors, searching for something in the fridge. Something to fill them up and distract them.

Black cabs circle the roundabout with their orange lights glowing in the hope of some journey. Adrian John chuckles from his empty studio. 'So, Everything I Do, I Do It For You is our new Number One. All you hopeless romantics have made Bryan Adams a very happy man. But of course, we all know the song was written for me.'

I switch off the radio. I hate that song.

So, this is my life. Stripping in a hostess club. Smoking dope with someone else's fiancé most nights. Sleeping with another woman's husband most Thursday afternoons. Oh yes, and a mother I haven't seen in years, and a father who has no idea who I am. I take a final drag of the joint. Oh and if we add in the nicotine addiction and the penchant for vodka then the picture is just perfect. I stub out the damp butt hard.

All this by the age of 21.

Excellent work, Tiggy.

Chapter Three
Scarlett

I woke up this morning with £20 notes stuck to my face, and thanked God for giving me great tits.

It's all about The Tits. I mean men can't help themselves. I know there are supposed to be blokes that aren't bothered, but I've never met them. Mine grew overnight. Honest. It was like one morning I woke up with these huge breasts, and suddenly all the boys in the sixth form were interested. It was pretty cool actually, at first anyway. There was other stuff that came with it, the obvious stuff, like the moment the older boys started liking me, the older girls started hating me and trying to flush my face down the toilet, but that only happened once, because after that I stopped going to school.

The teachers had this big thing about how important it was to get an education. If they were living proof of where a few A-Levels could get you then no fucking thanks, what a bunch of losers. There was this science teacher who actually cried in the lessons. He sat there with his bald head buried in his hands and sobbed. We were all like – 'Um... hello... aren't you meant to be teaching or something?' People threw rolled up paper at his head and he didn't even flinch or tell us off or nothing. After that, I figured that there had to be a better way.

Mum said she had no idea where The Tits came from.

'I'm as flat as a meringue.' Then she patted the space where her breasts should be.

She tried cooking a meringue once. A recipe from *Women's Weekly* or whatever and in the picture it looked gorgeous, like cream and fruit on a plate of sugary heaven. She was separating this and that, getting sugar on her face and the floor, whisking up a storm, and then she put it in the oven and we only had to wait a bit, not long and we both sat there salivating. Mum was practically wetting herself and normally I would have told her to calm down only I was pretty excited as well. Well it made a change from bloody rice pudding and the other slop she usually served up from a tin.

Then she pulled it out and it was just a biscuit really. This chewy hard biscuit thing that got harder as it got cooler.

'Oh,' she said, 'it doesn't look much like the picture does it?'

But it did look like her chest, flat and brown, like it forgot to rise. So by the time I was 14, I was five foot seven and a size eight, with these gigantic tits on me. I didn't have time to hate them or think about whether I looked like a distorted freak because it was like being Supergirl, like the moment they arrived I got the power.

Men think they're a miracle. They moan and stare at them; they lick them and nuzzle them. They push their face into them wobbling them from side to side (I have to stop myself from laughing when they do that). But mostly they like to talk about them to me.

'Your tits are amazing.'

'Ooooh... yeah... push them up... God you're majestic.' (They mean my tits are majestic, of course.) And I'm like, 'Thanks.' Except I'm not really sure that it's me they're complimenting and The Tits can't speak. I'm not responsible for them, they just happened. It's not something I achieved through 'talent and application' (My drama teacher's favourite phrase). But I say thanks anyway, because saying, 'everyone says that,' would sound bigheaded. So I have to pretend like they're the first person that has ever said my tits are nice, you know look a little surprised and flattered.

It's funny what men want you to do for them, funny how they need you to pretend. They think that them suckling away is the most original bit of lovemaking I've ever encountered.

Tossers.

This bloke last night was called Guo and he was Chinese, though he said he'd never been to China in his life and wasn't interested in going either. He was so jittery. I'd been sent over to his table, and we were getting on all right, but he kept going on to me saying, 'You're so young.'

And lots of them do that, and some of them say it in a dirty way, like they're excited, some of them aren't bothered, too busy looking at The Tits, and some of them, like this Guo, get nervous. He was real jumpy.

'I'm... um... I'm... you see... the thing is... um... you seem like a nice girl...'

I said 'I can be a very nice girl.' And I accidentally let my nails drag over my cleavage as I leant in to him. He went bright red, and sort of crossed his legs and ran his hand over his chin.

'Um... and... you see... the thing is... you're lovely... very young... and well... golly... um... the thing is I'm sort of looking for a bad girl.'

Then he looked away which was good, because I thought I was going to giggle, because this poor bloke, Guo, was like obviously wanting to be spanked or have a threesome or something, and terrified of asking, and it was kind of sweet because some men are just like 'do it' and 'suck it,' and all of that, and they assume that you're loving it.

'I can be very naughty,' I said placing my hand gently onto his inner thigh, which we're not supposed to do.

Mario has some nonsense rule about no physical contact in the club.

And he soon perked up at that.

We had to wait till Viola Viola had finished her number. She removed her bikini top with the same fake blush she uses every night. A good trick that, knowing how to blush on cue, I might practice that. She's a funny one her, always blushing and fidgeting. Her body's okay, and she's an okay dancer, but she's nothing special. She's a type, like those girls that live in the decent houses in Islington, the ones that didn't go to my school and didn't know how to punch properly. The thing with her is that blush, just before she takes off her top she always hesitates, as though every time she makes the decision right there and then.

When Dan Dan the Piano Man came on I asked Guo to order me another bottle of champagne. So I got my commission, and he got pissed enough to be misty eyed at all that soft shit old people's music that Dan plays, and Guo looked at me like *A Nightingale Sang in Berkeley Square* could have been written for me. Like picking up a teenage girl in a shitty place like Valerios is how all true romances blossom.

We left from separate exits. I waited at the back of the club for his taxi. He tried to jump me the moment I got in the cab. He'd been all nerves and politeness in the club and it was like a personality transplant happened.

'Wait,' I said, in a way I hoped sounded breathy and sexy.

In the hotel he got nervous and started offering me drinks and asking me where I live, like he gave a shit. So I went through the usual story of how I live in Primrose Hill with my best friend Tanya. That Tanya is a stripper and a lesbian, that we're best friends, and a little bit more sometimes, when it suits. That I prefer men, and women are just for fun. I pretended not to notice that his eyes were popping out of his head or that his nose was snorting like a bloody dragon, which was about right with him being Chinese and all.

I asked him what he wanted and, after a few false starts and embarrassing silences, he told me.

Some people are fucked up.

It was after 3am when I left with Guo's £500 thrust in the bottom of my handbag. I checked it properly in the cab. Some blokes try and give you £20 or £40 less, like now they've got what they want they still want to feel like they got a bargain, but Guo had given me the full whack, a big pile of notes.

I love feeling that big clump of money in my hand.

On Upper Street I shoved it back into my bag in case anyone mugged me before I got home. I mean, this is the dodgy part of north London.

I'd lost my key again so had to wake Battleaxe the landlady to get in. She always makes this big hoo har about the whole thing, like no one ever locked themselves out, and goes on about how this is the third time she's had to let me in, the third spare key I've requested. She doesn't mention that she charges me a tenner for each new key when I know it only costs 60 pence to make a copy. Or that the B&B is a cockroach infested hole and that actually she's bloody lucky that anyone stays there, or pays any rent or doesn't have the building condemned.

So I apologised and she shrugged angrily at me and gave me some bullshit about this being the last time, and where the fuck did I go every night anyway and what was the world coming to etc. Then having made sure she'd woken up everyone in the building with her bloody lecture she took her fluffy slippers and fat sausage legs off down the corridor to bed.

She's a manky old bitch.

There was a dark dry patch of maroon on my red dress, a speck of Guo's blood. What kind of person gets off at the sight of their own blood? I thought about washing, brushing my teeth, changing my clothes and all that. But I don't like walking along the corridor at night.

There are another five rooms off this landing and too many dark corners. When I'm in the bath all I can think about is that there is only a bit of mouldy chipboard between me and the next room and that no one would come running if I screamed.

So I emptied out my bag, smoked a fag and counted out my cash, laying it out in piles of tens and twenties on the bed. £500 from Guo, plus the £50 tip from the bloke earlier, with the commission that's about £600 in one night minus cab fares of course, but still, not bad for one night's work. And I didn't even have to fuck anyone.

The Tits are worth their weight in fucking platinum. In the last six months they've earned me nearly £70,000.

Just another £30,000 and I'm good to go.

Chapter Four
Tiggy

My father is already there.

I take a deep breath and let the waitress (size four, fragile and feisty) lead me to the table.

Walking behind her I feel self-conscious, like a heffalump or some other ridiculous creature. It's not that I'm overweight, but I'm tall and my co-ordination is terrible. Compact women always agitate me into pathological clumsiness. I'm relieved when we get to the table and I can sit down.

'You're late.'

My father kisses me on both cheeks, his lips not quite meeting my skin.

My father is one of those men who've matured well. At 46 he has all his own teeth, a full head of hair and an even fuller wallet. In spite of his love of good food and fine wine he never gains weight. My own toe curlingly slow metabolism must come from my mother's side of the family. My father is always impeccably turned out. His clothes are tailored in Jermyn Street. Every few months he takes a taxi to Favourbrook or New and Lingwood and lets obsequious staff pander to him. They flatter him into spending a small fortune. He is a creature of habit and routine. His world is safe, ordered and sanitised. It makes me want to scream.

'Nicole, a glass of red wine for my daughter.'

The waitress pours me a drink dismissively, not reciprocating my smile. My father is overly solicitous. He gets flustered around pretty young girls, fusses with his shirt straightening it out and then twiddling his cufflinks.

Why does he irritate me so much, sitting there fiddling with his cufflinks? He's an ordinary man. He's only five years older than Tony. But somehow it's as though my father is from a different age.

I sip my wine slowly. Daddy wouldn't approve if I had more than two glasses. He worries. Because of course he still thinks I'm 14.

The stereo is playing Dexter Gordon, *The Blue Note Years*. Tony loves mournful Jazz, wants me to appreciate it. Recently I've been buying up the jazz section of Tower Records, collecting stacks of records and cassettes and reading sleeve notes in anticipation of future conversations.

I browse the menu. I try not to listen to the girls at the table next to ours. They're talking in loud plumy voices about the *probs* they are having with their boyfriends.

'Yah, darling, Matty's great, but last time we were in San Trop he was just seriously châteaued the whole time.'

'Yah, babes, he's an absolute mess when he's smashed, total shocker.'

This is the type of daughter my father would have preferred. The woman I'm expected to blossom into. I tug on the sleeves of my blouse. I take another deep breath.

'So, I see you're still starving yourself. Any point me buying you lunch or will it all go straight back down the toilet?'

I sigh. Meals with my father are all about moving him swiftly through benign topics and then taking the cheque. I always hope that this time it will be different. That we will find some common ground and learn to relax around each other. But it's never different. I remind myself to be calm. I try to be nice.

'What would you recommend I eat Daddy?'

'Well, the duck is excellent.'

'I'll have that then, shall I?' You see I am polite and well behaved. I am a good daughter.

'Well. If you can't make your own decisions.'

And my father is a cantankerous old bastard. Dan's right. I shouldn't put myself through it. I wonder whether I could feign sickness and leave early. Except I did that last time.

'So, Reg Durrant-White was saying that Amelia has some kind of drug habit, apparently they're all at it, snorting God-knows-what.'

When my father isn't fussing about my weight he's nagging me about drugs. He's convinced I'm taking cocaine.

'I don't want you hanging around with that crowd.'

What is he talking about? I would rather put pins in my eyes than spend time with Amelia Durrant-White and her horrible friends.

'I don't even know Amelia anymore.'

'I distinctly remember you being friends.'

'Not since prep school, Daddy.'

'You went to her party.' His glass is empty. He looks hopefully around the restaurant for the waitress. 'I remember taking you.'

'I went to Amelia's pool party in 1978. I was eight years old.'

'I knew it.' The waitress passes and he nods at her, raises his finger and then points towards the bottle of wine. 'So you're not friends now?'

'No Daddy.'

'Huh. Go off with someone a bit more fun did she?'

How does he do it? How does he always manage to

pepper conversations with tiny snubs? I don't answer him. Instead I look around the restaurant. All the tables are now full. There's a queue waiting to be seated at the bar. All the women have the collars turned up on their stripy shirts. Is this a uniform or do they phone each other before they leave the house? 'Yah, I'm wearing Mumsy's pearls, my Benetton trousers and a pink Alice Band, you?' Heaven forbid they look different; or have an original thought.

I should be more gracious. These women have done nothing to me. But this is enemy territory.

'Well,' I say, smiling nicely at my father, 'it's busy today isn't it?'

'Waitress solidarity eh?'

My father thinks I'm working in a café. He finds the idea appalling, that a daughter of his should have sunk so low. Fortunately the pocket-sized waitress arrives with more wine and haughtily takes our order.

'I simply must come and visit you at work one lunchtime... but Shepherds Bush, eh?' He frowns.

Here we go. He's always saying that he *simply must* come and visit me at work. Just like he *simply must* come over and see my flat, or we *simply must* do lunch more often.

So many things we *simply must* do, that we never will.

'How's Margaret?'

His second wife. The woman who stepped in after my mother walked out.

He folds his napkin onto his lap. 'Busy, all the time. I keep telling her she should give up work and let me take care of her, but oh no some notion of wanting a career, load of feminist tosh.'

My father sees women as cerebrally unsteady and liable to fits of inexplicable emotion. He adores

Thatcher (a woman), and threatened to leave the country when she was ousted from power last year, and replaced by Major (a man).

He doesn't see any inconsistency in his views.

'You keep telling me to have a career.'

'That's different, you're bright.'

He takes another sip of wine.

'Margaret would love to hear you say that.'

'You know what I mean, Tiggy. Margaret doesn't need a career. She's got me. I've told her, whatever you want darling you can have, just ask... wants her own money in her own bank account... nonsense.'

'I think you should admire her for it. Be proud of her.'

'Feminist tosh.' He repeats.

Over dessert he nags me again about going to university.

'I thought women didn't need careers,' I tease. 'Maybe I'll just marry someone rich.'

He fills his mouth with another spoonful of ice cream.

'No, you're not the sort.'

'Oh what sort am I, Daddy?'

'Too dark and brooding. Rich men want a happy woman on their arms, don't want to be dating a rain cloud, do they?' He booms out a long laugh, I'm about to object to being a rain cloud, but he's off already.

'Percy's ex-wife was like you, except she was German. Gorgeous though, legs longer than your imagination, but you couldn't get the old thing to smile. Never once laughed at a joke, miserable humourless bunch the Germans... still her divorce settlement was very generous... she's probably laughing now... Ex-wives eh... hell hath no fury eh.'

He is a pompous pig, and I don't know why I play

the good girl with him. Percy is ten times worse than my father. I vaguely remember him trying to put his hand up my skirt when I was 13.

'Daddy, I'm sure she deserved whatever money she got if she was married to Percy.'

'Bloody women, they always say they're not interested in the money, and then the moment things sour a little it's all they care about. Your mother was like that.'

The mention of my mother always irritates me beyond comprehension.

'And no doubt I'm the same, is that what you're saying?'

My father's face falls. He has a line of melted ice cream dribbling along his chin. He looks like a small remorseful boy and I am immediately ashamed.

I wanted this to be nice, to go well. He shouldn't have brought her up. We fill the rest of our time together with silence.

After coffee he takes a chequebook from his blazer pocket and tears out a cheque for £500. At last!

'It's payable to cash. I've called ahead and arranged things. You just pop into Coutts and Co.'

'Daddy, you shouldn't have.'

He bloody should, he owes me.

'See you in August then, do call if you need anything.'

He kisses me on both cheeks and I watch as he strides away down Kings Road. A cheque and a meal and his fatherly duties are complete for another month.

£500, that's what I'm worth.

Chapter Five
Tiggy

I walk along Argyll Street, bypassing Liberty's and shopping the length of Carnaby Street. Two stray punks pass me, maybe still looking for the 1970s.

I thumb through some black and white postcards, buying one of Louis Armstrong blowing his cornet, and a larger poster of Billie Holliday; her desperate eyes fixed on someone in the crowd, smoke filtering into the picture. Tony will like it.

In the second-hand market I choose a pair of bright purple flared Levi's and some black buckled biker boots. I pass a shop selling fetish gear, called Kinky Malinky. The mannequins in the window are trussed in leather chaps and rubber strap garters.

I turn back and go in. Ignoring the sickly stale incense and the brooding eyes of the shop assistant. She stops chewing her blue hair extensions long enough to stare at me and make a lacklustre attempt at conversation. I leave the shop the proud owner of two new wigs. One long and purple, the other a short blonde bob. I also have some new boots and underwear for my act.

I'm feeling good. I stop at a phone booth and call Tony.

The phone rings twice. Then *she* answers. Shit. I replace the handset, my ten pence piece still in my hand.

Damn.

'Nice look.' Dan says when I get backstage. I'm

wearing the purple wig with thigh length rubber boots and a rubber basque.

'You like it?'

'Not really.' He wrinkles his nose. 'You look like a cartoon dominatrix... you're on in five.'

After my first show I drink a glass of water in one of the private booths near the stage. In my boots and basque I am still Viola Viola. Somehow stronger than Tiggy, more in control. Dan is laughing at me over the top of his microphone, I swish my long purple hair and pout at him and he giggles mid word, fluffing his lines.

A waitress comes over to my booth carrying a bottle of Cristal Rose champagne.

'Viola, the gentleman over there asked that I send this to you. He would like you to have his number.' She hands me a gold embossed business card.

'Jonathan Lloyd. Managing Director. Lloyd, Doyle and Smith.'

'Thanks.'

I nod to the red-faced man waving at me.

'I've explained that you're not a hostess, so you're not allowed to talk to him.'

'Thanks doubly.'

I am genuinely grateful. The last thing I need is some chinless wonder trying to chat me up. The champagne is delicious, I lean back into the booth, crossing my booted legs in front of me. Sipping from the glass.

I don't feel like myself at all.

Dan sings *I've got you under my skin.* He doesn't take his eyes off me for the whole song.

I am sassy, sexy and an object of desire.

Then I remember the phone call and the tenor of her voice. Tony's told me a thousand times not to call him at home. He's going to be so pissed off.

I'm a disaster.
I drink the rest of the bottle.

Chapter Six
Scarlett

I missed breakfast again, slept right through. It really pisses me off that SHE insists on having breakfast in the middle of the fucking night. 6am 'til 8am that's it. How am I supposed to get up and get downstairs after four hours sleep? I should get a discount. I've missed breakfast at least five mornings a week for the last five months. I shouldn't have to pay for 'Bed & Breakfast', just for 'Bed'. The breakfast is disgusting anyway. It's like fake food, rubber sausages and snap hard cardboard bacon and these eggs that give off a vile smell and you just know they have been hanging around for ages and probably aren't even from a chicken. The coffee tastes like dishwater and the toast, you wouldn't think that someone could mess up toast, but the toast is damp and soft in the middle and still burnt around the edges. What kind of a fucked up toaster can do that?

There's a toaster I saw in this kitchen shop, it takes four slices at once, it's got a silver basket thing in it that you lower the toast in with and it costs a fortune. When I'm sorted, I'm going to get me one of those toasters and a juicer and have breakfasts like people in homes magazines, a rich bitch breakfast. I'll wear a silk robe and buy one of those fancy dogs, a poodle or something with pink ribbons. I'll be Audrey bloody Hepburn.

My tummy is trying to get some message through about wanting food or wanting something but it's not happening. I've got three miles to run first, nothing's going into me until after that. I love my tummy, it's so flat you could bounce a ping-pong ball off it. I love sliding

35

my hand along it and feeling the bones poking out at the sides, looking at the bony arch that leads down to my pubes. Sometimes I try and push it out in front of the mirror and imagine that I'm fat or pregnant. I think about what my body will be like when I get old, if The Tits will droop and my stomach will grow out and sag or if they'll meet somewhere in the middle. But all I can see is me pretending to bloat myself out and it makes me giggle. Anyway I'm not going to get fat, pregnant or old, I won't let it happen.

I run down Essex Road and then cross through Halliford Street, and down to Southgate Road. I debate whether to go up to Vikki Park or down towards Angel tube. I jog up and down on the spot a bit, deciding, then I make a deal with myself. If I run an extra few miles today then I can go on the shorter run tomorrow.

The canal is full of shit, shopping trolleys, prams, plastic bags all wrinkled and ripped against the wall. The path is way too narrow. If a bike comes past or those couples that insist on holding hands like they're glued together, I end up scraping along the wall. But Vikki Park is nice enough, ponds and ducks and dogs chasing sticks, if you like that kind of thing.

My thighs are aching and I'm beginning to think about turning back as I pass through the main gates but a group of lads on bicycles start wolf-whistling me so I speed up. They cycle alongside for a while calling out.

'What's your name?'

'Oi gorgeous, come on talk to me.'

'Hey. Come on, you're breaking my heart here.'

I increase my speed and end up sprinting the whole distance of the park with this convoy of bikes surrounding me. Legging it back down to the canal, I blow them a kiss, leaving them stuck at the top of the steps. In your dreams lads. I'm not giving anything away for free.

Once they are out of sight, I have to stop. My hands on my knees, panting and gasping for breath. When I shake my head, beads of sweat fly off me in different directions. I wipe the sweat from my eyes with my T-shirt, which now has a dark damp V down the middle. I love it when I have to wring out my clothes because they're so full of sweat. That's a good run. I can smell the alcohol and cigarettes oozing out of me. 'Better out than in,' as Mum used to say. I walk for a bit, then slow jog back through the streets to the B&B. I ignore the look from Battleaxe who is always on at me about not dripping my sweat over the lino in the hallway. She's a fat bitch.

Chapter Seven
Scarlett

There's a queue at the building society, and the woman in front is making this big old hoo har at the counter about what a disgrace it is that something or other hasn't been done. I'm looking at my nails and wondering whether I should get another manicure. I'm thinking that maybe a shocking pink would be better than red when the woman behind me nudges me.

'Oi.' I turn round with my hand ready to slap. I hate that.

'The counter's free, so you can go now.'

Yeah all right, fucking hell, who made her boss of the world?

'Yeah. Well don't touch me, alright?' I push her hard to show her what it feels like, and her face is this gigantic 'O' which makes me giggle. I go over to the counter really leisurely, like slow motion just to piss her off.

I've got Mustang Sally today. 'Good Morning Miss.' She flicks me a fake smile, she fucking hates me, hates that I have all this cash and she doesn't know why.

'Can I put this in?' I hand her my book and the pile of notes. She knows better than to try and have a conversation with me. She presses a few keys on the computer and slides my book into the stamper.

'Thank you.' She hands my book back.

'No bother,' I say. I bet she's wetting herself wanting to find out where I get my money.

I buy fruit and sandwiches at Cullens and eat them on a bench in the green. The Screen on the Green is showing *Robin Hood: Prince of Thieves*. On the billboards it says 'The best movie of the year'. I mean, how do they know? It's only bloody July. Who wants to watch men prancing about in tights anyhow? The sun is warm and other than the drunk on the bench opposite me, the green is empty. I crunch into an apple as the red buses creak to stop and start, loaded with losers who are wasting their lives in shitty jobs that will lead them nowhere.

On Essex Road I stop at the only hairdressers that has a half decent sun bed (a good 20 minute sleep) and get myself a quick manicure (deep plum) so by the time I get back to my room it's 5.30pm and there's just enough time to watch *Neighbours* on the telly before I have to start getting ready. I lie on my bed, my ashtray in front of me watching Madge complaining to some other wrinkly about a supposed break-in at The Waterhole. Naggy old bitches those people. Then they do that thing that they do, when Madge pretends to get a phone call from Charlene saying she can't come to the wedding or whatever. Like we're not supposed to notice that actually Charlene hasn't turned up at all or visited her family in years and that she's meant to still be alive and living with Scott in Perth or whatever. It's a bit unbelievable that she wouldn't have even come home for Christmas. Then again, I haven't spoken to my mum in months.

I miss Charlene. People shouldn't be allowed to leave soaps. They should have it written into their contract that if they leave, they still have to come back for big family occasions, weddings, Christmas, funerals or major events. Because at some point no doubt Madge will be in a car crash or on a life support machine for some reason and Charlene won't even visit her which is bollocks. Half the bloody cast are living in London these days anyway. Jason Donovan is on the radio, as I get ready to go. *Any Dream Will Do*. That song is mental. All those aaaah ha haaaas. I mean I liked it when I was seven and I was happy enough singing along with it, but now I listen to it and it just doesn't make any sense. His brothers should have buried him and his technicolour coat in the ditch when they had the chance!

On the estate where I grew up there were the flats where I lived, and then the maisonettes round the back. The maisonettes were meant to be posh because they had gardens, although the gardens were just litter trays for pit bulls and staffs. Half of them were graveyards for burnt out motorbikes and old fridges. The 'flat kids' had this battle going on with the 'maisonettes'. My favourite game when I was nine years old was called Jason. The game was that we'd walk about until we spotted one of the maisonette kids on their own, then we'd jump on them and give them Chinese burns and stuff until they yelled the magic word. Sometimes it was 'Surrender,' sometimes they had to yell 'I'm a poof,' or 'My mum's a slag.' Then we'd have to get off them. Once they said the words, you had to stop. Most kids would take the punching rather than give in. But this lad Jason, the moment he saw us he'd start pissing himself and yelling out, 'Surrender... my mum's a slag.' Like before anyone had even touched him. He wore rainbow home knitted cardigans, and had NHS Elastoplast pink framed glasses and always smelt of his mum's perfume.

Even after he and his mum moved off the estate, everyone still knew what it meant to be called a Jason.

That Bryan Adams is a right Jason. I can't believe that's number one. I mean do people actually fall for that soppy shit? *Everything I do, I do it for You*. Bollocks to that. Everything I do, I do it for myself, no one else is going to do it for me that's for sure.

I sing along with the *Neighbours* theme tune then switch

the telly off before the news. News is boring and besides it's getting ready time so I have a little fashion show for myself to make up my mind which dress to wear tonight. I've got it down to three, the gold, the black or the blue.

I try the blue first, but it's too big and hangs off me, like when I was little and me and Nina used to play dress up with her mum's clothes. Nina's mum had the best clothes, like whatever was in the latest catalogue, she already had. Every time I went round to Nina's, there were new packages with all this stuff in, it was like her Mum didn't even want the stuff once it arrived, she just liked ordering it and opening up the packages.

Nina loved gold dresses. She always wanted to wear anything shiny or anything that made her look like a princess. She had this white blonde hair and these grey eyes so it was almost like she was invisible. The kids on the estate called her freak girl for a while, and then dummy girl on account of how she never took her dummy out. Even when she was nine years old, before she left for good, she still had that dummy in her mouth. But Nina was sweet, you know, and the only person I ever met who would save you half her chocolate bar rather than scoff the lot.

The black looks better, classier, but I wear the gold dress anyway. Not only because Nina would have liked it, but because you've got to stand out in the club, make sure you get booked. Lola and Georgia and the other girls, they pretend like they're all mates and girls to-gether, linking arms and sharing lipstick and all that crap, but the truth is if a rich punter comes in waving his cash about then any one of us would dig our stilettos in the back of the others to get in there first.

The gold is too strappy for a bra and just thin enough to show off The Tits properly. I take out the sponge curlers from my hair and twizzle the strands into ringlets.

I try bare legs first but then decide on pull up stockings that stop an inch below the dress, leaving a gap of firm thigh. A final touch of lipstick and I shake my hair back over my shoulders. I am fucking gorgeous.

Battleaxe is sweeping the street outside the B&B. She gets a right face on her when she sees me. I lift my arm above my head and click my fingers for a cab, which screeches to a halt at the curb. Battleaxe is tutting and leaning on her broomstick like the old witch that she is. I spit my gum out at her feet and wink at her before I get in.

Chapter Eight
Tiggy

'I'm sorry.'

Tony has negotiated the fourteen floors to my flat to give me his 'Don't call me, I'll call you' lecture. There's a George Michael track I love on the radio, which is happily distracting me. I figure he's about three quarters of the way through.

It's raining again. It's supposed to be high summer, but lately it just seems to drizzle. I pretend to hang my head apologetically. Tony requires me to show remorse. I wonder what Andrew Ridgley is doing without George, whether they are still friends. I think that my carpet needs cleaning.

'I've told you so many times.' Tony clutches the air in exasperation.

I have the urge to giggle nervously at being told off. It's like Tony and I are still at school.

'I just wanted to talk to you.'

'Tiggy... look... you know how difficult this is for me and I can't have...'

'What? You going to give me detention?'

Tony pushes his hands through his hair and glares at me.

I am so bored with this.

'I thought you were going to tell her, anyway.'

I don't believe that anymore.

'I am... it needs to be in my own time... okay?

But I want to.

'Okay, you're right... I'm sorry Tony.'

We get so little time together and when we do, we

fight.

'Sandra's fragile, okay... we need to be careful.'

Oh is she, poor Sandra, how awful for her. I'm being unreasonable. I should try harder.

'I know, I'm sorry.' I get up from the sofa and move to hold him. He pulls away. Punishing me just a little moment longer.

'What was so urgent anyway?'

I just wanted to talk to him. A different day I might be indignant. Why shouldn't I call my boyfriend? But today I don't have the energy for a row, who am I kidding? I never have the energy for a row.

'I was out shopping and I was... well... having a nice time and I just wanted to talk to you. I'm sorry.' I try to look sorry, but I'm not sure that I am. Tony shakes his head and then must decide to be magnanimous.

'Okay, but let me call you alright... baby?'

'Alright. I'm sorry.'

I move towards him and this time he lets me. I stroke his cheek and run my finger over his lips, relieved as he takes my finger and slides it between his teeth. Biting it gently.

Tony and I have been lovers for six years. If you do the maths it means that strictly speaking, he is guilty of a criminal act. Add in that he was my form teacher at the time. And he's twenty years older and married. The whole thing looks unbearably icky, but it wasn't like that, not with me and him. It was true love. It's like Tony says, 'You can't choose who you fall in love with, can you?'

He tugs on my T-shirt pulling me close to him. 'You silly thing, come here.'

And I come.

I never questioned that Tony would leave Sandra once I'd left school. But it's been three years now. And still no movement. I keep wondering if there is something more that I should be doing. Some other method of persuasion that I could be using. He says that he needs time. That I should be patient. That one day soon he will leave and we will be together.

We both know he's never going to leave.

After Tony has gone home I pour myself another drink then take out the shoebox from under my bed. It's filled with letters and cards. The poems he used to write me. There's a strip of pictures of us in a photobooth. I'm so happy in that picture. I flick through the pages of my old diaries, yellowing already, covered in stickers and doodles.

I wonder how we got here. How I got here. To this flat, this job, this life. This half-life.

Tony was the teacher that everybody liked; the one no one had a daft nickname for. The boys thought he was cool because he was brilliant at every sport and swore when he was fed up with the class. The girls liked him because we all thought he looked like Magnum PI and he had this way of making you feel like you were the only person in the room.

And he chose me.

On May 25th 1985 I've written: 'TW and I did it!!!! Oh my Gooooood!!!!' I've decorated the page with tiny red hearts and pink felt tip kisses.

I smile.

I lie back on the bed and I think about how scared I was, how excited. How once Tony noticed me I felt that finally something was going to happen.

Something good.

It began in the old library. After my mother left I'd started hiding out there in the evenings. The old library was rarely used because it was too cold and there was a rumour that it was haunted. But I liked it, because no one bothered me. I could read, listen to my walkman, be alone. I liked the smell; mildewed books, dust and stale cigarettes, it had its own story. I imagined centuries of schoolboys sneaking over the grey tiles to smoke illicit cigarettes. On winter evenings I kept the lamps off, reading by the sharp line of light from the hallway window. In the dusky corners I'd created my own version of hide and seek. I could hear the life and routine of the school beyond the doors, but they couldn't find me here. I was invisible.

But that February everything changed. I was reading in my usual corner when the doorknob turned. I shrank back behind the shelves and watched the door open through my makeshift spy hole. Sometimes sixth formers came in here to kiss or escape a patrolling teacher. If they saw me then I was dead. I made ready to bolt. But Tony Welsh came in, reaching for the light switch then pausing and leaving it off. He browsed the library shelf in front of me. I watched the rise and fall of his jacket as he picked a book from the shelf and read a few lines. He replaced it and chose another one, seemingly at random. Then he walked the length of the library and took the seat opposite mine. I thought my heart might burst out of my chest and land on the table in front of him.

He opened the stiff pages and without lifting his eyes from the page said, 'So, what are you reading?'

I held up my book, my hands shaking.

'Little Women eh? You enjoying it?'

I nodded.

'Nice here… nice and quiet isn't it?'

I nodded again, wishing I could think of something to say.

He continued reading, every so often he looked over at me, and I looked away.

My face was burning like I'd swallowed a mouthful of hot coals. At first I couldn't concentrate on my pages knowing he was near me, but as the minutes passed by I started to manage entire paragraphs.

The footsteps on the flag stone corridors outside the room tip tapped past from time to time. But nobody came in. Nobody tried the door. It was our universe. Just me and Tony Welsh, and the sound of the clock ticking away the taut seconds. Like time could snap.

'Any news from your mother?' Tony asked and I shook my head.

'Must be hard for you,' he said gently.

'I'm fine,' I said quickly, embarrassed at how my eyes were welling up. I tugged on the ends of my cardigan, pulling the sleeves down over my wrists and then stared down at the table. I was determined not to cry. When I looked up again he was gone.

After that he came to the library most evenings. Sometimes for a few minutes, sometimes for an hour. He'd bring books for me to borrow. Recommend things to me. 'The Great Gatsby… wonderful book, Tiggy.' Or 'Tess – try it, she's a little like you, I think.' I'd stay up long into the night reading his suggestions. Reading too much into every line and wondering what I was supposed to be thinking or feeling. What clever insights I could find for the next time we met.

When he didn't come I'd miss him. I'd listen for the sound of the door creaking open. My heart beating. My hands shaking. After weeks of meeting in the library, weeks of half finished conversations, I finally asked him why he came. He'd looked at me for what felt like forever.

'I don't know,' he eventually replied. 'I like your company, Tiggy,' he said quietly. 'You intrigue me.' I could barely breathe.

'But how about we meet somewhere a little warmer. My flat say... tomorrow evening... after tea,' his finger stroking his cheek.

'Um... okay,' I said in the smallest whisper.

'Good. Sandra's away, so it will just be us.'

My stomach pitched. I brought my hand to my mouth but my fingers couldn't contain my smile.

I push the shoebox away and curl into a ball.

I stare at the ceiling, at the little swirls of artex, the nicotine stains hanging on their tips, like a cancerous chocolate topping. I wish that I was 15 again, and that everything was simple as it felt in that library.

My life and this bloody building are the same. Neither red nor green, stuck in yellow. Waiting for something to change. Whatever this is, it doesn't feel like my life.

I don't seem able to make any decisions. Some nights after the club closes, Dan and I drive around aimlessly for hours. We don't talk, we just drive. Dan chooses cassettes and plays bits of tracks, half songs. I lean my head against the car window and watch the streets pass us. We drive everywhere, along the back lanes of east end warehouses, past the bright bluster of Leicester Square and Soho. The night buses, cardboard boxes in doorways. The dark streets of Dalston and Stoke Newington.

Some people belong to these streets, to these road names. They have families, neighbours and a sense of home. I wonder how that must feel.

Sometimes it's just us and a few taxi drivers left. One time Dan filled up the petrol tank and we drove right out of London. For a few moments I felt like Tracy Chapman in that song about the fast car. I thought Dan should keep on driving, never stop.

I wanted my ticket to anywhere.

Chapter Nine
Tiggy

Dan and I are playing chess.

It's 5am and we're both too awake to call it a night. Sunlight is coming in through the curtains. I guess it's already tomorrow. He can take either my knight or my queen with his rook. He chooses the knight. I pick it back up. 'Not my horse!'

'It's a knight Tiggy. They're called knights.'

'Well don't take my knight then... please.'

'Well it's either the knight or your queen.'

'Well take the queen then.'

He rolls his eyes.

'Tiggy, with the queen you still have a chance of winning.'

'No I don't.'

I don't. I've never beaten Dan at chess.

'I'm not going to take your queen. Sorry. Why you like the horse so much I don't know. Is this some latent middle class need to keep hold of your cavalry? Say goodbye.' He sweeps the knight off the board and slips it into the box.

'Noooo... he's my favourite.'

He laughs.

'Your go then.'

I move my bishop.

He puts his head in his hands.

'You can't move there.'

'Why not?'

'Tiggy, you are putting yourself in check.'

'Oh.'

I really don't care.

'Go on, think about it, try and strategise... Jesus woman, I've never known anyone with less competitive spirit... at least try and win. Can I put a record on?' He flicks through the pile of records on the floor.

My record collection is my pride and joy. The culmination of days spent browsing in second-hand record stores. I will travel miles for the right EP, the perfect import, a collectors' edition picture disk. It is also my great shame; revealing more than I would like. Exposing me as a slush-brained nerd with next to no discernment.

Stacked against the walls of my flat, in vertical piles, are hundreds of albums. A quick look will reveal the covers of Happy Mondays, Charlatans, Inspiral Carpets, Carter USM. You could be forgiven for assuming that at weekends I can be found at Brixton Academy, gigging my life away, stage diving into the arms of the great unwashed.

'Sure,' I say. 'But um... some of the ones at the back are very old.'

Behind all the baggy Indie records is a whole other story. I like to think of my taste in music as eclectic. That my choices are democratic and unencumbered by the need to be cool.

'Bloody hell you've got some crap here, Tiggy.'

Or crap. I have a whole lot of crap records. An innocent enough vice. Listening to The Osmonds never killed anyone did it? Abba is comfort music for me – *Voulez Vous, Arrival.* Just looking at the covers takes me to a happy place where I believed I would grow up to be Annafried and marry Benny.

Dan is holding up my copy of *Rock and Roll Juvenile.*

Oh and Cliff Richard. My dirty little secret pleasure.

I stare at the chessboard trying to think of a way to move my king out of danger. I'm going to have to cheat.

'Tiggy, I'm sorry but I can't just let this pass. This is like a collection of crimes to pop music.

'I like Cliff Richard.' It seems pointless to deny it.

'Obviously, Jesus there are over twenty Cliff LPs here. Tell me you're joking. Tell me it's a statement against the rise of indie music, this is your subverting of the monopoly of Madchester bands.'

'I do... I used to dream he was my father... in fact I wrote to him once asking if he would be my father.'

'I'm going to pretend that was a joke... oh thank God for that... The Smiths.' Dan places the record on the turntable.

'He sent me a picture.'

It comes out at the wrong speed. Morrissey sounds almost perky. He changes it.

'Who did?'

'Cliff.'

'Oh God. I'm trapped in this flat with a mad woman.'

'Black and white. He's standing by a gate, in a plaid shirt. It said, "With love." Do you think he really meant it?'

'Tiggy, if you don't shut up about Cliff then I might have to rethink our friendship.'

'Sorry... *Mr Music.*'

'Listen it's people like you that are ruining pop music. You and Stock, Aitkin and Waterman. The more you buy the crap, the more they make it. It's a vicious cycle.'

'I was about nine when I bought those. I can't be held responsible.'

'Exactly, Tiggy, and this is the problem. The people buying records are nine year old girls, and nine year old girls should not be the arbiters of the music scene. This is why PWL are stuffing our charts with Sonia, Sinitta, Rick Astley and bloody Big Fun. When I rule the world the first thing I am going to do is ban anyone under the age of 21 from buying records. It's the only way we're going to get music back from the brink. They look like bloody children's TV presenters most of them, miming infantile rhymes along to music that a three year old could compose on a Fisher Price toy. Since when was a musician required to dance and not required to learn a bloody instrument?'

And so he continues. I hope that he doesn't find my Bros LPs.

Dan forced his friendship on me when I first started working at Valerios. That's the only way to describe it. The club was empty, the hostesses were staring at their nails and reapplying lipstick. I was sat on my own in the staff booth when Dan came off stage and took the seat next to me.

'Hi, I'm Dan. I know what you're thinking. You're thinking, what is a talented fantastic musician like you doing in a dive like this?'

Which sounds like a corny chat up line. Except that it was actually what I'd been thinking. The fact that he's gorgeous didn't hurt either.

'Well, I'll tell you then.' He took a sip of my vodka before I could protest. 'It's a travesty, a terrible oversight. Right now I should be playing Hammersmith Odeon or Earls Court. You should be sick of the sight of my face on billboards, the side of buses. Already you should be wondering whether my third album is going to see me return to the form of my first, after the terrible self indulgence of my experimental second.'

'Should I?'

'Yes Viola Viola, if there was any justice in the world you should.'

'Okay, I believe you. It's... um... I'm called Tiggy.' I held out my hand, which he shook with both hands and one eyebrow raised.

'Oh... okay then *Tiggy*. Fair enough. So what's with the Viola Viola name thing? Are you a fan of Shakespeare, Twelfth Night your favourite play is that it?'

'No, no, I kind of stole it from a girl at school.'

'Well your friend must be very flattered.'

'Hmmmm, maybe not, school bully, made my life hellish. I... um... well, it's my sort of revenge I guess.'

Which Dan thought was very funny and so offered to buy me a drink, which I refused. But he insisted on account of how he had drunk half of the one I already had. So I gave in and our friendship slotted into place right there and then. Not that I had any choice in the matter.

Later that week, having established that he wasn't psychotic or perverted, I accepted his offer of a lift home.

I retrieve my knight from the box and put it back on the board in front of my king. I turn it to face the king and say, '*Neigh* your highness,' and then giggle. I think I might be a little stoned, and I'm not feeling even slightly paranoid. This is cool.

Dan is standing at the window, looking at the sunrise, and singing *Heaven Knows I'm Miserable Now* in a dreamy way.

He looks like a rock star.

A David Bailey black and white photo.

'You could still do it, you know, leather trousers, rolling about on some sofa, groupies at the door wearing T-shirts with your face on them. We looove you Dan.'

'Hardly.' He laughs half a laugh.

Dan is rarely serious. But already I like him best when it's before sunrise and he lets his ghosts join us.

'Why not? I mean, you're only what 30 or something, it's hardly over the hill.'

The guitars swagger round the room and Morrissey makes being miserable sound just perfect right now. I get up and take the joint from Dan's hands.

'Seriously Dan, why not?'

I go to sit back on the sofa. I nearly miss it. I'm definitely stoned. Dan sits next to me.

'I'm done with dragging myself around record labels begging for my chance.'

'Someone might sign you... you're always telling me to try things.'

'Been there.' He stares at the half-smoked joint as though it may be a crystal ball. I want to photograph him like this. Troubled and vulnerable. I don't believe that anyone sees this side of him. Well, maybe Jackie.

'So... what happened?'

'You really want to know?'

'I absolutely, really want to know... come on I've told you my story.'

'Okay then, we got signed, everyone at the label loved us – we had a release date, but it kept on getting pushed back, something to do with the artwork. Then there was some problem with distribution, then our contract ran out. Then nothing. Which is a shame, because I was looking forward to spending all my money on drugs and loose women and then buying a trout farm.'

There's a knock on the door of the neighbours' and for a second I wonder what would happen if Tony was to turn up here right now. What would he think if he saw me with Dan?

Dan waves his hand in front of my face.

'Sorry, am I boring you?'

'No, go on, I'm interested really... sorry.'

I am. I'm just a little distracted.

I pour us both another drink and fold my legs up onto the sofa. Turning to face him, giving him my full attention.

'Well, okay, if you're sure... well the A&R people were suspicious about why. Thought maybe we were *difficult* or something. So we tried something different. We had this ferociously ambitious woman representing us, our manager. *Rachel.*'

He winces as he says her name.

'I think she wanted us to make it more than we did. Anyway she got us this other deal with a small independent label, not much money, but her plan was that we would have a one single deal with them, then once our single went into the top 20, we would be more marketable... we could sell more product. *Product*... I hate that word... anyway, Rachel thought that once we got the single released, the plaudits, the five gold star reviews... then we could hold out for that three album deal and go 'stellar.' But as you can see I'm not playing a stadium right now. So Rachel's little plan went belly-up.'

'Did you get to make your single?'

'Oh yes.'

'And?'

'And, NME said that it was 'innovative rock blend fusion.'

'Rock blend fusion? Wow! What does that mean?'

'No idea, but they got us in for an interview and this bloke Ralph with red hair and green trousers, asked me all these art school questions about my motivations for writing songs. He actually said at one point, and I remember this clearly. 'Dan do you feel that Luna Zeitgeist are rediscovering the inevitable transit into spiritual melange.' Dan giggles. 'I remember thinking, shit, I'm never going to manage any interviews if I don't understand the questions. It was the first time I understood why so many rock stars have private educations. Where else would they learn all that pretentious crap?'

'Luna Zeitgeist! Dan, you're not seriously telling me that you were in a band called Luna Zeitgeist!'

'Don't blame me, blame Mickey, the drummer... It was the late 70s... everyone had daft names. I mean what were you listening to in the 70s? What were you rocking to at seven then Tigs? Oh no, you're going to say ABBA aren't you? Or was it Bay City Rollers?'

I see myself at seven years old, sat at the dining room table eating Sunday dinner. My father would be silently chewing his food, occasionally making affirmative noises. My mother's unhappiness and minimalist approach to conversation no doubt clashing with the floral wallpaper. I can't hear any music. No one was rocking to anything.

'Yeah, something like that,' I say. 'So what happened with the single?'

'It went straight in at number seventy nine.'

'That's not a bad start.'

'The following week it was one hundred and sixty seven.'

'I'm sorry... can I ask what it was called?'

'No. No, if you didn't buy it then you don't deserve to know.'

'Come on, please.'

'Absolutely not.'

'So what happened to the band then?'

'Ah… the band. Well the band reformed under a different name. With a different lead singer. *Rachel,* Rachel felt that it was me… I was the problem, I was holding them back, ruining her chance of vicarious stardom.'

'Bitch!'

'Hmmm… I'm too nice apparently. Nice doesn't sell.'

'She said that!'

'She certainly did.'

'Bitch!'

'Nice is boring, which is probably why she left me for Mickey.'

'Sorry?'

'Rachel, the ferociously ambitious manager… was also my wife.'

I look at Dan, who is looking at me, waiting for some kind of reaction. I don't know what to say to him.

'She broke my heart,' he says then grins.

'Bitch!'

He laughs. 'Exactly Tiggy, though you might want to vary your vocab a little.'

'No really, that's awful… she went off with the drummer?'

'I know. I mean no one ever fancies the drummer. It was horrible actually Mickey ended up in casualty. Rachel threatened me with an injunction… but Jackie, well… you know… she sorted me out. So… anyway, come on let's finish the game. Did you have your go?' He sits back down on the floor, signalling that the conversation is over.

I'm wondering why Mickey ended up in casualty but decide it's best not to ask.

Dan reveals himself to me in staggered stages. Some evenings we gossip about the club, the girls and

Mario. Other nights he's more distant and I don't like to push. Those are the nights when we drive in silence. Men are puzzling. He's my first male friend. I take my lead from him. I speculate about Dan and Jackie, about why he spends time with me, when he could be with her. But I never have the nerve to ask him. I'm worried it might break the spell. Anyway a man like Dan wouldn't want to be with a stripper. Jackie is probably a nurse or a superhero or something, the sort of person who actually does something useful with her life.

'So, you had a wife?'

'Yes, I had a wife.'

'And she left you for the drummer?'

'Yes.'

'Of Luna Zeitgeist?'

'Again, yes... and I went doolally.'

I laugh. I don't know why, I start to apologise through my giggles but it doesn't work and then Dan is laughing too.

'It's really not funny you know.'

'Oh come on Dan. It is kind of funny.'

'She broke my heart!'

Then we are both laughing. It must be the dope. Dan leans back on the sofa next to me and his shirt rides up a little and I have to stop myself from reaching out to touch his stomach. He looks at the board, laughs then looks back at me. He is holding my freshly resurrected knight.

'Duplicitous lot you women... can't be trusted.'

He puts the knight back in the box.

'Come on then young Antigone... make your move.'

And I wonder what he would do if I did.

Chapter Ten
Scarlett

I'm stuck at a table with Lola and one of the ugliest men ever. I mean I'm not trying to be nasty or anything, but when I was a kid I hid behind the sofa when things like him came on the telly. He's like a slime ball, and every time he speaks he spits everywhere and the table is practically swimming with saliva. I'm pretty good at faking things but every time he touches me, it's all I can do not to scream, and not in a good way.

But he's bought the vintage Krug and treated both Lola and me to a 50-pack of fags each so I guess we have to grin and bear it.

'So how old are you?' he sprays at me.

'How old do you want me to be?' I resist the desire to splutter this at him and manage my much-practised purr. He raises a hairy eyebrow at this and his eyes sparkle with the glint that those monsters on TV used to have just before they ate their prey.

'Put it this way... I like my meat tender. Veal, duckling... the younger the better.' He leans a little nearer to me, up close his skin has the texture of a reptile, crackly and scaly and it looks like it might smell. He reaches out to stroke my face. I pull away, I can't do this but thank fuck for Lola who quickly grabs his hand.

'We're not allowed to touch in the club.' She smiles sweetly at him.

'Here, Max, have another glass of champagne.' She pours him another glass while I quickly gulp down the glass in front of me. This is one evening where being pissed might make the job more bearable. Champagne rolls along the folds of Max's chins and he wipes it back with a linen napkin.

'Well, ladies, if there's no touching in the club then I guess we'd better go somewhere else.'

There is no way I'm going anywhere with him, I'd rather stick electric eels up my giblets.

'I can't,' I say quickly. 'I'm sorry, but it's not allowed.'

Lola flashes me an angry glare. She's been having a slow night and I haven't seen her leave with anyone in weeks. Corporate hospitality slows down in the summer months, and at 35 Lola is considered old in this game. Like I said, they want to believe that they're the first, and with Lola that's a lot of self-delusion.

'Girls. Girls,' Monster Max slithers his hand into his wallet. 'I think you'll find that I can make it worth your while.' He flashes a wad of cash at us.

There is no money in the whole world worth it mate.

'How much?' I can't believe Lola's even considering it, but she is definitely on her own with this one.

'A thousand.' Max squelches back in the chair and smiles.

'For us each or between us?' Lola must be desperate to even ask.

'Each,' he replies quickly. 'But I want both of you. You and the lovely young Scarlett here.' He looks at me and licks his lips.

My stomach turns over and I pull the black velvet of my dress down a little, trying to stretch the fabric further. It's short this dress, a velvet stretch mini, maximum exposure of The Tits and thighs in fishnets. Right now I feel like hiding underneath the tablecloth.

'I just need the toilet for a second,' I say. 'Please excuse me.'

'I'm coming with you.'

Lola follows.

'Scarlett, please.' Lola is sat on the toilet, her dress hitched up around her waist, the cubicle door wide open.

'You have to be kidding me Lola. I'm not touching him.' I take a lipstick from my bag and re-apply the pillar-box red.

'Scarlett. A grand. It'll only take a few minutes... come on... close your eyes, please.'

'You do it, if you're so keen. There's no way that man is getting his scaly skin anywhere near me.'

'You heard him. He wants us both. Look I'll do most of the work, I promise. But it's you he's after... we both know it.'

'It's *both* of us he's after. Three is his magic number alright. And sorry, no.'

Lola grabs a sheet of loo roll and wipes it between her legs then chucks it into the bowl.

Standing at the sink next to me I wonder whether thirty five is a lie. In this light, she looks closer to forty five and the grey routes of her peroxide blonde hair are beginning to show, she should stop coz she's beginning to look mangy. Then again, next to her I do look spectacular. She's right; it probably is me he's after. Well, he's going to have to whistle.

'Scarlett.' Lola's hand touches my lower arm, her fingers squeeze it real tight. 'I really need this money... and I promise you won't have to do anything.'

I don't like it when people touch me without permission.

'Get off me Lola. I'm not doing it.' Lola removes her hand but stays close to me. 'That man is not putting any part of himself inside me.'

'He won't,' she takes a small pill bottle from her clasp bag and shakes it. The tablets rattle cheerily from side to side. 'I can guarantee it.'

Monster Max is staying in a suite at the Ritz, which is something I suppose. He spreads himself out on the giant gold sofa and grins greedily at us. The room is full of huge vases filled with lilies and hand painted bowls with the most gorgeous fruit. Max has filled a silver bucket with ice and opened a Magnum of Veuve Cliquot champagne.

'For my ladies, I want you girls to enjoy yourselves.'

He pours three glasses and Lola and I take ours and sip at them slowly. I've drunk enough and I really want to go home. Not many people would want to leave a suite at the Ritz for a mangy room with a broken sink in a Cannonbury B&B, but my room with its shitty mattress and dirty carpet seems like heaven in comparison to the gigantic slime ball rolling about on the sofa and fiddling with the front of his trousers.

Sometimes this job is like proper work. Mostly it's a laugh. Mostly I'm paid to look fantastic and drink champagne, and then at the end of the night it's just a case of switching off and letting your mind go somewhere else. There's nothing difficult about sex is there? I mean you don't need a university degree or anything to work it out. But with the punters like Max, well I wouldn't normally bother. It's like how in other countries people eat snakes and eyeballs and elephant testicles or whatever. You just close your eyes and swallow and it's over in a matter of seconds. Close your eyes; think about the cash and just about anything is possible. I create shopping lists in my head. I calculate how much each lick, thrust, kiss or whatever is earning me. And pretty often you can distract them enough to be too pissed or too tired to do anything anyway.

Max seems pissed but not sleepy. I'm beginning to really hate Lola.

'Let's see if there's something on the TV that will

loosen us up a little.' He presses the remote and the video starts playing some predictable porn film where women are licking at each other and 'Ooohing and Aaaahing,' calling for God to help them.

He pushes his hand down the front of his trousers. 'Scarlett, tell me my sweet young thing. Do you like this?' He nods at the film.

I see Lola reaching into her bag. Come on Lola, move it on a bit.

'I love it.' I say moving over to Max's right hand side, leaving Lola a clear line between herself and his glass. 'I love watching women.' I lick my top lip with the tip of my tongue.

Lola clicks open the top of the case with a pop, and Max turns to her just as she slides her hand behind her back.

'Lola, did you hear that? Scarlett loves women. What about you Lola? Think you could bring yourself to enjoy the pleasures of young Scarlett here?'

'It would mean a little extra,' Lola replies. 'But show me your money, and we'll show you whatever it is you want to see.'

Max nods towards his wallet.

'Take it all. But from now on I direct everything.'

Lola stares at the thick rolls of notes in his wallet.

'They're all fifties darling. But I expect to get my money's worth.' And then he laughs and it makes me think about the noise the sink plunger made that time Mum blocked the whole thing up with chip oil. I gesture to Lola to get a move on.

'Lola, come here.' Max beckons her away from his wallet and points at his dick. 'I think I'd like you to have a little nibble on that, while our little friend here strips for me... then we'll see.'

The women on the TV are shrieking fake orgasms now

and Lola walks forward, kneeling in front of Max, her hands clenched behind her back. I get up to stand behind her and she unclasps her hand showing me the fistful of tablets.

'I haven't got all day. Unzip me.'

Lola drops the pills into my palm then puts her hands out and reaches under Max's belly to undo his trousers. He sighs and throws his head back, 'Oh yes, that's a good girl.'

I take my opportunity because if I have to watch anymore then I may have to burn my own eyes out.

'You watching this Scarlett?' he splutters from somewhere guttural. His yellow eyes feasting on me, Lola is pulling his penis out of his trousers, and the thing is huge, like a creature within a creature.

'Oh yeah,' I say, deadpan. 'It's getting me really hot.'

'Strip for me baby... show me those titties of yours.'

The Tits again! It's always about The Tits. The pills are melting in the palm of my hand and my panic levels are beginning to rise.

'Can I just have a little more champagne?'

'Scarlett, I hope you're not scared.' Although by the tone of his voice, I think he'd love it if I were.

'A little, I wouldn't mind another drink.' I reply cute as I can and Lola looks back desperately at me over her shoulder. Max looks down at her. 'Show Scarlett there's nothing to be scared of.'

Lola opens her mouth and moves forward and Max pushes his hand hard on the back of her head. I feel myself gag. But he's distracted for a few seconds, his eyes focus on nothing but Lola's painted mouth moving up and down.

I shove the tablets into his glass and gulp down my own then turn sweetly to face him holding two full glasses.

But Max isn't going to make this easy. He doesn't want to drink, he wants to watch, then he wants me to strip. He's paying he says, so he decides. I think about leaving Lola there on her knees with this gigantic monster man who will make her do everything. I'm wondering if there is anything she would stop at, it's like in my mind there are hookers, like me who shag blokes for money, but I choose who, and then there are whores, the ones who are so desperate that they will do anything with anyone. I figure she's not my problem anymore, she needs to look after herself. I should just leave her to it, but I suppose I have to work with her.

'Max,' I say as soft and deep as I can, 'the girls on the TV are making me horny, stop hogging Lola, I want a go... here.' I push the glass towards him and swallow mine down in one. 'Why don't you lie back there and watch for a few minutes, it's not fair to leave me out.'

I hand him the glass and lift my dress over my head, revealing The Tits. He takes a giant gulp and bubbly narcotic liquid pours between his thin mean lips.

'Great idea.' He pushes Lola's head away. 'We'll get back to that in a minute. Now go play with Scarlett.'

Lola and I stand face to face in front of each other while Max watches, his semi hard penis creature crawling from his trousers. Lola pushes her hands into my hair and pulls me towards her.

'Is it sorted?' she hisses.

'Too fucking right it is.'

'Come on girls. Strip.' Max makes that plunging laugh again. He can fuck right off.

'How many did you give him?' Lola makes a low moaning noise and reaches for the clip at the back of my bra.

'Oooooh... all of them.' I step back lifting my hands to let Lola lift my straps over my arms and my bra falls to the floor.

'Aaaaah... giiiiirlss...,' is the last thing Max says before he crashes from the sofa onto the floor, his penis squashed beneath him, its beady eye pushed to one side still staring at us.

'All of them! Scarlett, that's enough to kill an elephant!'

'Good,' I pick up my bra and pour myself another glass of champagne, handing one to Lola. I survey my catch, face down on the carpet, I feel like David against Goliath, like George slaying the Dragon. I want to do it again. I will re-live that moment over and over, I start giggling.

'It's not funny Scarlett. That amount, he could be dead.' But she's laughing too. She picks up his wallet and separates out the notes, dealing it into piles. 'Two for you... two for me... Scarlett, this is a lot of money.'

Lola counts the cash while I pilfer notepads, toiletries, an ashtray and a couple of hand towels from the room.

Then, just for good measure, I write 'Tosser' in lipstick on Max's exposed arse.

Chapter Eleven
Scarlett

We walk down Park Lane towards Piccadilly Circus still giggling, our bags bursting with Ritz goodies, each of us has earned £1500 tonight. I've hit my weekly target in two nights so I'm feeling good. Then Lola's like, 'Fancy a drink. I know a place.' When Lola smiles she looks much younger, less manky.

'All right. Fuck it.' Lola's old enough to be my mother, and we've never gone out before but what the hell, I've made my target, for the second night in a row. I didn't even have to take off my knickers. Plus, I slayed a monster man and it doesn't get much better than that.

Lola leads me up Regent Street, stopping outside a blue door where she knocks and gives her name through the grill. A giant bouncer bloke opens the door for us and she kisses him on both cheeks saying 'hello darling'. I kind of shrug at him and say 'alright?' because I don't know him from Adam do I? Then we go down this staircase and through another door, past another bouncer that Lola insists on fussing over and then finally we are in. Lola turns to me as she pushes through the last door and says 'Welcome to Club Velveteen.' I follow her through the door and suddenly we are in this whole underground club world that I never knew existed, and couldn't have even made up in my wildest fantasies. There are Magnums and Jeroboams of champagne, plates filled with caviar and little itty bitty foods. I recognise some of the blokes from the telly and *Top of the Pops*. The waitresses carry giant trays with pills and lines of different powders on them, like this big old drug buffet and people are just helping themselves.

The men are wearing black suits and bow ties and the women are dressed in glamorous beautiful white dresses. They make me think of all those old movies, like this is the set of some Fred Astaire film or something and if I yelled out 'action' then everyone would start dancing.

'The women in white... they're all whores,' Lola whispers. I look again properly. All the women in white dresses have blonde hair and are giggling and laughing enough at everything the men say to be sure that they're working girls.

On stage, three black blokes are playing some of that jazz crap that Dan Dan the Piano Man does, but better. There's a grand piano, a bass and a saxophone, and these blokes are really grooving it out. I grin at the bass player who's slapping away at the strings and chewing gum, like he's cool as shit. And when the sax player starts, it's like you can see musical notes floating out and swirling round the club.

'God, it's beautiful,' I say, still taking it all in and Lola laughs and then she links her arm into mine, and points to a table. 'Come on Scarlett, this is where we sit.'

I'm sat down gobsmacked, feeling like that first time me and Nina got pissed and saw stars. Then a silver ice bucket holding a bottle of Bollinger arrives at our table without us ordering it.

'What's this?' I ask.

'Oh, this is Roberto's place, didn't you know?' Lola ushers the waitress away and opens the bottle herself, laughing as the cork flies off over the dance floor. 'Let's just say I do favours for him from time to time, so he keeps me sweet.'

Then she opens a wrap of cocaine, cuts a couple of lines and snorts a row right there at the table. 'Want some?' she wipes the powder from her nose then licks her fingers.

'No. I'm fine on this.'

She shrugs, pushing the coke to one side.

'More for me then.'

'Lola. Who's Roberto?'

'Over there in the middle, that's Roberto, the other men with him are his minders.' She nods towards these blokes sat in a dark booth by the side of the dance floor. Roberto must be the fat Godfather lookalike.

'He's a bad boy.' She laughs, 'Very bad actually... makes Mario look like a schoolgirl.'

I don't know the names of the TV people, but I recognise housewives choice, Jed Carter, who is snorting himself happy. Mum had his calendar one year. I swear she used to kiss the pictures coz they were all sticky and gunky round his face. So I'm watching Jed when Roberto catches my eye and he stares right at me.

'Is it okay that we're here? Is he dangerous?'

Lola has white powder on her nose and darting eyes. 'Maybe so, but I go where I want to Scarlett... you?'

'Yeah. Sure. I'm my own boss.'

Lola is like a walking example of why this game is no good for your complexion, late nights, alcohol and no fucking sunshine.

'What's the story with Roberto then?' I ask. The coke is getting to Lola, so she's talking fast, like someone has a stopwatch to her mouth.

Seems that Roberto and Mario got off to a bad start when Mario bought The Blue Sunset club from under his nose. Roberto had seen himself as the main man in the hostess world and from nowhere Mario appeared and outbid him. Lola says that most people wouldn't dare go after something that Roberto wanted because 'his boys can be seriously psychotic'. But Mario's nerve had sort of half-impressed Roberto at first, and even when Mario turned the place into a hostess club and named it Valerios after himself, Roberto let it go. He figured that maybe a little bit of competition wasn't such a bad thing. But then Valerios starting charging less for entrance, less for drinks, less for girls and that's when Roberto got mad.

'Roberto's old school,' Lola says. 'He's a big old suck-ass. He loves upper classes, rich people, celebrities, the politicians. He doesn't care about the money or the fame, he's in it for the prestige. Roberto would never dream of naming a club after himself. He says it's vulgar and common. Whereas with Mario...'

'It is all about the money and the fame?'

'Absolutely, Mario has a business plan and a business mind, Mario thinks big you know, he's seen the future.'

I figure that Lola must be a little in love with Mario because she starts gushing like a broken toilet about how brilliant he is, and how Mario this and Mario that. I can't help thinking that it's a shame I didn't get a job here, because there is something sort of wonderful about Club Velveteen. Valerios is only a cheap imitation. Lola is still fixated on Mario.

'Mario wants to go for corporate groups, stag nights. He wants to make Valerios a chain, a Valerios on every corner of every street.'

She rubs a little extra coke onto her gums with her fingertips and licks her lips, her pupils widening and contracting madly.

'And I'm going to run that chain for him,' she says rubbing her nose a little. 'But Mario, you know, I'm not sure that I can always trust him, so you know, in the meantime I keep Roberto a little sweet. I'm sort of a double agent.' I can tell that I'm supposed to be impressed. 'And Roberto rewards me. He rewards me very well.' She starts laughing so loud that I want to smack her, but it's not such a bad plan she's got, running the club for Mario. Seems to me that that's where the big money is, but it's got to be dangerous playing these two men off against each other.

'But Lola... if Roberto is such a big gangster, then why don't his people finish Mario off or something?'

But Lola's concentration has gone and she's staring at the dance floor now and jigging along to the music like a mentalist.

'Lola wants to dance,' she says. I knock back the glass of champagne. I'm about to say I've got to go, but she drags me onto the dance floor and I kind of think, 'Oh well why not. After all, all work and no play makes Scarlett a dull girl.'

We find a space on the dance floor and try to dance to the end of *Dub Be Good To Me*, which is too slow to dance to and too fast to just hover, and I'm wondering why I came here when the opening beats of *Groove is in the Heart* glide out from the speakers. I make a whoop noise and I spin round and round, my bag is filled with cash and I feel pissed and happy.

That chick from Dee-Lite is singing about how she couldn't ask for another and I'm loving it. It doesn't even bother me that I'm singing at the top of my voice and I have no idea what the lyrics mean.

I realise that Roberto is having himself a good old look at The Tits, so I kind of play up to him a little. And it's not long before he sends one of his muscle bound lackies over to ask me to join him.

Chapter Twelve
Tiggy

There's a message on my answer phone. I press play and hear my father's voice. I stop still for a moment.

My father's phone manner is usually hasty and businesslike. His messages sound like a monthly chore. But today he sounds hesitant.

He says, 'Give me a ring would you. It's important. Okay, Tigger.'

He hasn't called me Tigger since I was six.

I listen to the message again. I try to call him but there's no answer. I smoke a cigarette. I wish I could speak to Tony but I don't dare call him. I try my father again. I run a bath. I sit beside the phone sipping vodka. I play the message over and over.

'Give me a ring would you. It's important. Okay, Tigger.'

I decide that he has cancer. I decide that Margaret has left him. I play the message again.

'Give me a ring would you. It's important. Okay, Tigger.'

It's hard to know whether it is cancer or Margaret. But definitely something.

I drink a little more vodka and take my bath. I call him again. Maybe he's at the hospital. Maybe surgeons are operating on him. They're making giant incisions into his chest. I see my father and Margaret, pale and terrified, listening while a doctor gives my father his devastating prognosis.

'Okay, Tigger.'

Perhaps he's lying with his wrists slashed open on the floor of his house. Perhaps I was the last call he made. I wasn't there for him and now he's dead.

I have been a terrible daughter.

I wonder whether he has left me a note or anything in his will.

I doodle on a napkin, half lines, songs, and words from the songs of my childhood. Then I start a letter for my dead father just in case he isn't dead. I tell him how sorry I am and how much I love him. Even in my vodka-enhanced state, I know I will never finish it. At that moment it feels incredibly important and profound.

Then I pass out.

I dream my favourite dream of Tony, of our first time together.

There is a 'Do not disturb' sign on the door. I turn the door handle. I am so scared.

Tony and Sandra's flat is part of the main school building, above the art rooms and along a private staircase. I've never been in this corridor before and I'm shaking all over. The carpet is red, threadbare and scratchily industrial. It smells of stale detergent. The magnolia walls have inky fingerprints and grubby marks. I find Tony's door and knock very, very gently. It's so quiet. What if Sandra answers the door? What if she asks why I'm there? I feel a little sick. Then Tony opens the door and smiles. He has a tea towel in his hands, a blue tea towel.

'Come in. I was just drying up.'

'Oh.' My tongue ties in knots.

I go through into his living room and I am enchanted. It's small and messy, piles of books and papers everywhere. The walls lined with shelves full of more books and records and cassettes. Tony's desk with its small typewriter and piles of paperwork. There's no obvious sign of Sandra at all. I'm secretly delighted. I try to retain everything. The framed photos and pictures on the walls. Abstract colours in blocks clipped into glass frames. On the main wall there are four posters of Shakespeare plays. RSC productions. *Love's Labours' Lost*, *A Winters' Tale*, *Hamlet*, and the *Merry Wives of Windsor*.

I hold my hands together and hope that he won't notice how much I am shaking.

'Make yourself comfortable.' Tony gestures towards the large sofa against the wall. I sit down, as though this is an order, trying to look relaxed. From the kitchen I hear the clanking of cups and the yawn of the fridge door opening. I want to be older, more eloquent, more like him. I sit on the edge of the sofa and stare at my fingernails. Bitten right down. I resist the temptation to put them in my mouth.

I sit on them instead.

Tony comes back carrying a small tray with tea and biscuits placing them gently on the coffee table in front of the sofa, and then he sits down next to me. I smile at him in a way I hope is adult and confident.

'So, you're here,' he says quietly.

'Yes.'

'And I'm here.'

'Yes.'

'And Sandra is away... so...'

My teacup wobbles and twists in my hands, as though possessed. I put it back down quickly. I concentrate on not saying anything stupid. On not being sick.

Tony takes his cup of tea and sips from it slowly.

'There's so much I want to discuss,' he says solemnly, 'I've been thinking, over and over... about... I'm not sure that I should... I...' Then he jumps up from his seat and claps his hands together. 'Um... music, we need music.' On the far left of the room there are shelves and shelves of cassettes, all copies, all labelled. In alphabetical order. Louis Armstrong, Chet Baker, Duke Ellington, Ella Fitzgerald, Dizzy Gillespie, Dexter Gordon, Billie Holiday, Sarah Vaughan.

'Anything in particular you want to hear, Tiggy?'

'No, anything, you choose.'

'I think something classical... what do you prefer... Mahler, Mozart, Mantovani?' And he laughs.

I laugh too, but I'm not sure what the joke is.

'Mozart,' I say, it's the only name I recognise.

'Mozart it is then.'

He slips a cassette into a giant black stereo unit and presses play.

'You've got lots of tapes.' I sound so stupid. I'm an idiot. I hate myself.

He looks at the wall of cassettes. 'Yes, I suppose I do... so... Tiggy, you found your way into my little flat alright then?'

'Yes, sir.'

I hate myself for calling him sir; it makes me sound like a dumb schoolgirl.

'Are you okay with being here? It feels okay to you?'

'Yes, sir. I mean, it's nice. I like it. Being here that is.' I am just one big blush at this point.

Tony sits back on the sofa, taking my hand and looking at my palm for a long time. Then he places his other hand over it.

'You make me want things I shouldn't want, Tiggy,' his face is sad, full of yearning. I am making this gorgeous, intelligent man feel sad. I want to make him feel better, feel happier.

'Sorry,' I say, 'I don't mean to.'

76

I want him to kiss me like the people on TV kiss each other. I want him to hold me and kiss me and tell me I'm beautiful.

'How do you do it?' he says softly. 'Make me feel all this?'

'I'm not doing anything.'

'I wouldn't be so sure. You've derailed me. I'm lost here. Such a longing... I see your sad face when... when I shouldn't. Maybe you're a Siren. That's what it is, you're a Siren.'

And I can feel it, like there is magic in me, calling him in. Tony moves closer to me and for a second I feel powerful. He is the teacher, and yet I am controlling him. His eyes are so black. Close up he has tiny dots over his chin where he shaves.

I've never kissed a man who shaves before.

I've never kissed a man.

He places a hand on my leg, just at the end of my skirt, his fingers on my bare skin. His other hand strokes my cheek, his fingers on my lips. I think I might stop breathing. I no longer feel magical. I feel excited, completely overwhelmed. And maybe a little scared. I am so in love with him. Everyone is in love with him and he has chosen me.

'Is this okay?' His hands move higher and higher. 'Should I stop?'

I don't answer. I am scared he will stop. I don't want him to stop. Don't want to remind him that I am too young.

I want him to own me.

I want to be his possession.

If I belong to him, then everything in my world will be wonderful.

'Should I stop?' he repeats.

I shake my head.

He kneels in front of me. The violin is playing a sonata. I stay silent. A tear dries on my cheek, my heart beating too quickly. I wish I knew more, wish I understood more. Then he moves under my skirt. The music rises and falls around us.

'Sir?'

'Call me Tony.'

'Tony,' I say quietly. 'This cassette is beautiful.'

And right then the tape clicks off, this loud clunking noise, and the room fills with silence.

I wake up alone.

My hair is piled into the ashtray and the napkin is glued to my face by sweat and drool. My profound alcoholic insights from last night are now stained along the side of my face in blue ink.

I miss Tony. I feel completely full of love and completely hollowed by his absence. This is how he has always made me feel.

I call my father and he answers. Nobody is dead, nobody is sick, but he wants to see me. Tomorrow, six o'clock at the Royal Court Tavern.

Chapter Thirteen
Tiggy

He's late. With each flick of the second hand I feel my insides vibrate. I've been trying to consider whether it is physically possible that Margaret might be pregnant. I've never asked her age and she has that earthy, unmade up look that could be anything between thirty five and fifty. I guess it's possible.

I've never asked why my parents stopped at one child because it always seemed so obvious. The more insistent question would be why did they have children at all? My mother displayed the maternal tendencies of a polecat. My father has always looked confused and diminished in the company of children. He's not entirely sure what they are for. In his defence, he doesn't bother with the effort that some adults push themselves through. He would never ask little Johnny or Suzie how things were going at school. It wouldn't occur to him to question new parents on how they were coping.

My father bought a yacht once. He was terribly excited. Couldn't shut him up about it. He joined an elite country yacht club, subscribed to Motor Boat and Yachting. He talked endlessly of lazy days on the water drinking gin and tonic, how for him, sailing was 'A challenge, of course, Tiggy, but ultimately rewarding and restful.' Then after a few summers of hauling sails in freezing sleet and haemorrhaging cash, the yacht was abandoned on its mooring. He kept his membership of the club. He drank Pimm's around the subsidised bar with his new yachting pals. But he never actually got back on the water. For my father, children are a little like that yacht. Nice in theory.

He arrives in a bothersome mood. Traffic and tourists and the state of the world are all apparently going to hell. He collects drinks from the bar and bangs his foot on the table leg as he sits down. I realise that he is nervous, but not angry.

He doesn't know about the stripping.

Margaret is definitely pregnant.

Maybe they are renewing their vows in lavish style.

Oh God. I'm going to be forced into some monstrous dress and paraded in front of photographers from *Harpers and Queen*. I take a deep breath.

'Father? What did you want to meet up for?'

I'm prepared. I have an excellent speech on my right to do what I want with my life and my body. A gentle supportive speech if he wants to tell me that he is having another child. I could have put together a small box of index cards with my responses. It's just a question of which one I'll need. I am certain that I must have covered every eventuality.

My father focuses on the wall behind my head, coughs and then refocuses on anything but me.

'It's your mother.'

I catch my breath. I realise that there was one possibility, one index card that I have forgotten.

'Mother?'

'Yes, your mother.'

We sit in untidy silence. I wait for him to speak but he doesn't seem to want to say anymore. Eventually I can't bear it any longer.

'Has something happened to her?'

Why am I panicking? So what if something has. It's not like I've seen her in years. It's not like she gives a fuck about me.

80

'Has something happened to her?' I grab his wrist.

'No. No, nothing like that.' He places his hand over mine. My heart creeps back into position and beats at a nearly normal rate.

I hate that I'm relieved. That I feel attached, that she can still hurt me. I hate that I am almost in tears already, and I don't even know what my father wants to say. I hate that this woman who has no love for me, no sense of me, can still get straight through to the emotions that I reserve for no one. She sneaks her way into my blood and poisons everything.

My father leans back on the chair. He watches me looking at him; I am sure he wonders whether I really am his child. My childhood fantasies mainly involved finding out that my parents were interlopers. That I was in fact the love child of Olivia Newton John and Cliff Richard.

'Your mother has written you a letter, she wants to see you.'

'Well she can fuck off,' I spit the words into my father's face.

'I'll get another drink.' He clicks his fingers at the barman, who delivers fresh drinks to the table even though they don't do table service here. Some people command respect.

I am breathing like I've just run a marathon.

'Right, so she's alive then,' I'm hoping that my father will let the swearing pass.

'Yes, she's very much alive. Sounds very content. She's worked a few things out.'

'Here.' He hands me the letter.

I open it too quickly, and start to read intently. Her handwriting is almost identical to mine. I skim over the words, trying to understand what she wants, aware that my father is watching me.

I chuck it down on the table.

'It's self-centred bullshit.'

'Read it properly, Tiggy.'

'Why?'

'She's giving you an explanation... *read* it... I think she's hoping, well, she wants to make amends.'

'Well it's too late.'

I was 14. She left me.

'She sent me a copy too, Tiggy. Said that she didn't want to do anything secretly, didn't want to undermine our relationship... come on... give her a chance.'

Undermine our relationship? Is he taking the piss?

'I'm not seeing her. I've managed the last six years without her.'

'That's your choice... I think you should at least read it properly.'

'Have you seen her?'

He shakes his head. 'That's not on the agenda. It's you she wants to see.'

We sit in silence digesting the information. I glare at the letter as though it might bite.

My father tries a different tack, 'Margaret thinks it would be good for you too.'

'Oh, for fuck's sake.' I push the letter away from me. It skims across the table.

'Don't use that language again. It's common and I don't want to hear it.'

'Can I go now?'

'*Antigone.*' The reprimand in his voice annoys me.

'Why don't you just rip it up Daddy? I mean it's just her trying to make herself feel better. Am I supposed to say that everything is okay, that it's fine to just bugger off. That I didn't really need her anyway. I mean who needs their mother?'

I am aware that I am ranting.

'You know what Daddy, I'm fine, and I don't have anything to say to her. Not a thing. I don't care if she's found God or Buddha or whatever she was looking for. She can sing *Kum by Aah*, with her hippy friends or whatever she's doing. I'm not going to hug her and cry and say that I forgive her when I don't. And I don't see why I should.'

My father sighs, 'Don't be ridiculous, Tiggy. You're behaving like a child. Overreacting as usual. You must be curious at least. I know she's curious about you.'

'Curious? I'm not a bloody exhibit.'

'No, that's certainly true.'

'Send her a photo. Send her one of those update letters that you send at Christmas. Filling her in on the last six years. Photos of significant events that sort of thing.'

'Think about it, Tiggy.' My father is using his selective deafness technique again.

'Why?'

'Why not? Why do you have to make such a huge fuss about everything?'

'Oh it's me is it? Making a huge fuss about my mother abandoning me. I'm sure a better daughter would have taken it in her stride.'

'Don't be this way.'

'I'll be and do what I want,' I say slowly. Then I pick up my bag and go to leave; only one of the straps is caught under my chair leg so that tumbles as I move away.

I turn the chair the right way up, it falls down again and so I kick it, hard.

'I'd forgotten about your temper tantrums.' My father sounds almost proud.

'I don't have temper tantrums.'

He leans back on his chair and laughs.

I run from the bar, slamming the door hard behind me.

Then promptly throw up.

Chapter Fourteen
Scarlett

That Chinese bloke came back to the club tonight. I hate that. I hate it when they come back and I have to try and remember what I told them last time. I can't be expected to remember everything, so when he came into the club I thought, 'Oh fuck.' But then I figured that if he wants to pay me to cut him up again, then that's his business. He was looking round the club, and when he saw me he lit up like a fucking firework. I kind of waved back and got up to join him at his table.

He was like, 'I came in last night, where were you?' Like he's my mother.

'I missed you Scarlett, have you missed me?'

No, do I look completely mental?

'I've been really lonely without you,' he says and I'm like, 'oh that's really sweet,' while I try to remember his name.

That's the thing with these blokes, they're all fucked up, but mainly they're lonely. Whether it's coz their wives don't think they're interesting or because what they want is too pervy or something. Basically they are sad lonely tossers who come here because they don't have lives.

So he ordered champagne, fags, the works and we were chatting on about all sorts of bollocks. I asked him how his work was going and what he'd been up to. He kept on saying how he couldn't stop thinking about me and trying to get me to kiss him and I was saying, 'The thing is, you know that I can't be seen touching you in the club.'

He was like, 'It's me Scarlett, Guo.' I'm like thank God

he said his name coz that was getting embarrassing.

'I'm not like the others.'

Yes you are mate.

'I care about you Scarlett.' His eyes fill with hearts. 'I want to help you.'

Oh for fuck's sake.

Now the thing about your Guos is that they are the scary ones. They're the ones who truly believe that the time you spend with them is more than just business. I mean they won't allow themselves to believe that the sex was just that, just sex. They gave me some cash and I gave them a blowjob or whatever. They have to turn it into something else so they call it 'love' and then because they think they love me, they want to rescue me.

'That's so sweet Guo,' I say, trying that fake blush I've been practising. 'But I'm fine really, thanks though.' He looks a bit sad for like a second, then he starts on this long old schpiel about how he'd been thinking – he could maybe buy me a flat or something. How we could spend time together – there'd be no pressure. That he wants to do this for me because he cares for me.

Except, of course, we both know that when he came to visit me he'd want more than a cup of tea and a biscuit.

'Can you excuse me Guo?' I say. 'I need to powder my nose.'

I sit in the toilets for longer than I should have done but I didn't want to go back inside. I was thinking that it used to be a laugh, a proper laugh. I don't mind the sex. Although I try not to do the kinky stuff if I can avoid it. It's just the listening to them bollocks. Same old, same old, shit. I'm like, 'If what you want to do is talk, then get a shrink or something. Don't come in here and expect me to have all the answers.' I'm a hooker, what kind of answers do they think they're going to get? Except, of course, they don't really want answers do they? They just want an audience, oh and a fuck.

When I get back to the table, Guo has drunk the rest of the champagne and he's ordering more.

'You know Guo,' I say, 'we had a really nice time the other night. But I think it's best if we just leave it at that.'

That's when he starts to flip, he's all like 'Please don't say that Scarlett, I love you Scarlett, what we have is special Scarlett.'

I try to be nice to him, to explain that I'm not supposed to get close to punters and that it was for the best, but he won't have it, keeps trying to grab my hand or touch my hair. I warn him over and over that it's not allowed.

In the end, I leave him at the table without even asking for my tip.

This other group of punters come in. I get booked with Georgia and Lola and some other girls. Guo sits at his booth drinking the champagne and staring at me with these sad eyes, making a face like his heart is breaking into pieces. I think I might have to call Mario or one of his boys to come and throw him out. But then he gets up, chucks down some money and leaves.

The blokes we are with are some office party nonsense, just out for a laugh, so I give up on the idea of earning decent money for the night and decide to get pissed. Dan Dan the Piano Man has moved on from his jazz shit for the evening and is singing Marvin Gaye numbers like *Sexual Healing*, and *Let's Get It On*. People are trying to dance to it, but they aren't sure quite how. And I'm thinking with the right sort of music this place would be a whole lot better. Dan Dan is making funny faces at that stripper, while he murders Motown numbers. She's all fiddling with her hair, drinking vodka shots and chain smoking.

I think I might stick my fingers down my throat. I mean Dan's like this total south London tosser that plays the sort of music granddads listen to. And Viola Viola needs to raise her standards.

Eventually Viola Viola comes on in this blonde bob wig, leather shorts, basque and this long whip like they use to train horses. She does her *Edge of Heaven* routine, which is a rubbish song for her normally, but tonight she really gives it some, cracking her whip along with the lyrics, like CRACK CRACK CRACK, and the blokes are all like 'YEAH!' Clapping, wolf-whistling and going 'WHOOOOO.'

She seemed to be having fun, playing up to the whole thing and enjoying herself. By the time she leaves the stage, she's sweating and smiling and she has that glow, you know, like I get after a good run.

In the toilets, changing to go home, Lola's licking up cocaine off a hand mirror and bragging to the other girls about how 'Scarlett and I had the most brilliant time at a secret place the other night. Didn't we Scarlett? We danced all night, we had such a laugh.' It pisses me off that she's trying to pretend that we're best mates or something.

So I say 'Lola, just because I went with you once doesn't make us mates, alright.' And she looks at me like I'm a total bitch, but I mean *what?* I'm just being honest.

'Well, you won't want to be going there with me again then.' She shouts and stomps off out of the club with that stupid Georgia running after her, yelling at her 'Wait. Wait for me.'

I don't need to go there with Lola again anyway because Roberto and I have a whole other understanding.

Then on the way home the cab driver is a bastard, takes me totally the wrong way, saying it was coz of road works and bollocks then charges me a fiver more than I normally pay and when I try to argue, he was all like, 'tell it to the police,' with this smug face on him. So I pay him, don't tip and slam the door real hard behind me.

Which was when this man appears outside the B&B. I nearly jump out of my skin. I mean one minute it's just me on the pavement scrabbling in the bottom of my bag for my keys, and the next there's this bloke there, like from nowhere.

And then I realise who it is.

'What the fuck are you doing here?'

I notice that he's crying. Oh please.

'I followed you... I'm sorry... I love you Scarlett.'

I just look at him and say, 'Go home Guo, I'm knackered.' He starts crying really loudly, almost screaming, like I'm hurting him or something.

'Scarlett, please don't do this to me!'

'Guo, get a life.'

I shut the B&B door in his face and go up the stairs to my room. A few seconds later, I hear him on the landing.

'Scarlett... Scarlett.'

What fucker let him in?

'Scarlett... I love you... talk to me.'

So I go back out to talk to him only SHE is already there, the fat Battleaxe, and she's staring at me and Guo is crying and holding up his wrists and I notice two things. One: they're bleeding. Not badly. He's cut them, but he wasn't meaning to kill himself or nothing, and besides he likes blood. But the other thing, the second thing I notice is that he is holding my old set of keys.

Battleaxe is saying, 'Did you give your keys to this gentleman?'

I'm like, 'No. I didn't. I don't know where he got them. I don't know him.'

Then I figure that Guo must have nicked them from

my bag that time and I'm like, 'You cheeky fucker.'

He's bleeding on the lino and crying, 'But Scarlett.' Battleaxe takes the keys from his hands and pushes him out of the door.

Then she turns to me, in her nylon housecoat with these disgusting flowers on it, and like, stains from God knows what. She's got curlers in her hair and cold cream on her face, like it's going to make any difference. You can stick a hat on a pig but it still grunts, know what I mean?

'I'm calling an ambulance,' she says all stiff like, 'and then the police.' There's this big grin on her fat, white creamed face and she says, like she's waited her whole life for this moment, 'And you, you little slut, you have five minutes to pack and get out of here... NOW!'

So, I walk out with the boom box, and my green suit-case and it's dead dark and like, 4am or something and sirens are coming up behind me.

Battleaxe is yelling, 'Never darken my door again.'

And I yell back, 'What is this olden times or some-thing? I mean, who speaks like that anymore you fat bitch.'

And Guo's sat on the pavement cradling his wrists and squealing 'Scarlett...' and muttering 'I'm not like the others. I'm not... I love you...'

He's talking to himself, I guess, because I'm not inter-ested.

He gets up and tries to grab me. I push him away and he's dripping fucking blood onto me. It's on his face where he's been rubbing his eyes, so he's all blood and tears and messed up. I'm like, 'Guo... please... go and get in the ambulance,' which is pulling up outside the B&B by this point, lights flashing, sirens wailing, and like half the street are peering out of their curtains.

People from the B&B are on the pavement staring,

and the police are going to be here any minute so I shout at him, 'Go on, FUCK OFF'. Then the ambulance siren stops, which is a relief as my ears were ringing and maybe the paramedics will make Guo go away.

Which is when I hear my name being called.

I look up and there's that Dan Dan the Piano Man bloke and he's running across the street like a big hero yelling, 'Scarlett, is that you?' and 'Scarlett are you okay?'

Guo's crying at me through his blood and there are more sirens coming, which definitely means police. I run to Dan, and say, 'Help... please,' holding out my suitcase, which he grabs off me, saying 'Come on then'.

And then we leg it to his car. He opens the back door, chucks my suitcase in and says, 'Quick then, if you're coming'. I clamber in after. Then we speed off passing the police cars coming in the opposite direction.

I start laughing because that is just about the most fun I've had in ages.

That Viola Viola is in the passenger seat and she says all posh like 'Dan, shouldn't we stay and talk to the police?'

Dan says, 'No. I don't think so.'

He sort of smiles at me in the rear view mirror, so I say 'Cheers, Dan.'

'Not a problem, I'm not a big fan of coppers myself.'

Viola Viola turns round, smiles and says 'Hi. Gosh what drama! Are you okay?' and reaches her hand back for me to shake. Like she's the queen or something. So I do.

'It's Scarlett isn't it? Hi. I'm um, Tiggy... Well... Viola Viola to you, I guess.' Then she blushes. It makes me laugh, because she even blushes when her clothes are on.

Chapter Fifteen
Tiggy

'Well how long is she planning on staying?'

We're in a window booth in a café near Liverpool Street Station. The commuters stream past in a rush. Disgruntled and disappointed. The tables are greasy. The service is slow. The sandwiches we ordered took an age to come and when they arrived they were soggy. I don't feel like eating anymore anyway. It's a beautiful sunny day. We should be in a park.

We should be lying in the grass reading each other poetry, making daisy chains or whatever. But we're not. We're sat in this grotty café. And once again Tony is pissed off.

'Well Tiggy, how long?'

'I don't know, a few days maybe, while she sorts her things out, a few weeks. I don't know.'

'A few weeks!!'

'What?'

'Tiggy, your timing couldn't be worse. Term is over, we can spend days together, or afternoons at least... and you take in some destitute... prostitute.'

'She's a hostess. It's not the same thing.' Tony looks at me like I'm stupid.

'What do you know about it?' I say indignantly. 'The hostesses talk to people, you don't know everything all the time you know.' Tony laughs, like I'm joking, which irritates me even more.

'Tiggy, you know what I think about that club. I think you just do it to annoy me. She'll rip you off you know. Anyway, more importantly, where are we supposed to meet?'

He's so bloody sure of himself, he's never even met Scarlett. Maybe I do strip to annoy him. But I've told him, if he leaves Sandra then I'll stop.

'Well, I could come to yours.'

Tony fires me a quick glare.

'Don't be silly.'

'We couldn't exactly leave her there on the street, could we?'

'No... I suppose *we* couldn't.'

Here we go.

'He's just a friend Tony. There's nothing going on.'

'Sure.'

'Oh for Goodness sake... *you're* married.'

'It's hardly the same.'

No, he's married to someone and Dan is only a friend. Whereas Tony shares a bed with Sandra every night.

'He's engaged to Jackie... I'm not having sex with him.'

Tony leans back against the red plastic booth and says very slowly; 'I'm not having sex with Sandra.'

He looks me straight in the eyes when he says this. It would be a perfect lie, except one of his eyelids is twitching.

'So you say.'

He raises his hands in disbelief.

'Oh, how did we get back here? I've told you a thousand times Tiggy that my marriage is a sham. It's over. Yes, we share a bed but we don't have sex. We hardly even talk to each other.'

'Then leave her.'

I hold my hands out on the table hoping he'll pick them up.

He doesn't.

'I will, Tiggy. But I can't right now. She'd well, she'd crucify me.'

I thought he said she was too fragile.

Poor fragile Sandra, who can't be upset. I hate her.

'She'd work out that this must have started when you were still at school. She'd get me sacked.' He puts his hands to his forehead. 'I just can't do it right now. But I will, I promise.'

I want it to be true.

'Okay, Tigs?'

Okay then Tony.

'So,' I say gently, 'we can't go to mine today, so what should we do?'

He takes my hands finally and smiles at me.

'Well?'

He's stroking the insides of my wrists. He knows I like that.

'Well what?' I say gently.

'We could check into a hotel?' He's searching for my smile.

'We could.' I grin and he leans over the table, kissing me perfectly.

I do love him.

He whispers into my ear. 'My treat... champagne... the works.' He bites the back of my neck.

Lord, the man is gorgeous.

'So, what are we waiting for?' I say.

We pay and leave.

And I try not to notice that before we pay the bill, Tony checks his watch.

Twice.

I try not to mind that before we check into the hotel, he makes a quick phone call from a phone box. Or that he leaves me standing outside on the street a little too long. I don't comment when he pays for the room in cash, even though we both know it's to make sure Sandra won't find a receipt. Or that the taps in the hotel room have lime scale. And the water comes out brown. That he buys sparkling wine, not champagne.

Because when you love someone, these things are not supposed to matter.

Chapter Sixteen
Tiggy

B ack at the flat Scarlett's left a chain of clothes and damp towels from the bathroom to her bedroom door. I hang the towels back on the rail. I fold her clothes, placing them outside her bedroom. I'm trying not to intrude on her space. It's important to respect people's privacy.

Plainly this concept is lost on Scarlett.

The door to my bedroom is open and the wardrobe door ajar. My red dress is missing. So I can't do my planned routine. I spend ages choosing a different outfit. I'm late for work, again. The tube is packed. I cram myself in. Irritating everyone in the carriage. There is a collective *tut*, which I could really do without. I say 'sorry,' sarcastically to no one in particular. The doors shut and we are all clamped tight. By the time I pull back the doors into Valerios my hair hangs limp and lifeless. I'm sure I smell of other people's sweat.

Scarlett's standing by the bar. She's wearing my dress. She's customised it, so that the cleavage is ripped daringly low. Her long dark hair hangs in ringlets across her otherwise exposed back. She's laughing loudly. Flicking her hair from side to side. She genuinely seems to be enjoying herself. Her customer is patently mesmerised.

My mood darkens.

She whispers something in the man's ear and then crosses the room, slinking towards me, smiling.

'Scarlett, I've looked everywhere for that dress.'

'God, I'm so sorry, Tiggy. You must think I'm such a bitch. I had absolutely nothing to wear. I mean, I must have left half my stuff behind when I was running from that maniac.'

'You could have asked, or left a note or bought yourself something new.'

'Oh, I know, I was in such a state, and I'm still really shaky about going out on my own.'

'Scarlett, I-'

She touches my arm. 'Listen I have to get on, but thanks so much Tigs, you're a real friend.' She strokes my chin and for a moment her eyes are apologetic and warm, then just as quickly they switch back to 'business'.

Before I can respond she is sashaying back across the dance floor. The dress hugging her curves possessively. Then I notice that Dan is watching her. There's so much colour to her. I don't like it. She looks like a fun fair ride.

I go to the bar and order a double vodka.

Chapter Seventeen
Tiggy

'So did you buy this when you were travelling then?'

Scarlett's holding up a painted wooden elephant. We're in my bedroom. She's giving me a manicure as an apology for stealing my dress.

'Oh yeah. I spent a couple of weeks in India, you know, like you do.'

'Do you? So is that where these spinny things are from then?'

'They're prayer wheels and they're from Nepal, or Tibet I think. When I was trekking in the Himalayas, the Sherpa... oh actually Scarlett, you know what... it's a lie, I've never been travelling.'

'But you said-'

'I've never so much as seen a yak, it's all a lie. Just don't tell my father.'

'Oooh, this sounds good, come on then spill.' Scarlett's pupils dilate and she rubs her hands together. 'Dirty little secrets are my favourite.'

So I explain.

About how my father and I have been in a power struggle our whole lives. How we've become expert at heightened politeness. How my mother gave up negotiating between us, absenting herself from mealtimes, staying in her room, drinking too much. That when I was 14 she absented herself entirely.

'So, your Mum left you?'

'That's right.'

'So, like your Dad's brought you up has he?'

'After a fashion.'

'So why did you lie to him about travelling?'

'Oh, I don't know... habit maybe.'

If I had concerns about what it would be like living at home after I finished school then my father must have been terrified. He'd immediately bought me a round-the-world ticket.

'Go have some adventures with your pals. I'll put a cheque in each month, so all you have to worry about is enjoying yourself.'

The ticket taunted me from my bedroom shelf. Another fabulous gift, which I was shamelessly ungrateful for. I didn't want to go around the world. I didn't have any pals. I didn't want to leave Tony. But there was the ticket, printed evidence that my father wanted me a few thousand air miles away from him and Margaret.

I gave in.

I made up the names of some friends, invented a few vague locations, found the lies tripping off my tongue and made my father happier than anything I had told him previously.

I never got on a plane.

Instead I sold the ticket through *LOOT* to an Australian in Earls Court. Then I rented this flat and for a few months, I rolled around on the bed, deliriously happy to finally have somewhere of my own. Somewhere I could smoke and have sex. Tony brought his own soap and aftershave and left it in my bathroom. A few months later he brought over some boxer shorts. Okay the movement was slow, but we were headed in the right direction.

Once a month, I used a payphone and called my father from a fabricated holiday brochure location.

'I'm in Agra, yes, Taj Mahal. It's amazing isn't it? An architectural masterpiece. The weather? Great.

Really sunny... anyway... must dash, you know how it is, museums to see, galleries to visit.'

And somewhere along the way time passed. School holidays ended, terms started. And Tony didn't tell Sandra.

'Cappadoccia. Yeah, glorious isn't it? I can't wait to show you the photos. So, Happy Christmas... no a bunch of us are getting together, it's going to be fabulous.'

I spent Christmas day waiting for Tony to call. Hoping that he might somehow find an excuse to get away for a few hours. I lit candles and I shaved my legs. The radio jingled out festive tunes as I valiantly tried to rally against the voices telling me that I meant nothing. That I was on my own. That no one and nobody cared. Tony called at 6pm. At 6.15pm I took down the tinsel and the mistletoe and all the Christmas trimmings and went to bed.

Two weeks later, I called my father and told him that I was coming home.

For the next three weeks, I spent my mornings on sun beds and my afternoons in shops full of hippy paraphernalia, buying sarongs and wall hangings and other evidence of my travels. I even lit incense and held it over my clothes to give the extra dimension of authenticity. I slept the night in my clothes. I left my hair unwashed. I filled two suitcases with dirty clothes and souvenirs and took the underground to Heathrow. From there I took a taxi all the way back into town and to Margaretta Terrace. I had a whole lost luggage story to explain the loss of the photos. On a cold February morning I stood on his doorstep, surrounded by suitcases. It had been 18 months since I had seen my father and I was strangely pleased to be home. I thought, when he comes to the door I will throw my arms around him. I will force him to love me.

I had to knock three times before I heard footsteps.

I put down all my bags and held out my shaking arms.

Margaret answered the door. 'Your father had to go away darling, on business, he said he's sorry.'

'Right... of course,' I said picking up my suitcases, following her into the house.

When he rang the next day, I heard Margaret prompting him, 'Do you want to talk to Tiggy? She's back, remember?' I pulled the covers over my head and pretended to be asleep when she called out to me to come to the phone. He hadn't missed me at all.

A few days later I told Margaret I'd found a flat and would be moving out.

Scarlett gestures to the batique cloth on the wall, 'So all this stuff in here is fake then?'

'Well, not exactly, it's 100% authentic Camden market.'

She rubs the silk between her fingers, 'Nice stuff... and your father has no idea that your journey was bogus?'

'Nope, he thinks I'm the most travelled waitress in West London.'

'Well, aren't you the dark horse, eh?'

She can talk. Scarlett's a master at changing the subject whenever I ask her about herself or her childhood.

'So, what about you then Scarlett... have you travelled much?'

'I took the Northern Line all the way to Morden once. South London. Yeuch.' She shudders exaggeratedly. 'Fucking nightmare place. Does that count?'

Chapter Eighteen
Tiggy

For a change I arrive early at Valerios. Mario's supervising a delivery of champagne, checking each box, counting every bottle.

I watch Dan's act. He's on good form. Inventing lyrics and acting up for the crowd. Dan toys with songs, changing words and adding verses. He tells me it is all done with 'massive amounts of respect.' My guess is that it's to stave off his boredom.

'You are all I long for – though your mother is a bore,' he sings, delighted with his interpretation.

I change backstage, and when Dan pushes the curtain back I hand him my cassette.

'I'll put the chair out.' He looks at the tape and he grins.

I am wearing a tiny school uniform. But that's not why he's smiling.

It's the song. Dan loves this song.

I don't know how many of the customers really get it. It's hardly a crowd pleaser. I think if I did it more than twice a month then Mario would sack me. But sometimes a girl just wants to lose herself in a song.

And this is the mood I'm in.

'Ladies and Gentleman... tonight... all the way from Los Angeles...'

Dan likes to ad lib.

'For one night only... please give a big Valerios welcome to... Viola Viola.' The crowd applaud and then the first few melodic notes of *At Seventeen* start.

I pick up the chair. I kneel on it. I drape myself over the seat. I swing it around back to front and straddle it. I put my finger in my mouth. I forget that I'm wearing a very small pleated skirt and that my blouse is a few sizes too small, my underwear red and visible.

I love this song.

Janis Ian is singing. Her voice is breathy, innocent and yet she sounds resigned to her fate as one of the non-beautiful. Sometimes music can transport you. While my body follows the rehearsed routine, my mind assaults me with well-worn memories.

And I am back at school.

The first time I saw the school buildings. The red brick. The turrets. The teachers in their black robes. How my knee socks kept falling around my ankles. About the flag stone corridors that creaked with ghosts in winter. About walking along snowy paths to lessons. About Viola spitting at me, tugging at my hair. I think of queuing to use the phone. I wanted to beg my father to take me away. Whenever he answered my voice seized up and I lost my courage.

'I'm fine,' I'd say. 'I'm fine.' And I'd put down the handset and run back to my room.

I'd cry because I was stuck there and I was so un-happy.

The song ends.

I find a smile and a bow from somewhere. Pick up my clothes and run back stage.

I can't stop shaking. I sit on the floor, my bra bunched in my hands.

Earlier Scarlett was asking me why I'm a stripper, and I couldn't think of an answer.

Basically it was the only job I was offered. Because after years of expensive education, I am too messed up to be good for anything else. I'd signed up with an employment agency as soon as I got back from my fake travelling. But other than a three-week reception job, every time they sent me for an interview I blew it. Nerves got to me. I was unable to say anything sensible in front of a panel. After another disastrous interview where I actually developed a stutter (I've never stuttered), I bought a sandwich, and sat in Soho Square chewing mouthfuls of ham and coleslaw. Trying to swallow enough pride to call my father and ask him again for money.

I closed my eyes and held my pen over the Evening Standard one last time letting chance dictate. And there it was, an advert saying 'attractive girls needed urgently.'

It was the *urgently* that made me call. I hoped that maybe the urgent need would override my lack of attractiveness.

Mario asked me a few questions and when it was obvious that I was blowing the whole thing, I started to cry.

'Hey. Hey honey,' he said like some 1970s B movie actor. 'Hostesses need to be able to chat. It's pretty much an essential job requirement. But... you're young, you're pretty enough... you can't dance by any chance can you? I really need a dancer.'

'I did... um... ballet for seven years... when I was younger?' I didn't mention that I was terrible, that people called me the dancing dumpling.

'Ballet? Okay, well how do you fancy ballet dancing in your underwear?'

'Stripping?' I blushed.

Mario looked at me with interest. 'No, dancing.

You'll take off your clothes, like stripping I suppose, but you can keep your underwear on. Look, you need a job and I need a dancer. What have you got to lose?'

And I had a choice; to dance in my underwear or to call my father and tell him I needed his help.

I was terrible of course, but Mario said that it was good that I was bad. That clubs were full of women dancing and stripping and looking jaded and that my embarrassment was sexy.

'It's good. You looking scared is different. It's sexy. The punters will believe that it's your first time and they're getting to watch. So, three times each night. Five nights a week. £50 per time... interested?'

£750 a week in cash was more than I could earn anywhere else.

Of course, after a few months, Mario was waiting when I came off stage.

'You need to practice. The virgin stripper thing isn't so convincing anymore, so you need to look like you love it. Like there's nowhere else you would rather be. That being up there in front of them turns you on.'

'Okay Mario.'

'Oh and tomorrow you can take off your top.'

He made it sound like a gift and I could have said 'no'. But the truth was I liked the club. I was undercover. I'd found this whole new world that had nothing to do with anyone from my past. Nothing to do with me. Antigone Arnold would never be working somewhere like this, but Viola Viola?

And Viola Viola wouldn't let a little thing like dancing topless bother her.

I used to think that the more often I take off my clothes, the further I'll get away from the scared child I used to be. That somehow the confidence I find on stage will spill over into my real life. I'll somehow assimilate the best parts of Viola Viola and all the nagging insecurities that I drag around behind me will stop.

Now I think taking your top off in front of strangers is probably a slow track to empowerment.

On the stage now Dan's singing *How Deep is Your Love?*

Beyond the curtains there's the drum of easy conversation, clanking glasses.

And I need to get up off the floor.

Chapter Nineteen
Scarlett

I go out for a run to try to work out where I am. I go the wrong way at first, alongside Shepherd's Bush Green which is essentially a campsite for bench alkies. Keeping the green on my left I carry on running along the high street, past the bargain tat shops and dodgy takeaways, then along past these shit stalls selling scourers and toilet brushes and plastic crap. It's like Chapel Market and all those outings with Mum when I was a kid. She'd give me five quid and tell me to 'run along'. Her holding some bloke's hand and laughing too much at his shit jokes, and me on my best behaviour, being as sweet as pie, because of course that was what the fiver was really for.

She paid me to act like a loving daughter, so that these sad old drunks that she picked up would think she was a nice woman, so I smiled, held her hand and called her 'Mummy darling'. I took the money and pretended to like her knob-head boyfriends, because even then, before The Tits arrived, I was smiling and grinning at men I hated, and getting paid.

I'm obviously going the wrong way, so when I spot another jogger going the other way, I follow him. He has this gigantic Afro hair with this sweatband through it, like an extra from *Fame*. I follow him back along the road and then we are running back past Tiggy's building, Daffodil Towers.

What kind of name is Antigone anyway?

Antigone is just a little bit confusing. She talks like that posh woman in *The Good Life,* but lives on the top floor of that scummy high-rise block. But compared to the B&B the flat is huge and light, and there's a great view over what must be loads of London, but mostly she keeps the curtains closed. Walking into the sitting room was like going into Reckless Records or one of those dodgy record shops in where fat men go to smoke and sweat. Tiggy has old time muso posters and piles of vinyl everywhere. I half expected some The Cure T-shirt-wearing lardball to spring up from behind the sofa, and try to force me to listen to Joy Division or some other miserable band with wrist slitting lyrics.

Her records are in some kind of order only she under-stands like indie/rock crap up front, then all this turgid girlie romantic bollocks at the back. But, at least there's plenty of space, you could fit all of Mum's flat into the sitting room, and then some. And she's got so much stuff everywhere, pictures and ethnic ornaments. There's an old brown velveteen sofa, a couple of saggy beanbags, one of which spills polystyrene balls onto the carpet when you move. The coffee table has a rack underneath where she keeps dog-eared back copies of *Cosmo, Smash Hits, NME* and *Melody Maker.*

A whole wall is dedicated to books, mostly the kind of boring crap they tried to make us read at school, and they're all organised in alphabetical order. Like she doesn't have time to pull the curtains or wash the dishes, but thinks it's important to put the Jane Austen before the Charlotte Bronte. I've never understood why people keep books after they've read them, unless it's for show or something, like, 'Ooh look at me I can read!'

She's like, totally apologetic and embarrassed about everything. I'd thought the blushing was to do with taking off her clothes, but I bet that girl blushes in her sleep. She was apologising even as she showed me around.

Like, 'Sorry the kitchen's in a bit of a mess,' and 'It's not much I know, but there's a bath and a shower and look,' she opened a mirrored wall cabinet, 'You can have this side for your things... I'll... um... make some space for you I mean...sorry.'

'S'okay, Tiggy,' I said, coz really it is, I mean, she's helping me out, so she doesn't need to apologise.

I'm in her spare room or the *boxroom* she calls it. It has brilliant white walls, a single bed and a chest of drawers. It's the only small room in the flat, and the only room without a window.

I said 'It's t'riffic. I'm really grateful. This is so nice of you,' though really it looks like a prison cell. Tiggy says not to bother with rent, that I should just chip in when I can. And I'm thinking that she just talked herself out of £50 a week there for no reason, and I'm kind of working out what kind of a lunatic would do that when she says, 'Oh and help yourself to food.' Which must be a joke, because the fridge is completely empty and smells like a bin.

Afro boy steps up his pace and so I have to run fast to keep up. He's at least six foot and has thighs like a bloody horse. He has a Walkman, I figure maybe I'll get a Walkman too, or borrow Tiggy's when I'm running. He strides over the zebra crossing in three giant leaps. I'm so caught up in following him that I nearly get turned into roadkill by a taxi. The driver beeps at me and starts holloring something out of his window, so I give him both fingers and then look to see where Afro boy's got to. There's a gate on the right leading into a huge park, I can just about make out his heels in the distance. And I'm thinking it's gonna be weird sharing a flat with someone again. So far I've lived with Mum and Clare, but they were nothing like Tiggy.

'The world doesn't revolve around you,' Mum said on the day I left. She lined my stuff up along the stairs in bin bags and stood at the door waiting for the taxi to come, she kept checking in the road like maybe it would be late or something. Then she looked at me and she said, 'Don't look at me like that. I'm entitled to a life as well you know.'

Her life? Jesus, if that was living then I wasn't interested.

She gave me a hug goodbye and then burst into tears, like this wasn't what she wanted, like she couldn't just change everything. Then she ran into the house and slammed the door behind her. Mum was always crying at stuff that was her fault.

Pete, her latest boyfriend, was watching at the window. He gave me this angry look like it was my fault, like, look what you've done now. So I just stuck my tongue out at him and gave him the finger, then I went to stay with my mate Clare.

Clare and me got on fine for the first year or so, smoking dope and watching old black and white movies or videos of *The A Team.* We could watch entire episodes and not get a line wrong. Me and Clare were our own little A team, you know hiding out from the big bad world. Then Clare met Kieran and then it was the same as with Mum. Once women get blokes, they don't want mates around anymore.

I phoned home and spoke to Mum, who said that her and Pete were doing really well *now.* As though the only problem before was me, or something. She said that it was my business what I did; I was all grown up now. Then she said that Pete was talking about having some more kids, some of their own.

'He says he wants our kids, you know, proper kids.' Like I was some kind of starter kid, the sort you practice on, then one day you do it for real. I mean, what a bitch.

'I haven't got any money if that's what you're ringing for,' she added.

'I know,' I said. 'You never have any money.'

The signs all tell me that I'm in Kensington Gardens, which is like a bigger posher version of Vikki Park. I'm doing alright until Afro boy breaks out into a sprint, and I know I'm fucked, there is no way to keep up with him. So, I relax into a jog and feel my body sigh with relief. I reckon that living near a park like this is gonna be excellent for my running. There's like, a million different routes to try. I was getting bored of Regents Canal anyways.

Clare lent me a suitcase, this big green cardboard thing, and we got just about everything in it. She swapped me my stereo for her boom box. I looked like Julie fucking Andrews in *The Sound of Music*. Clare asked me where I was planning on going.

'Here,' I showed her the advert.

'You do know what a hostess club is, don't you?'

In my *interview* I gave Mario some old bollocks about being 19 and living in a flat-share. He said I should think of a different name, something classy. He asked me to give him a twirl and he must have liked what he saw because he said I could start straight away.

'But baby, your hair? It's too bleached, your clothes are too tarty. But if you buy something pretty, do something with your hair and think of a new name then... yes, okay I'll give you shot.'

I dyed my hair dark brown and nicked a posh red

dress. When I looked at myself with my new dark hair, my skin looked even paler, and my eyes almost purple. I'd never worn a dress like that before, not one with a tag saying £250.00. I figured I looked a bit like that actress in *Gone with the Wind*.

I jog slowly along enjoying the sunshine until Kensington Gardens turns into Hyde Park, where they are putting up all these bandstands and speakers. This roadie bloke in a Meat Loaf T-shirt yells out at me, 'You want some water gorgeous?' I stop for a second and drink practically the full bottle. He watches me like I'm even more fascinating than his latest tattoo. When I hand the empty bottle back to him he's like, 'You wanna see Pavarotti?' Snorting like a donkey when I say, 'Who's she then?'

Turns out that Pavarotti is a fat Italian who sings songs about Cornettos. The roadie bloke was reckoning that he could get me in backstage, telling me that there would be 'loads of famous people' and 'champagne and free food' and that 'all the beautiful people will be there'.

I was gonna ask how come they'd let a fat, tattoo-obsessed Meat Loaf like him in, when he said like he was hoping to persuade me, 'and Charles and Di are coming... you could see Di right up close'. Which was kind of desperate, like he thought rubbing shoulders with some pedigree humans was my idea of a good time.

'Cheers, but I get more than enough dim Sloane at home,' I say flashing him a giant smile. 'Don't need to go out for more.' Then I pound off down the gravel.

I sprint hard back to Daffodil Towers, where Princess Tiggy will be waiting for her handsome prince to arrive on his white horse and save her. Seems to me that Lady Di might have swallowed a crock of sentimental, because I've seen a few Disney films on video, and the princess almost never has to sit in the park in the rain watching some fat Italian singing about ice-cream. And the prince is almost never big eared and bald.

Chapter Twenty
Scarlett

I t starts to rain just as I get back to the flat. I figure I'll take the stairs, as the lift works about as often as Lola. I crash into the flat knackered and sweating, the booming of blood thumping round my body making me invincible.

Sloane reject Antigone is still there on the sofa with a book. Like she hasn't moved a muscle. A gorgeous sunny day and she's curled up on the sofa, a cigarette in one hand, book in the other and this concentrated face on her, like there's life-altering information on the pages that she needed to understand.

'Hi,' she says, and looks at me with those Bambi eyes of hers.

I wave, because I can't quite speak yet.

The phone rings and when she answers it she goes all soft and like, 'Hello stranger.'

'Hang on a sec,' she whispers into the receiver, cradling it on her shoulder. Taking the phone into her room and closing the door. Then all I can hear is her murmuring real low and then occasionally laughing and stuff. I get a glass of water from the kitchen, trying not to trip over the bloody phone cord. Then I pick up the book to see what is so worth reading and it's this soft shit love story where all the women are sleeping with other people's husbands, and they all spend loads of time agonising over it. Seems to me that if it bothers them that much then they should stop and that to spend a whole afternoon reading a book is a waste of time.

When she comes back out of the room she's all flushed

and happy.

'So was that your boyfriend then?'

She blushes, like this is really personal question, 'Well sort of.'

Then I get it, the book, the phone call, the mooning about and looking lame. She's shagging some married bloke and she's not even getting paid for it. I think maybe I should say something to her about how I spend night after night with married blokes. That if he's telling her that his wife doesn't understand him then she's being a mug. If you're going to waste your days mooning over something then it should at least be something worth mooning over. The men that I talk to divide women into two categories, women you marry and women you shag, and if you're one then you can't be the other.

'I'm desperate for the toilet,' she says blushing again and running out of the room, 'been crossing my legs for ages... sorry.'

Well, it's her life, and if she wants to waste it then it is up to her. If there's one thing that Mum did teach me it's that some people don't want to be happy. Some people prefer to spend their lives doing nothing. It's like they set their sights on something so small that they achieve it on the first day and then sit back and get pissed for the rest of their life.

Mum once said to me that all she wanted was a bloke.

'I just want someone to come home to, someone to chat to in the evenings, you know, watch TV with.' And I thought that was fucking pathetic. I mean, is that it? Her one big goal was to find someone to sit on the sofa with her and watch the TV. Get a fucking dog!

Then there are the people who waste their lives on something they can't ever have, like someone else's husband. It seems to me that it is just as pointless.

Tiggy's left her cigarettes on the coffee table, it's practically a full pack, so I pull a couple free, sticking one behind my ear for later. If she's gonna leave them out like that, then she's got to expect a few to go AWOL, I mean I'm an addict aren't I? I can't be held responsible.

Each time Mum brought a bloke home it went the same way. A few weeks of them snogging about all over the place and giggling in the bedroom, then it would turn into fights. Then he'd stop coming over so much. Mum would spend days sat by the phone, not leaving the house or when she did coming in and saying 'has he called?' and looking like the world was over when I said 'no'. Then weeks of lying in bed, moping into dirty sheets and doing her head in over what she was doing wrong and then being pissed and crying and saying 'why does everyone leave me?' with mascara over her face and her breath smelling like a tramp.

I was like, 'Do you really need to ask? They leave you Mum because it's too easy. Because however much make-up you wear, however good your legs are, you're desperate. Once they've shagged you in all the positions their little minds can think of then they get bored. Because the only thing you know anything about is soap operas and TV quiz shows.'

She'd stand there in her manky grey leggings, her hair bleached to the point of snapping, looking at me like I was this complete bitch.

'You don't understand about love,' she'd say when she came home from the pub all excited because she'd just met another bloke, who I already knew was going to do exactly the same routine on her. And I'd think, no, maybe I don't. But what I did understand was that whatever she was doing with these blokes didn't have anything to do with love either. She just called it that because she thought it sounded better than sex.

116

Tiggy comes back into the sitting room. She turns on the TV, stopping the channel on some soft shite movie with Barbara Streisand in it. She turns the volume down and picks up her novel, settling down into a beanbag. Like that's her sorted for the day.

I go back into the kitchen for another glass of water.

Mum's life is in that TV set, watching pretend people get married, have babies and argue with their family. Like watching life on the screen is better than getting out and having one of her own. On her beanbag, Antigone is lighting herself another cigarette and flicking over another page of the stupid novel, smiling. One bloody phone call from some married bloke and she's grinning like an idiot.

I'm thinking that she's some kind of a Muppet, because all it took was a few lies about being 21, and my real name being Charlene, and she's practically saying, 'ooh, live with me for free and be my best friend'. I mean she's gonna end up in bin liners under the floorboards if she's not careful, she's lucky I'm not a psycho.

Women are so bloody crap, it's not surprising that people take the piss. Women are hopeless, but then men are just as bad, they're all fucked up in one way or another.

I worked that out years ago.

Life should be about going for something you can trust, like cash.

Chapter Twenty One
Tiggy

I'm holding the letter like it's a grenade, wondering
if I should pull the pin.

My father has sent it on to me. His instructions on a
post-it.

'You should read this.'

I don't want to read it. I should just throw it away.

She walked out on me. She didn't even say goodbye.
I was 14 years old.

When she first left I assumed that she would come
back. For a few months I waited constantly for her
phone call and an explanation. I experimented with
hiding in the toilets between lessons staring at my
reflection, my body and skin betraying me. Concluding
that if I was thinner and had longer hair, no spots,
then maybe I would have friends, maybe my mother
would come back.

At home for the half-term break, 'Mummy' became
an abstract concept. Neither of us dared to discuss her.
When my father looked at me his eyes filled with guilt.
And I swelled with shame. It seemed easier to stay in
my room, to avoid him.

He insisted that we should share breakfast together. Already stiff with discomfort, conversations
between my father and me became staccato.

'Not going out today?'

'No.'

'I don't know what you do in that room.'

'Nothing much.'

'Well, I'll be in the office all day if you want to come?'

'No.'

'Okay, Well, um, I'll leave you some money shall I? In case you want to call your friends and go out.'

Back at school things didn't improve. I missed her. I was angry, resentful; emotions tumbled from me when I least needed them. I cried in class. I broke down in the middle of a hockey match. I developed a rash across my face and neck and spent two weeks in the school sanatorium smeared in cream that smelt of chlorine. Scratching at myself.

'I'm fine,' I'd say when my father called. 'Everything is fine.'

I turned to the usual suspects.

I promised myself that I would never eat again. A promise I didn't keep: a promise that morphed into forcing myself to vomit up my meals; taking laxatives and scoring her initials into my arms in the hope that it would kill my longing.

I spent my father's money on vodka and cigarettes. My hair grew, my spots cleared up. By the time I turned 15, four months later, I had lost two stone. I traded my size 14 school skirts in for size 10 at the school shop.

The girls at school still called me Piggy Tiggy.

My mother still didn't come back.

But now there was Tony, and he made everything feel more bearable. I stopped cutting myself, I didn't want him to know.

But I started being sick without the help of fingers down my throat. I fended off my anxiety by dreaming of Tony or of my mother. Imagining her in different scenarios. She might be sat on Ayers Rock. Or riding elephants through the streets of Bombay? Or had she been taken hostage and imprisoned somewhere hot and dusty. Was she right now digging her way through the sand, trying to tunnel her way back to me? Perhaps armed soldiers were sitting at her door? I would have her charm these rebels, seduce them and outwit them. She would find her way back to me across the deserts.

I needed a reason for her abandonment. I found an easy target in my father. Perhaps he had been violent or threatening. Was he keeping back the letters that she wrote to me? My life became a succession of inventions.

'That's okay. I'll be fine here,' I said when he called to say that I needed to stay at school over Christmas. He had to work and with my mother gone there wasn't anyone else.

'You'll have more fun there with your friends than with your boring old father won't you?'

Fun? Friends? What was he talking about? There was only Tony and even he was leaving me immediately after Christmas day. Spending New Year with Sandra's family somewhere miles away.

'You know it's such a relief to know that you're happy and settled. I'll be away working so it's such a help.'

'I'll be fine. You're right, it'll be fun... see you next year then, Daddy.'

School was a throng of activity. Parents quickly detailing holiday plans, skiing here, Disneyland there. In spite of myself, I still hoped my father's car would come up along the drive, if perhaps there had been a change of plans. Range Rovers, Mercedes and Jaguars filled up the driveway and then emptied urgently back out again.

As the last car pulled out of the drive I wrote 'fuck you all' on the misted condensation on the window.

Four of us ate dinner in the canteen.

We sang carols around the Christmas tree in the Foyer.

None of us made eye contact.

I played Cliff Richard records at top volume and rocked back and forth on my bed crying. I thought; if Cliff were my father, he would understand. I walked up and down along the school hallways hoping to see Tony. I saw him with a group of teachers, pulled myself up tightly into the wall. The sound of Sandra's laughter echoing sharply through the corridors.

Christmas Eve I took a three-hour bath. Topping up the temperature every ten minutes, my toes curled around the taps, a razor blade in my hand.

I saw myself floating in a sea of red.

I wondered who would find me, who would contact my mother, whether my funeral would be enough to bring her back.

I cut into my arms gently, calmly, a salutation. Feeling pleasurably sinful as the hot blood dribbled along my hands and down my fingers. I wrote my parents names on the bathroom tiles in my blood.

Later I bathed my wrists in TCP and clenched my teeth against the stinging.

Tony met me in the music rooms to give me my Christmas gift, a silver bracelet. He turned over my wrists and stroked my cuts.

'Oh baby,' he said. 'It's okay Tiggy. You've got me.' He put his arms around me while I cried. He kissed away my tears.

He lay me down on his sofa and undid my blouse and lifted my skirt.

He filled in the hollows and empty spaces where my parents should have loved me.

And now she's back.

I wave the letter in my hand. I put it in the bin. She's too late.

I take it back out again.

I don't need her anymore. I put it in the shoebox under my bed. She had the chance to be my mother and she didn't want it.

I take it back out again.

I waited every day for weeks for a letter. Each morning when the prefects handed out the post I waited. I was certain that there would be something. Whenever I saw the blue and red of airmail letters in their hands my heart skipped a beat and I waited.

She didn't write.

On my 16th birthday I felt sure that there would be a phone call, a present. I thought maybe something anonymous. Something cryptic. I thought there is no way that she can forget that I am sixteen today.

Or my 18th.

Or my 21st.

But there was nothing.

I should burn it.

I take a lighter and hold the letter over the ashtray and light the corner. It catches and glows red and gold.

I blow it out quickly.

The edges are singed and warm. I open the letter. Reading it again won't change anything.

I read it.

I throw it in the bin. I lie on the sofa and chain smoke.

The key turns in the door and the front door bangs open, slamming against the wall. Scarlett is in the building.

'Wow that was fab. Bloody fab.'

She's wearing red lycra shorts and a running vest that has a long dark V of sweat between her breasts. Her long hair is pulled back into a ponytail and her face is makeup free. Her eyes are smaller, her face younger.

I'd forgotten about Scarlett.

'You ok?'

I can't deal with her right now.

'I'm fine. Absolutely fine.'

She cocks her head to one side.

'You sure?'

I nod. She shrugs.

'Okay then. Well I'm going to have a shower. I stink.' She shoves her nose under her armpits. 'Yuck. I smell worse than Lola's giblets. Hey, do you fancy some company on the way to work? Walk in together?'

'Sure... absolutely... yeah... let's do that.'

'Great.'

Then she heads off to the shower.

I wait until I hear the water come on and then I take the letter from the bin. I unfold it and put it back into the envelope.

Chapter Twenty Two
Tiggy

On the way to Valerios, I glimpse what life is like for the beautiful. We walk in a symphony of wolf-whistles, smiles and lascivious stares. Scarlett chats on oblivious, her arm linked through mine, her hand resting on my forearm.

'Scarlett, is there anyone who isn't in love with you?' She laughs, her hair tumbling along her back. I swear I hear the sound of cars colliding.

'They're looking at both of us. And it isn't anything to do with love, babe.'

'It's definitely just you. No one ever looks at me.'

'Well, you're not exactly inviting them to are you? You are dressed like a lezzer.'

I'm wearing black DMs with thick black tights under cut off Levi hot pants. A little black T-shirt and a red woollen beret. Scarlett is wearing a low cut gold baby doll dress with red strappy stilettos and attitude.

'I do not.' Well, perhaps a little. 'Anyway, even if I dressed differently, men wouldn't look at me the way they look at you.'

'Tiggy, men pay to watch you night after night, you think they don't want to look at you on the street for free?'

'Well-'

'Seriously, if I was a lezzer, I'd fancy you. Definitely, you're smart, pretty and when you make the effort you're sexy. What more could a young girl want?'

'Sexy... me? I hardly think-'

'Yes Tiggy, sexy. Blimey how do you get up on stage

every night?'

'It's pretend, I pretend, you know... it's... well, not the same.'

'Can I ask you something?'

I nod.

'Why be a stripper when you're so shy?'

'I... well... I.'

'I'm waiting?'

We're outside Valerios by now and I grab at the door and swing myself through it, almost knocking into Mario as I do.

'Eh, eh careful. Watch where you're going will you.'

'Sorry, sir.'

I practically scuttle out of the foyer. Scarlett follows me into the club.

'Sir?' She's biting her lip with glee.

'It's a school thing... how embarrassing. God, I'm such a disaster.'

'Tiggy, lighten up will you. It's funny. Oh come here you.' She holds my face in her hands. 'It's funny... *sir!*' She kisses my nose.

'Scarlett.' We're receiving curious glances from the other hostesses. Scarlett and I are creating a good deal of gossip right now. Usually strippers, waitresses and hostesses don't mix outside their groups. And no one seems to mix much with Scarlett. Dan says that there is probably a good reason why. I'm not so sure. I know what it feels like to be left out. Besides, I'm proud to walk in with her.

Well, unless the looks are about something else.

'Scarlett, I'm not a lesbian or anything. You know that right?'

'Shame.' She kisses me again, this time on the mouth. 'Laters. Gotta go work.'

'Scar... Scar... let,' I stammer. 'Are you?'

She smiles and places her hand on the back of my head, gently pulling my face towards hers, her lips brushing my cheeks. She smells of wine and roses. I stand frozen as she whispers into my ear.

'Tiggy, for the right money I'm whatever you want me to be.'

Chapter Twenty Three
Scarlett

I'm in the money. Oh yes. I am going to be so rich.

This evening started out really badly. I had this punter, this moronic stingy bastard. We were watching Viola Viola. It's weird now I'm living with her, she's not half as interesting as I thought she looked. So, I was sat with this bloke, the moronic stingy one, who said his name was Herbert. I didn't believe him, I don't think there's anyone called Herbert under the age of 75. And he was hard work.

'Can I call you Herb?' I said.

'No... call me Herbert.'

'Sorry.'

'Good. Because I'm paying you to do what I want you to do. Alright?'

So I said, 'alright' although to tell the truth, I wasn't in the mood. Some of them obviously think they don't get enough respect at home or something. They get off on coming in here and making you act like their servant. They call you a whore to your face, say that what you do is disgusting.

He told me only to talk when he said I could talk, only to drink when he said I could drink. Stingy bastard. Only one bottle of champagne between us and he made it last nearly an hour. Then when he said he was leaving and I politely reminded him about the voluntary hostess tip he tutted.

'I told you. Only talk to me when I give you the word.' He picked up the laminate card from the table and made a big show of reading it out. 'Customers are reminded that it is polite to leave a tip for your hostess. The club recommends a tip of at least £50, however this is entirely at your discretion... entirely at my discretion you see, Scarlett.'

I smiled sweetly. Tosser.

'Here.' He opened his bulging wallet. Making sure I could see how much cash there was and taking out a fiver. 'That's for you. Try and learn to be a bit more obedient in future.' Then he heaved his fat arse up off the seat and strode off out of the club.

I was just beginning to think that I am never going to make my target by September when one of the waitresses came over and said that Mario wanted to see me upstairs.

Now the thing you should know about Mario is that he thinks he's the main man. Even though he's a new name in the world of hostess clubs, he's making his mark real quick. Mario acts like he's your actual Don Corleone of the sex industry. He fancies himself as a proper gangster, someone you can't say no to. Saying no to Mario is like personally deciding to quit and making sure you never get work again. Oh and possibly saying goodbye to your legs/arms/tits. Whatever he feels like cutting off.

If he had half a brain, Mario could be a big time psychopath.

I go round behind the bar and up the stairs to Mario's flat. I haven't been in there since my first week. Mario likes to 'introduce' himself to all his girls, if you know what I mean. It's an initiation test, a rite of passage and I've never heard any of the girls complain because Mario is so smooth that actually we're all a little in love with him. There was a rumour that Lola and him were together for a while. I guess it must be true, because there's no other reason why anyone would have a manky old tart like her working in their place.

But anyhow he's the big cheese and he asked for me. ME!

Chapter Twenty Four
Scarlett

Mario loves to dress in black. Black leather trousers and tight black T-shirts. Everything in the flat is black or silver. It's that whole bachelor pad minimalist shit that he does. He beckons me over to the leather sofa next to him. Leaning back and smoking his cigarette and leering at me. I'm a bit shaky coz he's not only the big cheese but he's pretty sexy with it. Mario has this whole Mickey Rourke in *9½ Weeks* thing going on.

'Scarlett, I need you to do me a favour.'

I say, 'Sure Mario.' Like I'm totally cool with it, when actually I'm more, 'I hope he isn't expecting me to shoot someone for him or something'.

He goes, 'This is important, okay?'

So I say, 'Okay' and fix him a look right in his eyes that says I'm cool with whatever.

He takes two cigarettes from this gold tin, puts them in his mouth, lighting them with one Zippo flick. He hands me one and then exhales and I swear on Mum's life that the smoke comes out of his mouth and makes the shape of a skull.

'I have this friend. He's shall we say a business colleague. A funder, you know what I mean?' I nod. 'His son, he's going to be 18 and my friend has asked me whether I have someone for his son for the night. Someone to be the girl on his arm at his party. A very private party, and this colleague of mine, he wants his boy to have a really *special* girl... someone exceptional.'

'Sounds fine.' I smile at him, my best genuine smile.

'And you Scarlett are the most beautiful girl in this

club.' He holds my gaze and I squirm a little, I mean this man is seriously hot.

'But there is something more Scarlett,' he adds, 'it's a classy do, silver service. You'll need to dress up, you'll need to fit in. I mean we're not talking about the sort of men who come to the club. This isn't about smoothing over anyone's midlife crisis. You need to be classy and you need to look like you are his girlfriend'.

'How much?' I say and he laughs, and I laugh too because he's the boss and he's gonna be a big name.

'That's my girl. Oh and the money is good. £5,000.'

'No problemo Mario.' My eyes are probably showing cash registers. He shifts nearer me on the sofa and then pulls me towards him, kissing me on the mouth, biting into my bottom lip a little. Because as far as he's concerned we're all his girls and he can do with us what he wants.

He tastes of morning-after Indian takeaways.

'Good girl, Scarlett.' He rolls his tongue over his gold teeth. 'I'll get someone to give you the details. Dress smart, you understand me?'

'Anything for you, Mario,' I say, my lips still tingling a little.

As I'm leaving he says, 'Scarlett, one other thing. These boys can sometimes be a bit rowdy. But this one, this is for me, you remember that. For me okay. You just think of me. And Scarlett, don't let me down.' He laughs again.

So I laugh too.

One day other people will laugh when I speak and hang on my every word. Mario can have his moment. I intend to have mine. I'm gonna show everyone. Everyone who ever looked down their nose at me, everyone who ever thought that they were better than me had better watch themselves.

I intend to have the last word and the last laugh.

Back downstairs the other girls were all looking at me coz they were jealous and they wanted to know what Mario had said. They can kiss my arse. Viola Viola came on for her second act. She did the number she does about being an old-fashioned girl who wants a millionaire. It's one of her better ones. She has this Marlene Dietrich thing going on, all old time movie star style. It's a cool look, like she could be a man or a woman. She wears a penguin suit and has a top hat and a cane. The cane spends much of the act sliding in and out between her upper thighs or across her chest, and when she gets to the part about wanting an apartment building with her name on, she opens out her shirt and she's naked underneath and she blushes. All the blokes' eyes pop out. Every single time. Even though they must have been expecting it. I mean, for God's sake she's a stripper, it's like they've never seen a pair of tits before.

I'm thinking £5,000 is not bad at all. Watching Viola Viola pick up her clothes from the floor, I realise that if anyone knows what silver fucking service is then she does. She might be as useful as a chocolate fireguard, but she knows her posh.

Chapter Twenty Five
Tiggy

'Hey baby, do you want to hear a joke?' Tony calls at 5.30pm. Scarlett is out on one of her ten-mile runs. I've been watching the news most of the afternoon.

It's all very emotional. John McCarthy has been released and the TV footage is making me cry. In a good way. A cathartic happy way.

'Go on then.'

I'm not really in the mood for jokes.

'McCarthy gets off the plane, he's been in captivity five years, and the police and the armed forces or whoever are there to meet him, you know the CIA, FBI and all that lot, well they say, "John, you must have lots of questions about the world, about what you've missed, who's the Prime Minister, how Arsenal are doing in the cup that sort of thing." And John replies, "Well, there is one thing." The men in uniform are there, the most knowledgeable men on the team and a group of psychiatrists etc. They've got their computers, newspapers and briefing notes clenched in their hands ready to update him and he says, "Is Bryan Adams still number one?"'

He laughs.

I hold the phone out in front of me peering questioningly into the receiver. His laughter is all tinny and distant.

'Tiggy?'

'I'm shaking my head.'

'No?'

He's disappointed.

I don't know what's more depressing, that Tony found the joke funny or that Bryan Adams is still number one. It's been a month or something now. Every time I turn on the radio Bryan Adams is there swearing to do all kinds of wonderment for his woman.

'Tony,' I ask, 'what is the difference between Islamic Jihad and Shiite Muslims?'

'Well-'

'Or Islamic fundamentalists and pro-Iranian militants?'

Tony's the sort of person who would know. He always knows everything.

'It's complicated Tiggy... civil wars are never simple.'

He's like my own personal reference section.

'Because I still don't really understand why they abducted him.'

On my 16th birthday.

But instead of giving me a lecture on the politics of the Lebanon he avoids answering the question and moves it back to my territory – the relationship stuff.

'I bet you're rooting for him to get back together with his girlfriend.'

It occurs to me that maybe he doesn't know the answer. Which would be fine if he could admit it. But he won't. Because our relationship is based on the fact that he knows everything and I need to learn from him. I would start to wonder if I am jumping to wrong conclusions except Tony is talking very fast and so transparently moving away from the question. As though it were a flame filled building. Desperately looking for an exit.

Then Tony leaps.

'And have you been crying at the footage?'

'Only when I think about him finding out that his mother is dead and that his girlfriend is with someone else.'

Straight into the frying pan

'Well it has been five years Tigs. I mean, he couldn't have expected her to wait around forever.'

And I shake my head.

Then there's background noise and a woman's voice calling his name.

He says, 'Right John, well thanks for calling and I'll get the papers marked and on your desk by next week. Cheers mate.'

And hangs up.

I chuck the phone at the wall.

Viola Stamford, the most popular, beautiful girl in the school had a picture of Tony in his cricket whites, on the front of her diary. Cut from the formal shot of the first team, she'd disposed of 14 perfectly passable sixth form boys, hurling them into her wicker bin. Choosing to save only Tony. Like all of us she spent her evenings giggling and fantasising about him. Underneath the heart-shaped photo she'd written in red metallic pen, 'Viola Stamford loves Tony Welsh' with some daft calculation where you get a score for every L then every O, V, E and S etc. By her rudimentary calculation she loved him 84%. A good score.

We'd all done the calculation one night in the common room. Turned out Tony loved me 16% which Viola thought was hilarious, 'Oh dear dreggoid. Oh dearie me.'

But I was the one he'd chosen.

Tony and I were a conspiracy against the school, against Sandra and all the other girls.

I loved the excitement of our secret meetings. The snatched times that we managed to escape out of school together. My heart soaring as I climbed into the back seat his car and hid under the blankets he left for me. Hearing him say, 'it's okay now' as soon as we were out of school range. Climbing through to the front seat and kissing his neck while he pretended to concentrate on the road ahead. I became so used to missing him, that even when we were together I was already missing him. Thinking about how long we had together this time and hoping for the next time.

Everything Tony said seemed articulate and meaningful. I would carry his words, his ideas with me. Hearing myself using phrases he'd said. Liking the feel of his words turning over on my tongue.

I don't know the moment that it changed. When instead of being blown away by his brilliance I thought 'hold on, that's not true.' Or what day it was when instead of being grateful for a scrap of his attention, I felt taken for granted.

'Be patient with me,' is all he ever says. And I do try. But how much longer? Like Tony says, I can't be expected to wait around forever can I?

I don't want to think about Sandra and Tony in their house, about what they talk about or what they do. I prefer to blank it out. I go back to watching the news and the TV is showing this montage of significant events since McCarthy was taken hostage. It's over the backing track of *A Different Corner*. The screen fills with images, Richard Branson breaking the Atlantic record, Voyager spacecraft reaching Neptune, the Guilford Four being released. They show footage of the Kings Cross fire and De Klerk saying that apartheid is over. They end with the release of John's friend, Brian

Keenan. Then they go back to the studio and show an interview with Jill Morrell that I've already seen.

She's talking about how awful it is to wait and to not know.

Even though I know it's different, I know what she means. There've been wars, space travel and extraordinary events. All I've done is wait. For Tony to leave Sandra, for my mother to come back. For my life to begin.

I turn off the TV and light a cigarette.

I may as well be blindfolded and chained to a radiator.

Love shouldn't feel like a gun to your head, should it?

Chapter Twenty Six
Scarlett

Running you see all the stuff that they never use in the tourist guides of London. Like the totally crap streets that are right next to the posh ones. The run along Cromwell Road is like Mr Benn's cartoon changing room. Like on Tiggy's side, there's Shepherd's Bush common and all the dilapidated buildings and boarded up shops, but the other side of the park is Knightsbridge, all boutique shops and tourists blocking the pavement. Round that way, the houses are all white with balconies and gated communal gardens. The streets are lined with BMWs and Mercedes and have names like Beauchamp Place and Belgrave Square.

In Shepherd's Bush the pavements are covered in pigeon shit and yesterday's kebabs. When you run along Kensington High Street the pavements are brushed teeth shiny white and flowers spill out over the sides of hanging baskets. And nobody nicks them or vandalises them even though they could because no one is watching. But just like on the estate, the mums still choose to get pissed rather than take care of their kids. Except, of course, they do it drinking champagne on tables outside little French named brasseries with their kids neatly packed off with some 18 year old au pair from Croatia or whatever. Like, Mum would have been drinking Malibu and pineapple in The Crown, me being watched by the neighbours glue sniffing teenager. These Kensington women have better clothes and accents like they've got pool cues up their arse, but it's the same. Why do people have kids if they don't want them?

The first time I went to Valerios I thought it was so classy. The red velvet sofas, the leopard print covers on the bar stools. I'd never been anywhere with so many chandeliers. I figured that this was a place that posh people went. But Roberto says that no one with real money would be seen dead in a dive like that. I asked what he meant by real money, and he was like, 'Real money is *old* money Scarlett, the one thing that you can't buy,' getting this misty eyed look on him. 'The Establishment, Scarlett, that's what I'm talking about. These men, the men that come to my clubs, they are men with old money, they come to me because they know that I respect them, and they respect me.' And he went into this whole spiel about how he's their friend and there is a bond between men, because for these men it isn't about the sex or the booze, it's about privacy and trust. Yeah, whatever you want to believe Roberto.

Tiggy's gone into some sort of stupor, that girl's life is one long daydream. It's like the more I find out the less I believe. I used to watch girls like her round The Green. They were always giggling over their *Smash Hits* magazines and making stupid jokes. And they had this really shiny hair, like they'd never had to wash it in soap or have their mums cut it all wrong. I thought that maybe they were living a normal life like the sitcom people on telly. Cab drivers go on at me sometimes with their rosy-eyed soppy stories about growing up around our way. They make it sound like, 'oh yeah, well we had no money, nothing but a bag of marbles and a satsuma for Christmas... but we had love... we woz family.' I'm like, are the government paying you to say that? Coz actually on my estate no one had any money but most kids got piles of everything at Christmas, like if they shoved enough plastic into our greedy little paws, then we wouldn't notice that there was no love, that everyone was too pissed or stoned to give a toss. Then on Boxing Day it was swappsies, we swapped whatever useless tat we'd got for someone else's plastic tat.

Summer was when everything used to kick off. The Flat lads would rampage their way through everything. Nina and me used to go to The Green just to get away from them and all their testosterone, or whatever it is that makes men thick. The Green was where the play area had been before they took the swings and round-about equipment away and put a giant padlock on the gates. The wire mesh around it was ripped up all over the place and we'd sit under the 'Keep Out – Strictly Private' sign and smoke. Smoking was the only time Nina took her dummy out.

But then Nina's Mum died. Sat on the sofa reading a catalogue, she stopped breathing. Everyone on the estate was saying how it was 'shocking' and telling the reporters from the local papers how they'd been her best friend, and how she was like, the best person ever, even though none of them had much to say to her when she was alive.

Nina stayed with us. Slept tucked up in my bed. She lay next to me, howling and bawling like you wouldn't believe. Then on the second night she wet the bed. The mattress went all warm and then chilled beneath me but I never said anything.

'They're going to take me away aren't they?' We all knew what happened to kids in those homes, the glue sniffing and the bedtime games with the perverts running the place.

'Nina. It'll be all right you know. It will.'

'Promise?' And Nina looked at me with eyes like wet windows and I nodded because I knew Mum and me could look after her.

In the morning Mum called the Social.

'What did you do that for?'

'Oh come on, you didn't think that she could live here with us did you? It's enough trouble trying to keep you on the straight and narrow without another one to think about.'

I begged and pleaded and I said I would do whatever it was that she wanted.

'Well you could start by going to school.'

'I will, I will, I'll go every day.'

'Go on then. Go on. We'll discuss it when you get home'

'Promise? She can stay. Really?'

'I can't promise Luv. Let's see.'

I spent the whole day in school. I went to every class. I wrote down everything the teachers said to write down. I only had one cigarette.

When I got home there was a police car outside the house and half the estate was outside their doors and staring. Nina was sat on the back seat of the coppers' car, her face tight and scared. When she saw me she gave me this little wave and I started running to the car but the bastard coppers pulled away right in front of me. I was running after the car and screaming at them to bring her back, but I had on these daft jelly shoes that meant I couldn't go fast enough, even when I kicked them off and ran like anything after the car screaming at them to stop. Nina must have heard coz she turned round then and looked at me. And the look on her face did my head in.

Then the car was gone and I stopped running. There was blood pouring from my feet. I walked back to the estate, and everyone had gone back into the flats. The balconies all empty, like the show was over and that was that.

I walked round the estate for hours. I kicked over

every fucking bin, till the every shitty part of it was covered in plastic food containers and beer cans.

Mum reached for my arm as I came in the front door. Like we could just hug and make up after she'd betrayed me like that.

'Luv.'

'Get off me, you bitch.'

'It's better you know.'

'No it's not.'

'Nina'll be happier. It's for the best.'

'I hate you.'

'You'll make new friends.'

'I don't want new friends.'

Nina'd left that daft dummy of hers on my pillow – a gift – like she knew her childhood was over. Everything else on that estate was bollocks and so tough and Nina was like this angel, this pure white light, so they had to take her away.

But that's people for you, everyone is after what they can get, it's just some people disguise it better than others. People do things you wouldn't believe, to their kids, their wives, their best mates. And the people who act the nicest, with their classy accents and their gentleman's clubs, close up they ain't no different to anyone on the estate. It's to cover up some kind of stench. At the end of the day everyone's got a bit of rotten fruit at the back of their stall that they're trying to pass off as something else.

Chapter Twenty Seven
Tiggy

'God Tiggy. You're not telling me that you actually believe that?'

Dan seems to agree with Tony about Scarlett.

'Do you really think? I mean I know some of the girls do... but Scarlett?'

Now he's doing it too, looking at me like I'm stupid.

'Tiggy do you wear a blindfold when you're at work?'

'No.' I feel petulant.

'Then what are you refusing to see?'

'I'm not *refusing to see* anything. Men come in and then Scarlett talks to them and then the men leave.'

'Right, and you've never noticed that often about five minutes after her punter leaves then Scarlett will usually follow.'

'That doesn't prove anything.'

'Hmmmm... I think you'll find that your sweet innocent Scarlett does very well for herself.'

'You really think she does that... I thought that maybe she went back to the hotel for more drinks.'

'Tiggy are you being deliberately naive?'

Possibly I am. Possibly I am working on an Ockham's Razor anti-theory, where the most complicated explanation is the right one.

'But hang on a sec, she never has any money, she's always complaining that she's broke.' In the last two weeks I can't remember Scarlett paying for anything.

Dan shrugs, 'Well, maybe she's feeding a drug habit or sending cash to starving Ethiopians, but she's certainly earning herself a good wage, you should hear the other girls talking, they have some pretty firm opinions on your mate too.'

'You think Scarlett's a drug addict?'

'People in glass houses, Tiggy.'

I put the joint down quickly.

'That's not the same. Besides, she doesn't look like a drug user.'

Maybe I should check the bin for drug paraphernalia, bits of tin foil and razor blades, maybe count my spoons.

'And what exactly do you think a drug user looks like?'

'You know... like that TV add, with dirty hair, white spotty skin, skanky and thin.'

'Tiggy, did you grow up in a different universe or something?'

A heightened form of reality certainly.

'She doesn't look like a prostitute either... maybe she doesn't go the whole way... I mean some of them don't right?'

Dan lifts his hands and then throws them down again in defeat. 'Antigone, the world was not meant for one as beautiful as you. Now could we talk about something other than Scarlett... you're obsessed.'

I tell him about the letter from my mother and of course he wants to see it. Then he wants to read it and make up his own mind. He says that he thinks I might be putting just a touch of bias on it and that maybe it isn't quite as bad as I say.

I'm having trouble convincing myself that Tony and Dan are wrong. Scarlett's only my age, and she's so pretty. I know that some of the older hostesses sometimes make private arrangements with the clients. But surely Scarlett doesn't need to sleep with men for money. The hostesses can make pretty good money from simply talking to men and their commission.

'Besides, she's got a date next week, she's got a formal invitation and everything.' I tell Dan victoriously. This proves something at least.

'Whatever you want to believe.'

'It's for Greens. I know the restaurant. Do prostitutes go on proper dates?'

'Uh-huh. They're like real people and everything.' Dan turns his head back to the letter.

I can't imagine how Scarlett would let the blokes who come in the club touch her, let alone, well, everything else.

I've only slept with two people and one's Tony and the other, well, that was a mistake, the obligatory unsatisfactory and embarrassing attempt to make Tony jealous.

I still feel horrible when I think about it.

I was working on the reception in an office. My one and only temp job. Just for a few weeks. Mike was a cyclist, a courier. About four or five times a day he would come in and pick up packages or deliver packages. I just had to sign them. Every time he came in he asked me to have a drink with him. Halfway through the second week I figured that 35 times was enough rejection for anyone. The only way to stop him asking was to say yes.

I also liked being able to tell Tony that I was meeting a boy for a drink.

We sat in this beer garden drinking and smoking. And every time I said I had to leave he insisted I stay for one more drink.

'Come on gorgeous. Stay, please.'

'I um... I really have to go...'

'One more, just one little one more. Please. You

have my heart in your hands here.'

'But-'

Somehow we ended up back at his flat and drinking even more. The next thing I knew he was all over me. It wasn't rape or anything. It's just it was a little unexpected. It hadn't occurred to me that people moved that fast.

Mike gave me money for a cab home.

The next day a different courier came to pick up the packages. I called the courier company and this woman said, 'Oh... he's moved his round. Hey, Mike the Bike didn't get you into bed did he? He's such a slut.'

I told Tony. I said it was because I thought that honesty was important. Only I sort of made out that Mike was infatuated with me, calling me all the time. And that I was thinking of maybe going out with him again. I figured that driven mad by jealously Tony would leave Sandra immediately. He listened quietly, took my hand and said sadly, 'Well, you're 20 years old Tiggy. Old enough to know your own mind. If it's what you want. If you think he'll make you happy. Then I won't stand in your way.'

'You know this is really quite a lovely letter, Tiggy.' Dan's reading my mother's letter for at least the third time, curled up on a beanbag, leaving a half-drunk cup of black coffee nesting in the carpet next to him.

I sigh, 'No it isn't. It's bollocks.'

'You going to contact her?'

'No.'

'Scared?'

'No.'

'Maybe you should... sounds like she'd love you to give her a chance.'

'Dan, this is none of your business.'

'Then why give me the letter?'

'Because you asked.'

'You didn't have to show it to me.'

'I wish I hadn't now.' I grab the letter back.

'Do you remember her?'

'Sometimes... I can look at the pictures and remember them being taken, but I can't remember much about what we were saying or what I was feeling.'

'Tell me about her.'

'She left me.'

'Tell me what she was like.'

'She's like... someone who leaves people.'

'Very funny. When I think about my Mum I always think of her cooking.' Dan's voice is husky with remembrance. 'Making roast dinners, poking at giant hunks of meat, dicing up parsnips, or fixing my Airfix models when my Dad accidentally broke them.'

'My mother would be more likely to be fixing a gin and tonic or packing a suitcase.'

'Okay, so what was she like when she *fixed the gin and tonic?*'

'I don't know.'

'Come on. You must. Did she have a belly like dough and thighs that wobble, you know, like the pictures of mothers in storybooks, apron on, a little bit of flour on their forehead from baking?'

'No.'

'Did she beat you and lock you in a cupboard?'

'No.'

'Did she dress you up as a fairy and make you sing songs to her friends?'

'No. Did yours?'

'Only when I asked nicely.'

'Ok. I'll try. She was quiet. I was frightened that if I talked too loudly or said the wrong thing that she would vanish. Which is a laugh really. I couldn't believe that I had once been inside her tummy. Other people's mothers had loud voices. You know the sort of thing. Don't climb too high. Slow down. Eat your greens. My mother stayed in her room mainly. She made me nervous. We didn't really speak.'

'She must have said something.'

'Oh I'm sure that she said things. She wasn't mute. But I don't remember anything. I used to think if I was a better daughter then she would say something. If I could make her smile.'

'Doesn't sound very happy does it? Did you ever think that maybe she's telling the truth, that she felt she was letting you down?'

'No. Oh I don't know. You know what I thought as a kid? Oh it doesn't matter.'

'Come on, what?'

'I thought. I thought that she was ashamed of me. That I was the reason that she was unhappy.'

'Maybe you should talk to her,' Dan says quietly. 'She does sound sorry... and it might clear the air.'

I look at the letter on the table. I don't know why she's writing to me now or what she's hoping to find. If I disappointed her as a child then the adult version is hardly going to impress her.

I imagine her long fingers on the pen, immaculate manicured nails holding the paper steady, perhaps a small tear in the corner of her eye.

But she left me.

'I don't want to talk about this anymore Dan,' I say and he nods and says, 'fine.'

'So, how are things with Jackie?' I try to concentrate while Dan gives me the update on his relationship, which rather disappointingly seems to be going well.

Turns out that Jackie is neither super-hero nor

nurse. She works in a recording studio, being some-thing called a Tape-op. When Dan talks about her his voice threads with pride. I find myself clenching my fists.

'I think she's getting broody though?'

'Kids?' I hadn't thought about that.

'Well, not straight away. But soon, definitely soon. I'd probably have to stop working nights.'

'Kids?' I repeat.

'Sure, you know a couple of rug rats hanging around my apron strings. It would be fun I think, I could teach them the guitar, force them to listen to my favourite music. Hold them upside down in the park, all of that. Hey, you could be Auntie Tiggy.'

'Kids, that's great.' I smile widely at him. 'You'll be a brilliant Dad,' I say cheerily, though I can't help feeling as though Dan is going to abandon me too.

Chapter Twenty Eight
Tiggy

S carlett is staring at me like I'm a freak.

'What?'

'Tiggy are you seriously saying that you don't like your Dad, sorry Daddy, because he bought you a pony on your ninth birthday?'

It was going really well until a few minutes ago.

Scarlett and I had been shopping in Soho. She'd insisted that the day was too beautiful to waste indoors. I had been looking forward to a long lie in but she came bounding into my room all hyper. All 'Come on Tiggy, let's do something together, it'll be a laugh.'

Turns out that Scarlett's idea of a laugh is shoplifting from every store in Greek Street.

'No way Scarlett.'

'Oh don't be such a baby, come on, think of something you want. Come on Tiggy, imagine I'm your genie.'

'No, Scarlett. I can't.'

She danced around me making chicken noises. That whole chicken thing has never worked on me. I'm worse than chicken. I'm scared of chickens. Just thinking about their shrivelled grey feet makes me shiver.

'Come on Tiggy, rub my lamp, you get three wishes... cluck cluck cluck... '

'Can't we just pay for things?'

She stopped her chicken dance and cocked her head to one side, 'You need to loosen up a little, but okay, you're the boss.' She looped her arm into mine. 'So where do you want to go. Oh I know. Clothes. I need new clothes. I can't wear your stuff forever can I?'

Scarlett has given herself full access to my wardrobe. I am engaged in a process of rediscovery watching her turn my clothes into fabulous outfits. Right now she's wearing an old paisley shirt wrapped high and tied in a knot under her breasts. Exposing her perfect tummy, with a pleated tartan skirt and gold high heels. It sounds terrible. She makes it look like an obvious combination. Scarlett leafed her way through racks of baby doll dresses and PVC mini-skirts. Her hand pecking at anything shiny. Other girls watched her, open-mouthed, mentally sketching down her style and looking through the racks for anything similar. I spotted a pile of jeans and searched for the baggiest pair. I know the whole indie thing is out of fashion, but a pair of baggy flares and a white shirt is my idea of classic.

'More jeans, blimey, another pair exactly the same as the five pairs you already own. Leave them. Now this would be great on you.' She held up a purple PVC boob tube.

'I don't think so.'

'Go on.'

A few minutes later I was modelling the PVC disaster in the communal dressing room. I couldn't bring myself to look at my reflection.

'Wow – what a transformation,' Scarlett clapped. The other girls looked over. I blushed. She was right, it was a transformation. I didn't look like a stripper at all. I looked like a transsexual hooker.

We continued from shop to shop with Scarlett somehow persuading me to buy things that I didn't want and will never wear. Only back at the flat as she was trying on the stuff I'd bought, she started asking me more about my father, what did he do, where did he live, what was he like etc.

'Mainly he spends his time being oblivious.'

'Oblivious to what?'

'Me... he doesn't even know what A-Levels I did.'

'Oooh A-Levels, aren't you a clever girl. Come on what else, what are his crimes? I'm not taking the piss Tiggy, I'm not, I promise, I'm interested.'

'Well, when we meet he just talks about golf or work or anything but me, he's fine, but you know we don't really have much to say to each other. He's always-'

'What?'

'Oh it sounds daft really. But he always seems to get it wrong, you know? So when I was nine and all I wanted for Christmas was a stereo system. He bought me a pony. It was really nice. This sweet little dapple, called Cinders, but no good for playing records on. Then there was this time at prep school. One of the girls invited me to spend a week in Andorra with her. It was the first time she'd ever invited me. I thought that maybe we would be friends. Daddy wouldn't let me go because he'd booked us on this other skiing trip. So, I had to do that instead.'

Which is how we got here. Scarlett's hands on her hips. Her looking at me like I'm a freak.

'I'm not meaning to be funny Tiggy, but getting a pony doesn't sound like a reason to hate your Dad.'

When she puts it like that it sounds ridiculous.

'No. I'm just saying that-' What am I saying? 'They were just examples of-' Now I'm confused. 'It's complicated.'

'So tell me.'

I tell her more about school. How after my mother left

152

my father hardly came to visit. And then I tell her about Tony.

'Yuck. Child snatching pervert.'

'It's not like that.'

'Tiggy, the bloke sounds like a creep.'

'No. He's not. I love him. I wanted him to.'

She makes a face, 'That's what he would want you to think.'

'He loves me and I love him.'

'And you're hoping he's going to leave his wife right?'

'I suppose.'

'Well yes or no?'

'It's what he wants too.'

'Well, I hope you get what you want.' She clicks her fingers above her head. 'A girl should always get what she wants.'

'Is The Pervert why you strip?'

Oh we're back on this again. Scarlett is obsessed with why I'm working at the club. It's her favourite thing.

'Does he ask you to? Is he one of those men that likes sharing his girlfriend?'

'No!'

'Is it because you like men looking at you?'

'NO!'

'Do you? Do you get off on the idea of all those men masturbating over you when they get home.'

'Scarlett?'

'Well I bet they do.'

'I don't. Well, it's simple isn't it? I work for myself. No one bothers me. I don't have to deal with anyone else.'

'It just doesn't make any sense to me Tiggy.' There's

challenge in her eyes, 'You just said you've got A-Levels, so you could get another job easily.'

'I suppose.'

'No doubt *Daddy* could help you with that?'

'He'd be delighted to. Probably have me working for one of his friends in seconds.'

'So, why strip?'

'Why do you... you know?'

'Work as a hostess?'

'Yes.'

'Because *I* need the money. My parents seem to have forgotten about my trust fund.'

'But there must be other things you could do.'

'Like what?'

'Temping or something?'

'I can't type.'

'You could learn. It's not so hard.'

'I can't spell. No qualifications; some of us didn't get to finishing school. What do you think of this?' She's admiring herself in the mirror, having changed into the purple boob tube with my purple Levi's. My old school tie is wrapped around her waist. 'Tiggy am I fabulous, or more like a mutated Duranie?'

'You're fabulous. So what do your parents do?'

She snorts, flicking the ash from her cigarette into my empty coffee cup. 'Mum doesn't give a fuck about me.'

'And your Dad?'

'When I find out who he is, I'll ask him.' She doesn't turn back from the mirror. 'But hey, it could be worse. I could have a daddy who buys me a pony. Imagine. What a *disaster*.'

I stare at her back, she hates me. My hands are trembling.

'Joking!' She turns away from the mirror, pulls a

face and blows me a kiss. 'Don't worry Tigs. At least we've got each other. Can I wear this top tonight?'

That's the thing with Scarlett, the moment I think I've got a sense of her she slips from reach.

Later, on the tube to work, she dances around the hand pole, yelling out across the carriage, 'You should get one of these for your act.' Like the other passengers I'm trying to read, but I can feel a million eyes looking at me with newfound curiosity.

'Can we talk about something else?'

'Sure. Let's talk about my low life as a hooker.'

'Shhh.' How can she be so brazen? We definitely have the attention of the whole carriage.

'Do you have a problem with that?'

'No.'

'Are you sure?'

'Scarlett, I'm trying to read.' I pull my book near to my face so my nose nearly touches the pages.

'Hey Tiggy, Tiggeeee,' I look up to see Scarlett wrapped upside down around the pole. Her hair dragging on the ground. Her gold heels tapping on the carriage roof.

'Look, I'm just like Lionel Richie, I'm dancing on the ceiling!' She giggles deliriously as her skirt flies over her head. Revealing the pink satin knickers she persuaded me to buy just a few hours before.

'Blimey... cool head rush,' she yells from under her skirt.

Chapter Twenty Nine
Scarlett

Tiggy is teaching me silver service. She's set out this whole arrangement on her coffee table. She has me learning salad forks and soupspoons and all that crap and it's pretty easy really.

I say, 'Is this what they teach you at boarding school?'

And she's all like, 'No, not really.' Then she starts talking about how different wine glasses are used for different wines. I'm like, I'm not completely stupid, but I smile and say, 'Thanks Tiggy you're really saving my life here. I want to get it right.'

She says, 'I doubt he'll care looking the way you look.' So I lift The Tits, 'You mean these?'

Tiggy blushes like she always does and says, 'No, I mean your face. You have really unusual eyes Scarlett. They're gorgeous. Like a young Elizabeth Taylor.'

That's kind of sweet, so I say, 'That's why I chose Scarlett?' Tiggy doesn't understand and I say, 'You know, Scarlett O'Hara in *Gone with the Wind*.'

And she says 'But that was Vivien Leigh wasn't it?'

I feel a bit stupid so I say quickly, 'You look a bit like that Winona Ryder.'

She laughs and shakes her head and says, 'No, I don't Scarlett. I've just got brown hair. I think Winona would be mortified if she heard you say that.'

'*Moooortified,*' I say and she looks at me.

'Are you making fun of me?' She's blushing again.

So I say, 'God No, I love the way you talk, I wish I could talk like that. *Mooortified.*' She sort of grins and shakes her head and says that I'm a funny girl. She is a bit like those characters Winona plays though, the teen girls who think it's cool to be all angsty and riddled with doubts.

'So, Black Tie eh? What are you going to wear?'

'I thought maybe my gold lame dress?' I say, even though I know it's wrong, but Tiggy has this fantastic white silk dress in her wardrobe and I'm banking on her generosity.

She sort of squashes up her face and says, 'I'm not being funny Scarlett, but I think it might be a bit too sexy. Do you want to borrow something of mine?'

'Gosh, really, that would be so cool, thanks Tiggy.'

She comes out of her room with a pile of really posh dresses and says to try them on. Two of them are the revolting meringues in blue and purple Taffeta, but then I spot it.

'Oooh, can I try this one?'

'Of course.'

The dress is strapless and The Tits are kind of spilling out of it, but in a good way. This is pretty spectacular on me. The kind of thing I'd wear if I ever got married. Like that's going to happen. Nina would have been beside herself.

Tiggy is like, 'Wow. Why Miss Scarlett, you're beautiful. Hold on a second'. She goes back into her room and she comes out with these long white satin gloves that go right the way up my arms and feel like heaven.

Tiggy can do French Plaits on account of her having a horse when she was growing up. She threads my hair in and out and when she's finished I look in the mirror, and we both smile.

'I look proper posh.'

'You look like a proper young lady.' She makes some joke I don't understand about how she feels like Henry Higgins and how I'm Eliza Doolittle.

'Tiggy,' I say, 'could you do my hair like this on the night? Before I go. It's just it's really important that I look good.'

'Of course,' she says and she looks really pleased and I think that even though she's a bit stuck up and self absorbed, she's all right.

£5k and I get to look like a princess. Not bad Scarlett, not bad at all.

Chapter Thirty
Tiggy

The conversations started as hushed whispers. Not that I needed to listen to know what was going on. I was always causing them problems. Making them argue. It didn't matter how hard I tried to be good, to stay out of their way. I never seemed to manage to be the daughter that they had hoped for. They called me a *sullen girl*. A *difficult child*. It felt like an accusation. As though they had been depending on me to bring joy into the house. I was to be their redemption. The glue that would hold everything together. Instead I was a reminder of their misery.

Most nights my parents would eat dinner in silence. Their knives and forks scraping at the china. The wine bottle clinking against my father's glass. I don't think that I ever heard them laughing.

Sometimes when they talked about my future my father would try to suggest going to Boarding School. My mother had always resisted.

'I'm not sure.'

'She can't stay like this.'

'But boarding school, Francis. She's eight years old. It's a little drastic.'

'It's you who wants your life back. It's you who wants space, who feels like a, like a bloody *hologram*. So have your space.'

'What will sending her away achieve?'

'I was away from the age of seven and it didn't do me any harm.'

'No. You're fine, aren't you? As long as no one makes

any demands on you. As long as everyone plays along by your rules.'

'I am doing my very best here Serena. What is it that you want from me?'

'Me want from you? I'm trying everything that I can to be the wife that you want, to give you whatever it is that you think you need. But I'm vanishing here, Francis. And quite patently failing to satisfy you.'

'This is you trying to make me happy is it?'

'Francis. I cannot put every feeling that I have, every need on hold for my whole life just to suit you.'

'Oh, heaven forbid that you have an emotion and don't express it Serena. I work hard and when I come home I want to see a smiling face. Is that too much to ask? I've got you looking at me with that reproachful glare. Her- '

'Her? Your daughter you mean?'

'*Our* daughter. She doesn't act like she belongs here.'

'She's a little shy, that's all.'

'She sneaks about the place like she's some kind of stowaway.'

'What if Boarding School isn't the right environment.'

'*This* is the right environment, is it?'

My mother doesn't answer and then my father says, 'Maybe it's us, maybe we're making her miserable. Maybe with other children her own age. She might blossom.'

I'm thinking that there are lots of 'maybes' in that sentence when my mother quietly adds some more.

'Maybe, Francis. Maybe it is us. Or maybe you just want your problems out of sight so that you don't have to think about them.'

'If only it were that simple. But my mistakes look at

me across the dinner table every evening.'

I told them the following morning, over breakfast.

'Are you sure, darling?' My mother took my hand and I knew if she held it for a second longer then I would start to cry.

'I think I'd be really happy there. I think that we'd all be happier apart,' I said the last bit quickly, so that she understood that I was doing this for her, because I loved her so much.

'Okay,' my mother sounded strange. Speaking more slowly than usual and wavering. Like the time she told me that Granny was dead. But her eyes were dry. 'Well, it looks as though your father knows you best after all. Okay, if it's what you want darling.'

A few weeks into term, after Viola had smashed up a few more of my LPs, and burned another file of my essays, when I knew that this wasn't what I wanted at all, I looked up the word hologram. I wanted to understand what my mother felt like. There was all this scientific stuff about split beams and coherent lights and it didn't make any sense to me.

It wasn't until years later that I understood what she meant. That she didn't feel real, she felt like a three dimensional reproduction of herself.

And one day she was gone.

All my studying, all my tiptoeing around the house trying to be quiet, trying not to be annoying or irritating hadn't worked. She left me anyway.

If my mother was a hologram then I'm a Russian doll with no sign of a centre. So stripping isn't a problem, not really.

Taking off my clothes is just taking off the top layer.

I don't know what happens when all the layers are removed. The true content of my character.

The night of Scarlett's big date I have the flat to myself. I prepare myself by setting out the living room table with a bottle of freezer-chilled Vodka. I add a pack of Marlboro lights, a pad of yellow paper and a Parker cartridge pen (with three spare cartridges). I'm anticipating that this might take a while to get right. I retrieve my shoebox from under the bed. Then I read through her letter again even though I know it off by heart. The pad stares clean and unstained at me, until eventually I try to write a response.

I write *Dear Mother* and then cross it out.

She's not my dear and I don't know if she deserves the title of mother, although Serena sounds strange. Perhaps I should write the letter and then work out how to address her later.

At sometime around 2am I realise that I'm out of cigarettes and I have filled in the entire ream of yellow paper. I still haven't got to my point yet. I still haven't found the words that I am searching for. I pass a few minutes curling each sheet into a ball and chucking them on the floor.

I don't know if there is too much, or not enough to say.

But I do know that I need cigarettes.

There's an all night garage further along Holland Park. So I set out walking towards it. Once I've bought the cigarettes I don't turn back towards home. Instead I keep on walking and walking, until I am standing in the Strand outside my mothers' hotel.

Chapter Thirty One
Scarlett

I'm feeling fantastic as I step out of the limo. I mean William Clarke-Price is a total geek. He's the sort of lad that used to stare at me on buses all sneery but you just knew was going to go home and wank over you. The sort that loses their virginity at 25 to some sad fat desperate 45 year old. Well he's just like that, but rich, *really* rich. He talks in this totally stupid voice that makes Tiggy sound like she's not even a little bit posh.

Wills spent the whole of the limo journey staring at The Tits but who gives a shit. I'm getting £5,000 for this, so he can look at The Tits as much as he likes. When we get to Kensington Church Street, I wait like for him to come round to my door, open it and take my hand. I step out really daintily and totally ladylike, keeping my dress folded between my legs and he offers me his arm and we walk into 'Greens.'

The bloke at the door says, 'Good evening Mr Clarke-Price.' He nods at me and says, 'You too Miss.'

So, I say 'why thank you,' in my bestest fake Tiggy accent. He leads us through to a room at the back of the club. The room is set like a posh TV drama dining room. Big oval table, flowers everywhere and silver candlesticks that might be worth nicking later. Four other couples are already there, the girls wearing meringue dresses and boys in black suits and bow ties. The room stinks of brylcreem, expensive perfumes and too much aftershave.

Wills holds my hand real tight and I can see that he loves the impact we make because all the girls are like, really staring at me and the boys are just practically devouring The Tits with their eyes. I quickly check out the competition and I am totally the best looking girl in the room.

Wills introduces me to the girls or *guurls* as he calls them. He doesn't bother introducing me to the blokes on account of how they are 'a dirty bunch of rotten beasts'.

'Scarlett, this is Becca.' Becca is about three stone overweight and wearing one of those fuck-awful cake dresses that Tiggy wanted me to wear.

'And Millie.' Millie actually looks like a horse; a horse in a dress. You could stick a rosette on her neck and she'd be set.

'And Sarah.'

'Delighted I'm sure.' She has the body of a broom and a face about as pretty as wire wool. She walks away while I'm still saying 'how do you do.'

'And last but not least, this is Persephone.' Persephone has short dark hair and this wide-open face and a huge smile. When I put out my hand to shake hers she kisses me on both cheeks.

'Welcome to our strange and sordid bunch. I hope we're not too intimidating. But don't worry I'll take care of you.' She loops her arm into mine and takes me off to a corner. 'Tell me you smoke darling. Oh wonderful. Can't trust non-smokers. What a fabulous dress, I wish I had your courage. Although with your body, well.'

The other girls are looking over at us and Persephone says, 'Oh God, Scarlett, I'm sorry but they're a frightful lot. I'm only here because my bloody father said I had to. Some bloody Golf Club nonsense. Still, let's make the best of it shall we?' She squeezes my arm again. 'I'm so glad there's someone for me to talk to.' Even though I don't like people to touch me unless they're invited, I let it go because I really need some help if I'm going to get through the night without letting Mario down.

The men all have these stupid nick names like Bonzo and Dogby and Winnet and they all look pretty much alike in their suits. I don't really bother learning their names although it is pretty obvious straight off that they don't believe for a second that I'm really Wills' girlfriend.

The dinner is okay. I mean thank God for Persephone who makes a joke of the forks and knifes. 'Oh who gives a fuck,' she says, eating her salad with her soupspoon. In between courses she lights up a fag, and at first I don't dare because even I know not to smoke at the table. But then I see that all of them have their packs of Marlboro out the whole way through dinner and the moment the food is taken away they are lighting up, saying 'absolutely' this and how everything is 'sooo hysterical'. Which would be fine if I could understand anything they were talking about.

Once you get used to the accents and can make out the words it still makes no sense. Millie's going on about a Point to Point which for a while I think might be ballet or something, but turns out to have something to do with horses. Every time they finish a sentence they say 'Yah'. Or 'Yah Yah Yah'. I thought that was a joke! I didn't think that girls my age would speak like that, not really. But they are like completely serious. The more I listen to the conversation the harder it is to tell one boy from another or any of the girls apart, because other than the colour of their dresses they are all like totally identical. Like, 'Yah, Yah, Yah... bollocks'.

I'm thinking that it will be a laugh telling Tiggy about this, because mainly I can't talk about the guys I meet, but I'll be able to talk about the food and the flowers on the table and how mine was the best dress there and everything. I must remember to thank her for her lessons coz when we get to the cheese and port part of the meal I remember to pass the bottle to the left. It doesn't bother me that most of the other girls are manky cows, or that Wills has his hand on my knee and his eyes on The Tits. As bookings go this one isn't that bad.

Then the meal is finished and everyone is talking more crap and the girls say they're going to go through to the main club and dance.

Persephone is like, 'Come on, Scarlett, let's go get horribly drunk and become best friends. I'm sure you've got lots of stories about Wills that we'd love to hear.'

But Wills won't let go of my hand.

'Persy, be a darling and let me have some time with Scarlett will you?'

Persephone says that I should come out and join them whenever I want adding, 'Wills, you know that you boys are terribly dull and Scarlett won't want to listen to you talking about bloody rugby for hours, so Scarlett whenever you want to you just come out and find us.'

She leaves and Wills locks the door behind her. I think of the £5,000 and I figure they're just kids. But Wills' face totally changes and he gets this dark glint in his eyes and he sits down at his chair and beckons me over to the seat next to him.

I sit down, which is when he grabs me by my hair and tugs my face up and backwards.

'Say you like it.' I look at the other boys for help but they're all laughing.

'I don't like it,' I say.

'I bet you do,' Wills and his mates are really laughing loudly now. Their eyes are all focussed on The Tits and I'm thinking I should scream when Wills places his hand over my mouth.

'SShhhh,' he says and grips my perfect French plait tighter. I try to stare him out, to show him that I'm just as tough as him.

'Daddy bought her for me,' he says all fucking triumphant. 'She's mine to do what I want with from eight till three. Isn't that right, Scarlett?'

He makes my head nod. I feel the braids loosen and it really fucks me off. My hair took Tiggy ages.

The boys have stopped laughing now, they're all leaning in though and there's something else. Like, I preferred it when they were laughing.

'Scarlett,' Wills says, 'is a slut and a whore. And we know what we do with sluts.'

I try to catch the eyes of anyone, but none of them are looking at my face. There's this fierce silence in the room. Even with the beat of the club next door.

'Get on the table... slut.' Wills voice has changed, deepened, like this is turning him into a man and I may be a slut if that's what he chooses to call me, but there is no way that I'm going to let some chinless freak with a ridiculous accent and monumental acne talk to me like that.

So, I'm like, 'Wills, it's been a pleasure but I think if it's okay with you then I'll go and join the other girls.'

I'm used to rough boys so it only takes a second to yank my hair out of his hands. Then I pick up my purse and head for the door. He must have pocketed the key because it's not in the lock. I remind myself that they're kids, that they're probably just having a laugh, that this is the same as on the estate. My throat's real dry now, I take a breath before I turn around.

'Okay Wills, jokes over, can you let me out please?' I try to be as pleasant as I can, remembering what Mario said to me, otherwise I'd be at that boy with my French manicured nails digging into his face.

Wills and his mates are laughing. Wills takes the key from his pocket and waves it in the air, 'Come and get it, slut girl,' the key swings from side to side in his fingers.

'Why don't you just open the door, Wills?'

'It's so much more fun to play, don't you think?'

I go over to him, but of course each time I reach for the key he pulls it away at the last second and then laughs even more. I go to the door and lift my fist to hammer on it.

Fuck the money, sorry Mario mate, but this is over and above.

Wills grabs my arm mid air and twists it tight behind my back. He grabs my hair again with his other hand and yanks it down hard. I feel my roots ripping.

I scream, 'Get off me.' I look hopefully at the door. But both Wills and I know that I'll never be heard over the noise from the disco. He brings his face right up close to mine and for a second I think he's going to kiss me, and I make ready to spit, but from nowhere he headbutts me really hard, just missing my nose and crashing into my jaw. I yelp. I think the fucker might have broken a tooth. Wills simply smiles and then yanks my arm back harder and his face has changed to a kind of arousal, like hurting me is what he wants. That's what this is about. This isn't some teenage boy wanting to fuck a hooker. And this isn't the first time he's done something like this. This lad is like the blokes in The Crown who get off on slapping their girlfriends around. The ones who don't think they've had a good night unless it ends with them holding a broken beer bottle into some poor bastard's face. He's just another coward bully bastard with no brains and even less balls. For him to feel big, someone else has to feel small. He pulls a swiss army knife from the inside of his dinner jacket.

And it's then that I know I'm fucked.

'I told you to get on the table... slut.'

I get on the table. Wills tells me turn around and go on all fours. I refuse. He flicks the knife near my face. Then he slides it along the front of my dress, following

168

the shape of The Tits. His mates are silent now, not in shock, but in awe of him. I spit in his face, and realise that I am spitting blood. I scream.

But quick as a butcher Wills cuts through the cleavage of Tiggy's white dress. 'Shut up or I'll slice your face next. Now on all fours slut.'

Wills pushes some of the crockery on the table to one side and clicks his fingers.

I turn over onto my knees. He pushes his hand hard on the back of my neck, then presses the tip of the knife against my cheek. 'Open your mouth.' Wills says. I don't at first but he presses the knife so hard that I can feel it's about to pierce my skin. I open my mouth and Wills shoves some kind of material into it. I guess it must be one of the napkins.

There's a fork sticking into my calf. I try to ignore it.

'Lift your skirt.' I don't. I can't. The force of his hand on the back of my neck means I can't really move anything. If I lift up my arms then I'll be face down on the table.

'Bonzo. You do it.'

Another pair of hands lifts my dress. The silk flies forward over my head. I'm shaking and the napkin in my mouth is filling up with blood. Wills starts slicing gently at the lace on my knickers. Then he cuts them off completely and waves them in front of my eyes. I'm going to fucking kill him. I concentrate on the fork digging into my skin. I watch beads of my blood fall onto the table.

'Be nice, or you won't get your £10,000.' Which is the first time it occurs to me that Mario must be taking a cut. I remember him saying how they could 'be rowdy'. I want to kill him.

Wills climbs up onto the table behind me and I'm almost relieved that at least he's stopped mucking about with the knife. I'm actually hoping that all he wants is a fuck. He grabs my arms and holds them like reins. My face is pushed down in the ashtray. I can hardly breathe because there's ash in my nose and the fucking napkin in my mouth and I can taste the blood at the back of my throat. I'm thinking 'Get it fucking over with,' concentrating on the fork.

'Is this what you want?' Wills thrusts his cock into me, tugging on my arms, so that he lifts my face in and out of the ashtray with each thrust.

He's not using durex, fucking use a condom you bastard.

He holds both my arms with one hand and starts clawing at my back, scratching at my skin.

There's ash in my eyes and it stings like fuck. My eyes are streaming and there's blood all over the table. I'm hoping my face is okay. I'm trying not to suffocate, trying to think.

I think about Mario and how he said that I should think of him.

Oh, I think about Mario all right.

Even as Wills orgasms, and drops my arms and even as he climbs off the table, I think about Mario.

'I rather enjoyed that,' Wills says, and I turn myself back over and wipe the ash and tears from my face. And I can see that Wills and his mates are laughing like aerosol-sniffing hyenas. I clutch at the table behind me and find the bastard fork.

'Oh, do cheer up Scarlett. Be a bloody sport. Not every girl is lucky enough to get the full Clarke-Price treatment. And besides,' he smirks this stomach plunging smirk, 'you're booked until three am. You may as well play nicely.' He picks up his glass and swirls his port from side to side, sniffing the top of the glass, and then breathing in deeply. 'Mmmmm... lovely,' he says. 'So... chaps... who

170

wants a go on Scarlett next?'

Which is when I jam the fork, with a strength I never knew I had, right between his legs, and as Wills lies howling on the floor, the fork still sticking out of his trousers, twitching, I grab another couple of forks from the table, swinging round to face to his bastard buddies who look like about a millimetre off wetting themselves.

'Yeah, chaps. Which fucker's next?'

Chapter Thirty Two
Tiggy

The Strand at four in the morning looks like that Phil Collins video, where he is living another day in paradise. The shop doorways are filled with boxes and blankets. Which, on closer inspection, turn out to be filled with sleeping bodies. Some of the sleepers have created small shelters from packing cases and plywood. Others are curled in Salvation Army sleeping bags stating optimistically that *Jesus Loves Me*.

I find an unoccupied doorway near the hotel and sit down.

I smoke cigarettes for two hours solid.

Between the night buses, black cabs and the home-bound clubbers still singing at top volume. Some still dancing. There's not much peace. No one in the doorways moves. They are either very deep sleepers or know that staying still is the best protection.

Everytime the bus to Shepherd's Bush passes I wonder why I don't get on.

I promise myself that I will take the next one. But 13 cigarettes later I am still sat in my doorway staring at the hotel bedroom windows opposite and wondering which one my mother might be sleeping behind.

Just after 6am my doorstep comrades start to move. In my sleep-deprived emotional state I watch their movements. As though it were an improvised dance.

Almost as one they start to fold blankets, sleeping bags and deconstruct their safe havens. Dogs shake their heads awake and woollen hats are pulled up, gloves removed. Some sleepers leave their blankets. Others stuff them into backpacks or bin liners. Then the road sweepers and the council wagons arrive and I am distracted by their hosing down of the flagstones.

I step up from my doorway as a skinny bearded man in a neon council jacket approaches me, attacking the pavement angrily with his broom and dragging his litter trolley like a burden behind him. I tuck myself deeper into my sweatshirt. He kisses his teeth in contempt as I pass him, sweeping his brush at my feet. I increase my pace and stare down at the pavement walking as fast as I can, not making eye contact, not looking up until I reach Piccadilly.

When I finally raise my head it's after 7.15am. The streets of London are no longer an outdoor hostel, the cardboard homes have been replaced by cardboard cups of coffee, the sleepy silence by bustle and business.

Between Scarlett's preparations for her date and my aborted letters to my mother the flat looks as though it's been burgled. I crawl fully clothed into bed. I switch on the radio. Simon Mayo's running through the show's line up for the morning and prattling on excitedly with Sybill Roscoe. I'm fast asleep before I they reveal what did happen *On this Day in History*.

Chapter Thirty Three
Scarlett

Valerios looks like the tatty shack shithole that it is in the daylight. At night, with the neon and the punters you could almost believe that it's a half decent club. Roberto's right about Mario and Valerios. They are both crappy imitations with no class.

I sit on the front step and wait. The white silk of Tiggy's dress soaks up patches of red. I chain smoke fags and then grind the butts down with the tips of my stilettos, imagining each one is Mario's face.

I don't think about Wills and his nasty, bully friends. I don't replay anything they did. This isn't about them. They just got what they paid for.

My nails are split and chipped, the edges sharp like little razors, there's a three pronged puncture in my leg, glass in my hair, but at least my face doesn't look too bad. And I've had worse beatings, I know how to zone myself out from pain.

Finally his BMW turns the corner. Every hair on my body stands on end. My heart pumps like a Hip-Hop bass line. Something inside drops and freezes. I'm thinking a small amount of petrol, a tiny flame and Mario and that car could be visiting a whole new galaxy.

He notices me, hesitates, then gets out of the car. I drag on my cigarette. Come on Mario, if you're such a big man. He pretends not to have seen me, and then reaches back in to the car to collect something. I'm half thinking a gun or a knife, but it's just his shit awful leather jacket, the sort Spandau Ballet stopped wearing in 1985.

'Late night was it?'

'You fucker.' My voice comes out deeper, darker than usual. It's the first time I've spoken since I ran from that restaurant. It makes it all more real and I realise that my hands are shaking. I dig my broken nails into my palms.

'Come now Scarlett, such nasty words from such a pretty mouth.'

'You knew, didn't you?'

'Calm down little girl. You should go home and tidy yourself. You look terrible. Like a cat in hell.' He laughs.

'I'll see you there, mate. Just admit what you did, bastard.'

Mario says nothing, taking a handful of keys from his pocket, stepping up to the door, brushing me away like I'm litter. He unlocks Valerios. He switches on the lights as he goes in. Before he has a chance to close the door in my face, I push through it.

'Lock the door behind you,' he says, like he's not bothered, like there's nothing I could do that could touch him.

He hands me a box of tissues, 'Here, for the blood.' I don't take it.

'Come through Scarlett, let's get you tidied up.' Like he's on my side. And I follow him in, holding my hands tight as fists.

We go into the club. Then we're standing there facing each other and staring. Me hating him and him smiling like there's no problem.

'Come on then, what is it that you want to say?' His eyes challenge me to take him on, and he laughs, like he knows I can't do anything. Like he's this big man and I'm just a little girl. Maybe Mario, but this little girl's hand is curled into a fist.

'You said this was a proper job.'

'I don't know what you're talking about.'

'Cut the bullshit, Mario. Those boys, they were more

than *a little rowdy*.' I point to my bloodied dress, Mario shrugs.

'It's an occupational hazard.'

'No. You told me it was an escort job. I trusted you. Give me the ten grand.'

'Or what? Scarlett, you get what I give you. You want money. Well, it's not always easy work. Perhaps those boys made you earn your money for a change.'

'Earn? Mario, he raped me!'

He grins, all gold mouth and cigarette-stained teeth. 'You can't rape a whore, Scarlett. Everyone knows that.' I hear hissing in the back of my head. 'Besides. My client is not happy with you. You didn't play nicely. You should always leave the client happy Scarlett, otherwise, no payment. Nothing.'

'Give me the fucking money. All of it, all ten thousand or you'll be sorry.'

'You know what? I think I might just keep all of it. What you going to do Scarlett? You going to sue me?'

That's when I know it's over. Mario's so over.

I move to punch him but he catches my fist mid swing, pulling my arm behind my back, hurting me, twisting muscles that have already been twisted enough. I yell at him to get off but he doesn't. Instead he starts licking at my neck, kissing it with big slimy kisses.

'Mario, get off me.'

'Come come Scarlett. You're still my girl.' He slides his hand under my dress. I stand frozen and rigid while he touches me, even while he whispers, 'Shhh, now, say sorry Mario, sorry Mario for being a bad girl.'

I'm so tired, so sick of fighting. Maybe I should give in to him, maybe Mario can win this one.

I think about Nina on the back seat of that car, her teeth biting into her lips until they bled. How brave she was and I think, no you bastard. You are not going to be

176

the one that breaks me.

'Sorry Mario, for being a bad girl,' I whisper.

He smiles, 'That's my girl.' He kisses me one more time, soft and long, his tongue lingering over mine, before he releases me.

Mario offers me a brandy and I say, 'Yeah, cheers,' because it's important that he thinks he's won and I could do with a drink.

'To you.' He clinks his glass with mine.

'To me.' I swallow the brandy in one gulp.

I take a taxi home. Tiggy's passed out on her bed starfished and fully dressed. She's curled up in a ball, her thumb in her mouth like a three year old. I close her bedroom door.

Looks like she made a bit of a night of it. The ashtrays are full and there's a carpet of yellow paper confetti. I pick up a record from the excuse of a pile that Tiggy calls a collection. Fucking hell, Tiggy. Cliff Richard! What sort of 21 year-old listens to Cliff Richard without a gun to their head?

I take a shower. I stand under the water for ages and ages my brain thinking so fast it almost overheats. The water punishes the rips and tears in my skin. I move myself around to get the full impact to see if I can stand it. I turn the tap to cold.

I look at myself in the mirrored bathroom cabinet and all I can see is this ball of fire, like, this whole fucking face of rage. But this amount of anger, it's delicious, it's fuel. It's better than any drug I ever tried. It lifts me up and makes me see everything so clearly. And Mario, I can see right through him.

And then it comes to me and I know exactly what I have to do.

Chapter Thirty Four
Tiggy

Scarlett and I live on a diet of alcohol, cigarettes and fruit. Or more accurately Scarlett bulk-buys fruit and eats gargantuan quantities. I find apple cores on the sofa, or the side of the bath. Or in the pocket of my favourite jacket. Days pass and the fruit bowl fills and empties. Scarlett runs and showers. On our nights off we go to pubs and sometimes boys buy us drinks. Scarlett does all the talking. Inventing a different name and occupation for every conversation. When I'm not with Scarlett, I read, play records. I wait for Tony to call.

Dan still drives me home when Scarlett visits *punters*. He's stopped coming in so often. He says that Scarlett makes him uncomfortable. He suggests that maybe we should meet up before work sometimes instead. Somewhere 'without snooping ears.' It's not like Dan to be so immediately judgemental, but I've stopped trying to convince him of Scarlett's virtues.

As he says, 'The horse is quite obviously dead, so please stop flogging it, Tiggy.'

Living with Scarlett is different to being in a dormitory. Other than the obvious stuff like we are allowed to smoke and there isn't room inspection every morning. It's just a whole lot simpler. When I shared rooms at school there were always rows about who had used what. And which shampoo belonged to whom. Some of the girls drew chalk lines down the middle of the room to define their space.

Scarlett and I have no problems in that area. She

helps herself to whatever she wants, whenever she wants and I say nothing. Because the truth is, I like it. No one ever wanted to borrow my stuff before.

My days have a rhythm to them now and whenever Scarlett is in the room there is noise and laughter.

Of course, sometimes when I come in to find all my albums out of their sleeves, when I reach for a cigarette and find the packet empty, when she finishes the vodka and then shoves the empty bottle back in the freezer, I do wonder whether I'm letting her take advantage. But she has this last minute reprieve thing going on. Each time I decide that I simply must talk to her about the mess. Lack of fags. Ruined clothes. Phone being left off the hook or whatever. She comes in with a bunch of flowers or a fresh bottle of vodka and says, 'I got this for you, to say thanks. You're such a great mate.'

And I think – What the hell.

When Tony cancels me on Wednesday I feel ambivalent. I want to see him, but don't want the same old conversations. I play back the message unconvinced that something has come up. Scarlett and I go swimming instead. Part of Scarlett's ongoing attempt to interest me in a fitness regime.

'But, I dance three times a night, five nights a week... that's plenty of exercise.'

'Undressing doesn't burn calories.'

'And I rehearse. I have to work out the dance routines and practice them.'

She raises a neatly plucked eyebrow, 'Tiggy, I've been here weeks and I've never seen you practice.'

'Well, maybe I do it when you're out.'

'Bollocks you do... here.' She chucks a plastic bag at me.

'What's this?'

'Swimming costume, towel, goggles – let's go.'

So we go.

The Porchester Centre is just along Bayswater Road in Queensway: one of those old Georgian pools with Victorian Turkish baths. And no doubt Byzantine cockroaches. I hate swimming. Swimming at school was ritual humiliation of overly-hormoned bitchy girls stripping off together before walking, goose-pimpled and erect-nippled, out onto the poolside. Then it was a few lengths of being kicked in the stomach or face by better swimmers and swallowing my weekly quota of water. And a lifetimes' allowance of chorine. I would lumber back to the changing rooms, pulling off my rubber bathing cap and wondering how this could be considered fun.

'Come on, Tiggy. What are you doing in there?' Scarlett is hammering on the changing room door.

I fumble into my costume as quickly as possible, banging my elbows on the side of the cubicle. Keeping a close eye on the floor for crustaceous beings. I read somewhere that cockroaches can swim. London pools and hospitals are full of them. Something brushes against my foot and I burst out of the cubicle. Slipping on the wet floor, tumbling delicately into a sprawl face to face with Scarlett's painted toenails.

'Shit, Scarlett, how did you get those?'

Her upper arms are circled with small bruises, her thighs dark with yellowing marks. She has scratches all down her back. Dried lines of maroon blood. She looks like she has been playing rough and tumble with a wild animal. Something with sharp claws.

'What?' She looks at her skin and shrugs, 'Who knows?'

'But-'

'I bruise easily alright, I must have thin blood or something, it's not as bad as it looks.'

'But... Scarlett... your back. Those are deep cuts. You should put something on them. Don't they hurt?'

'Tiggy, you're annoying me now. So, you can have a slap or you can shut your mouth. Joking! I'm fine. Now, come on, let's swim.'

Of course Scarlett isn't wearing her boarding school Speedo. She's wearing an itsy witsy red bikini, her toe nails are painted a matching red. She splashes through the footpool and out to the poolside so unselfconsciously that I half wonder whether the scratches are real. I tip toe over to the steps and start climbing down into the pool. I'm halfway into the pool when I hear Scarlett yelling excitedly.

'Oi, Tiggy!' Scarlett is bouncing up and down on the end of a flexible diving board. The bikini looks dangerously close to pinging free. 'Watch this!' she yells. So I watch while she catapults herself into the air and then belly flops back into the pool. She surfaces a few seconds later giggling. 'You diving?'

'No, I'll just do a few lengths.'

'Suit yourself.'

Scarlett insists we try the Turkish Baths afterwards, 'I used to go to them in Hackney, they were cool, come on, come on.'

I wish I knew how to use the word 'no.'

'Brilliant... women only.' The tiled corridor passes a plunge pool, showers and a heated rest area. The whole place smells of sweat, essential oils and prawn cocktail crisps.

Scarlett whips her bikini off and strides along the corridor pulling open the steam bath door, 'Fucking yes.'

I choke back a mouthful of steam.

The steam bath is more like a misted market place. A flesh market at that. Women from every ethnicity and origin are squashed together on the stone benches. Three roly-poly Jamaican women are sat on the floor scrubbing each other's backs, eating crisps and chocolate.

'Squash up,' Scarlett says and then squeezes in between two women and pulls her head back, closes her eyes and smiles.

I stand with my back to the wall. The air burning in my throat. Waiting hopefully for someone to move over and let me in. More women come in and yell at the others to make room. Until I am almost flattened behind the door.

I leave. I'm not finding the experience relaxing.

Twenty minutes later a naked and sweaty Scarlett finds me wrapped in a towel and sat on a stone bench beside the plunge pool, outside the steam room.

'Wow, that was fantastic.' Her eyes are bright, her breasts defying gravity. She seems oblivious to her injuries. I'm wincing just looking at them.

'Plunge Pool. Fucking yeah.' She jumps feet first into the water. I scream as freezing water splashes me. Scarlett treads water grinning like it is pleasure.

'Come on in, this is the best bit, this is where you get the gain, it's meant to be really good for your skin. It'll keep you looking young forever, come on Tigs, no pain no gain.'

'I'm fine here.' I move my feet away from the side of the pool. I don't want Scarlett pulling me in.

I shouldn't have worried about her pulling me in. Within seconds she is out of the pool and behind me.

Pushing. My feet slip on the mosaic tiles.

'Please Scarlett, no Scarlett... SCARLETT... I'm Scared... NO. PLEASE. NO!'

I fall. Headfirst. Limbs akimbo. The sound of her giggles ringing in my ears as freezing water hits my body and for a moment I think my heart has stopped.

The lesson for the day is that 'no' seems to mean different things to different people.

Chapter Thirty Five
Tiggy

I'm meeting Tony in Kensington Gardens.

I get there deliberately late. He can wait for me for a change. He is carrying flowers. I take them without looking at them.

'Feeling guilty?'

He wrinkles his forehead, perplexed, 'No. I just bought you flowers.'

'Right,' I say. 'Thanks, I suppose.'

We walk into The Orangery, where I scowl at him. I refuse to order anything other than a black coffee, regardless of how many times he tries to cajole me into having a Danish pastry.

The Orangery was our discovery together. This magical tearoom behind Kensington Palace. The perfect place for an affair because no one seems to know it's there. It's a proper Merchant Ivory location. A gravel pathway through landscaped gardens leads to the pale marble steps and Corinthian columns. Inside it's all white walls, high ceilings and long sash windows. We took afternoon tea. Choosing from a decadent cake trolley and drinking Earl Grey from a silver pot. I thought for three hundred years lovers have come here and had felt everything that I was feeling. Tony and I sat hand in hand looking out onto the lawns. I felt like royalty.

Today all I notice is the pigeons trapped in the eaves. How they flutter from one joist to the next. Never choosing to escape through the open door.

Scarlett and I have been talking about married men. She's got this theory that they have affairs because women are dumb enough to let them. She says it's funny how women are always saying that men are unfaithful. Because, 'They're doing it with someone right. Unless there's one very busy women in Pimlico.'

Scarlett says that married men should use hookers if they want some excitement. She says that at least it's honest. And that the women who sleep with blokes knowing that they already have a wife and kids might as well have T-shirts with 'I think I'm worth less than shit' printed on them.

I pointed out that some affairs were about love, not just sex. That Tony and I have a connection. That we talk about everything. She made a face like I was suggesting ripping the skin off live baby seals was a pleasant hobby.

'Oh come on, Tiggy. You think *Sir* was interested in you for your mind? What is it that you think a 15 year-old can offer a bloke 20 years older? Don't be a dumb schoolgirl all your life.'

At which point I walked out of the room. She pisses me off.

'So are you going to be like this all day?' Tony catches up with me. I'm pacing along the path, stamping the ground down. I don't answer him. He's wearing cords, shirt and a tie, his brogues freshly polished. I'm wearing baggy jeans and a pink vest top, my hair in plaits, my feet in flip flops. People look at us curiously. A strange match. I wish he would wear something cooler, or something less, well, like my father.

The weather has lured everyone out of their beds: people of all shapes and sizes crawling out from the nooks and crannies, finding their way to the park. It's

like a children's storybook. *Tiggy goes to the Park.*
People roller skating, boys on skateboards, skinny men
wearing Sony walkmans, cycling, jogging, families
lying out on blankets, dogs catching balls, couples
holding hands. On the lake there are boats bobbing on
waves. I bet if you lifted up the surface, opened it up
like a tin can that there would be brightly coloured fish
swimming in the water. All *Bed knobs and Broom-
sticks.* It's like that, a perfect picture.

I want to rip it up.

Tony tries to take my hand.

'You know by rights, Tiggy, I should be the one
who's angry with you.'

What a surprise. Tony is spinning the argument 180
degrees. He shoves his hands into his trouser pockets,
his neatly ironed shirt tucked in, the sleeves rolled up.
Ever the teacher. 'Calling Sandra, stirring things up-'

'I've already apologised.'

'I don't know what you're thinking sometimes. Do
you think that by making my life difficult we can spend
more time together? Well let me tell you that it's not
going to work. I had to spend the whole weekend
running around buying Sandra white goods just to
keep her happy. I'm using up my savings myself over
this new kitchen.'

What is he buying a new kitchen for if he's leaving
her?

Only he isn't, is he?

'You're never going to leave are you?"

'Oh here we go.'

Tony pulls me from the path onto the grass. I drag
my heels and walk along in pigeon steps. I'm being told
off. Any minute now he's going to wag his finger in my
face and tell me how he's 'not so much angry as
disappointed'. How he 'expected more from me'.

I fold my arms across my body and tap my foot.

'You said you were leaving her.'

'So you thought you'd hurry things along a little?'

'No.'

'We talked about it. I thought you understood. That it wouldn't happen again.'

What is he talking about?

'You know I hate it when you push me, Tiggy. When you try to manipulate me.'

This is the thing with Tony and me. We have circular conversations. He talks faster and faster until I'm spinning with confusion. Then 'POOOF.' There's smoke everywhere and he's going 'Ta Dah!' And I'm wondering if I'm the woman being sawn in half, or the rabbit being pulled out of a hat. I guess what I'm saying is that sometimes it seems as though Tony tricks me into agreeing with him. However determined I am not to.

I don't know why he's bringing up an argument that we've already had. Maybe he's looking for a fight. Maybe he's trying to trick me into saying or doing something I don't want.

'I told you I was shopping and I wanted to speak to you.' I watch closely for the sleight of hand.

'Not that time, after that, why did you call?'

'I haven't. I haven't Tony, I swear.'

'Sandra says she's been getting anonymous phone calls. Sometimes two or three a day.' The statement is an accusation.

'Well don't look at me.'

'Well who else is it going to be?'

'I don't know. Anyone. Kids? It's the school holidays. They do that. Why would I do that?'

'She says it's definitely a woman. She can tell from the breathing.'

'That's ridiculous. From her breathing. Well, anyway, it's not me.'

'Tiggy, it has to stop okay.' He's using his 'controlling a class' voice. Tony talks to me about how when you're teaching you have to show the class boundaries set your limits and keep to them. Once you let someone cross over the line then its game over. He says that the hardest part of being a teacher is learning how to handle the children. I am being handled.

'Come on, Tiggy. I'm not angry. I know it's difficult for you. But please, please don't do it again.'

'Is it impossible for you to believe that it wasn't me?'

He doesn't answer. He kicks a tuft of grass on the pathway. He won't look at me.

'You think I'm lying. Tony, it wasn't me! Maybe Sandra's making it up.'

'She's not like that. She wouldn't do that. She's really upset.'

Oh of course. Poor fragile Sandra who can't be upset.

'Maybe she's testing you. Maybe she's invented these calls as a reason to-'

'She's not like that. If she has a problem then she asks me. She wouldn't lie.'

'Oh but I would, is that it?'

'Tiggy, we both know that everything hasn't been great between us lately.'

I glare at him. If Sandra is so perfect, so fragile, what is he doing here? He kicks the grass again and pushes his hands back into his trouser pockets. Sometimes the way he dresses, the way he talks to me is infuriating. He's an old man.

'Well maybe I've had enough of *this*.'

We have been here before. We have stood silently facing each other many times in the last few years. There's a conversation that we always return to.

Recently with an alarming frequency. We talk about how difficult it is to love each other and not be together. How maybe it would be better to stop. But whether it's due to love or laziness, we always slam the conversation into reverse the moment we get near its natural conclusion.

I don't know why anymore. It's obvious that we're steadily moving towards admitting it is over. We're both being cowards. At the end of the conversation we will hold each other and kiss. We will apologise for the hurtful things we have said. But we won't be sorry.

I am bored of my indecision, of hearing my voice say things I don't feel.

I'm going to be strong.

It will be different.

I will ignore the telltale twinge of nausea and speak my mind.

'What's really happening here, Tony?'

'I'm not sure. Come on let's get a drink and talk about it.' He takes my hand stroking the insides of my wrists.

Does he do that to remind me? To take me back to that Christmas, keeping me small and insecure. Caressing the veins I was too chicken to cut. That was a long time ago. I was a different girl then. Like my father, Tony refuses to let me grow up.

He lifts my wrists to his mouth and kisses the faded scars. 'What are you thinking sweetie?' His lips on my wrists, his face concerned.

'You want to know what I'm thinking? Because it's my mind you're interested in isn't it, Sir?'

'What's that supposed to mean?' He drops my hands.

'You know exactly what I mean.' I stick my chin in the air, delighted to finally be standing up for myself.

189

'Don't be childish and don't talk to me like that.' There it is again, *be good and I'll love you.*

'Isn't that the way you like me, Sir? What is it? Am I getting too old for you? Maybe you should find yourself another little girl to play with. Maybe I'm no fun anymore, Sir. Still there's plenty more where you found me, I suppose.'

I've never spoken to Tony like that. *Never* accused him of taking advantage of me. As soon as I've said it, as soon as I see his face, I wish I had a rewind button.

I'm damned if I'm going to give in. So I bite my lip while my insides list like a cross channel ferry

'Fine,' he finally speaks and nods, as though in agreement with himself. Then he nods again at me. 'Yes, okay Tiggy, maybe you're right, I mean, if that's what you think of me.'

It takes me a few moments to filter the information. To understand that he is changing the rules. Or the rules are the same, but the game has shifted.

I will hold my ground.

'Fine,' I say defiantly.

'Okay.' His hands are out of his pockets now and clenched in decision.

'Right, well then... Good luck.'

He turns and walks away.

Just like that!

After all this time. Bastard.

Then I realise what I've done.

'Tony!' I'm yelling, running along the path after him. I throw my arms around his neck and burst into tears. 'I'm sorry, don't leave me... I didn't mean it... please.'

He has been my parent, lover, friend. He is everything to me.

He kisses my face, 'It's the right thing, you know it too. You deserve more.'

Tony was the only one who could make everything feel better. Could make me believe that there was something to wish for. I know that something had to change, but it aches and it hurts. It feels easier to stay here in the park. To beg him to stay, to keep his arms locked around mine. To pretend that everything could be okay.

'No... no... don't,' I sob and he strokes my hair, kisses my face and whispers over and over that he is sorry. That this is the right thing to do.

Eventually he pulls my arms from his neck.

He kisses me one last time and then walks away.

With every step he takes away from me my heart splits another fragment. I am faint. I splinter from myself and stand shocked, watching myself watching him and thinking, 'so this is how it ends.'

He has never looked more beautiful.

I have never felt so alone. I have to stop myself from screaming at him to come back. I kneel down. I hold on to the ground. Because the world is spinning and I am coughing up tears, emotions and gasping for breath.

Like that possessed girl in *The Exorcist*. Choking out dreams onto the grass.

Chapter Thirty Six
Scarlett

How can someone be so downwardly mobile?

For starters, how many strippers have four A-Levels at grade A? But what really gets me is her bankbook, her cheque stubs, there are monthly payments of hundreds of pounds coming in from 'Francis Arnold.' Daddy I guess, and she pays the rent and that, but all the rest of the money, earnings whatever is spent in Tower Records, WH Smith and Oddbins. You don't have to be Quincy or Columbo to detect Tiggy's favourite things.

It's like money means nothing to her. In the last six months Tiggy has earned nearly £6,000 and if you include the £4,000-ish from Daddy that's up to £10,000, which is a long way off my earnings but not too bad when you look at it. And where I've got over £80,000 in the bank, Tiggy has got herself an overdraft of £2,452. Not that she needs to worry, a quick peek through last year's statements and it's clear that from time to time Daddy bails poor little Tiggy out. Her overdraft was paid off in full last year, a cheque for the perfect amount arriving a few days before Christmas. Francis Arnold is obviously someone worth being a bit sweet to.

I fish under her pillow and bring out her diary. Like genius hiding place Tiggy, took me seconds to find that. If people wanted to keep their secrets then there's no way they'd write them down, and besides who keeps a diary? I mean, I guess maybe if you're on some North Pole expedition there are things worth noting, you know the number of penguins waddling about, the polar bears you've shot or whatever, stuff for other explorers and that, but what the fuck does Tiggy have to record? 'Today I read a book, smoked some fags. Listened to music and then took my clothes off.' It's hardly the same as that diary they made us read at school where the girl is hiding in the attic from Nazis and everyone ends up dead anyway.

And Tiggy is no Anne Frank, you can't help some women you know. She's got money, looks, posh family, the whole thing – like, everything I wanted when I was a kid, yet on every page, it's just like Mum. It's all about the bloke. Pages and pages of navel gazing and arguing with herself about every move she makes. Most entries are exactly the same as the day before. Like she could have just written down *Lame* and it would have covered her whole life.

Still, I've not peeked for a few days, something major might have happened in her life, you never know. Miracles happen every day.

Dan Dan the Piano Man gets more attention than he deserves, the bloke is your ordinary south London tosser. Tiggy writes about him like he's special or unique or something. 'Dan drove me home tonight'. 'Dan is so supportive, he really understands me'. Oh fuck off Tiggy, Dan is like every other bloke from south bloody London. '*Sarf London*' pisses me off, I mean what is it for?

I ended up on a bus that went that way once, I swear it was like London but mutated. I got as far as Old Kent Road and that bloody ugly pink building with an elephant on top of it that was supposed to be a shopping centre. I went inside coz I figured that I was like Captain Kirk arriving on some strange planet, and I should at least have a look before begging Scotty to beam me back North.

Boldly going where only pissheads and deadheads have gone before me I discovered that south London is where people go to piss in the street and smoke crack. There were like hundreds of people in that shopping centre and every single one of them was wearing a nylon tracksuit matched with a tight curl home perm, including the men who had a range of mangy mullets, their fake gold-ringed hands dragging along the floor behind them.

South London is God's way of telling people not to build bridges. They stay their side of the river and I'll stick to mine.

If Tiggy's not careful she'll end up stuck in some shitty estate in Peckham with howling babies and that Dan Dan the Piano Man making terrible jokes. By the time she wakes up it'll be too late.

It's like she's started with it all, you know, the rich parents, the big house, the pony, the posh school but she's determined to flush her life down the toilet. She's a strong argument for a sharp slap to the face.

She's only just got shot of the cradle snatching pervert and she's lining herself up for another disaster.

Thinking about disasters reminds me of Mum, so I give her a call.

'Oh you woke me up.' Bloody three pm and the lazy bitch was still sleeping.

'Hi Mum.'

'Where've you been love?'

'I'm in Shepherd's Bush... I'm fine... I'm sharing a flat with this girl.'

'Well you could have rung-'

'Yeah, yeah.'

'Aren't you going to ask how I am?'

'I was about to... bloody hell, give me a chance.'

Then she's off on one about how I should have called and how she's been worried sick (unlikely). And how her and Pete have some news that they want to tell me and do I want to come over one evening. I figure she's pregnant isn't she. So I say,

'I can't this week.'

'Well, next week then... we have something-'

'Yeah, yeah – you knocked up or something? You going to keep it this time?'

She pauses for a second and then says, 'Of course we're keeping it.' She starts going on about how *her and Pete* wanted to tell me first, and how *her and Pete* are going to ask the council for a bigger place, because the flat isn't big enough for the three of them. And it's not really the right place to bring up a child (although it was good enough for me apparently) and how everyone at The Crown is saying that she's glowing and that Pete's hoping it's a boy and so on.

'I thought you wanted to tell me first?'

'We did love, but we didn't know where you were did we?'

She goes on and on about the party that they're having for the baby and I stop listening to her because it's all bullshit, all bollocks plans that I've heard before and which are never going to happen.

Pete's in the background going all like, 'Who is it Linda?' Mum must mouth to him that it's me, coz then he's on the phone, straight away saying 'You've got a bloody nerve. You selfish cow. If it's money you're after then you can forget it.'

Which is when I hang the phone up and then rip the cord from the wall.

Fuck them.

I go back and re-read a bit more of Tiggy's diary but it's so depressing that I start wanting to go over the tragic bits with a highlighter pen, and write stuff in the margin like *'Oooh poor me, I'm such a victim.'* I find her Polariod camera and a few boxes of spare film, so I rifle through her Viola Viola costumes, settling on the schoolgirl one and then take a few snapshots. I line them up one by one and look for something to do while they develop into proper pictures.

I put on the *Best of Blondie* LP and dance like a mental Muppet to *Rip Her to Shreds.* Then I stick on a blonde wig and do Tiggy's routine. I stand on the sofa, pretending it's my stage and dance.

When I was a little kid I had all these stupid dreams about my dad. I figured he'd turn up in a Porsche or something one day. Take me away to his mansion in the country, all that bollocks How all the other kids would have to eat dirt while he drove me around the estate calling me 'Princess'.

By the time I got to 13, I'd worked out that going on Mum's last 25 boyfriends it was unlikely that my dad was rich, handsome and caring, or even just an average bloke, coz Mum is a wanker magnet.

I didn't need a CSE in Maths to work out that the probability is that my dad will be a hopeless loser who thinks signing on is a career choice.

'You're so like him,' Mum'd say, except for when she said shit like, 'I think we row so much coz we're so alike.'

And I was like, 'Which one is it Mum, am I like my dad or like you?'

Truth is that I doubt she knows who he is. Mum's not one for keeping secrets, so if she'd known him long enough to get a name then she'd have told me by now.

I climb down off the sofa and find Tiggy's B52s LP and then play *Dance This Mess Around* over and over. I pogo around the flat, over the furniture and back into the lounge where I perform a perfect Tiggy routine to myself in front of the mirror. I could pass for Viola Viola. I go back to the bedroom and look at the new bedspread gallery of Polaroid pictures. I look hot, completely fuckable. And then I get it, the 'why' of 'why she does it'. In this get up I feel totally powerful, like nothing can stop me.

Whoever my dad is he's not going to be taking me skiing, buying me ponies or paying off my credit cards.

That's where she is now, sucking up to Daddy dearest, no doubt at some fancy restaurant where lobsters swim in tanks and the waitresses all look like supermodels.

Viola Viola is a whole lot more jazzing than Tiggy is ever gonna be.

Poor Tiggy, life's been so hard for her. Don't get me wrong, I like her, but she's such a Jason.

It's lucky for her that she has a new best friend to offer her a little assistance. Give that girl a silver spoon and she'll just use it to dig her own grave.

Chapter Thirty Seven
Tiggy

Y ou actually said that to him. Blimey. I wish I'd
been there, I would have loved to have seen that.'

I've just told Scarlett that it is over with Tony. I've
done a little editing on the story. I'm not lying as such.
More omitting a few of the minor details. Scarlett
thinks that I met Tony at the park, accused him of
taking advantage. I told him it was over, that I deserved better. I didn't mention the public vomiting
incident. And it's possible that I skipped over the bit
where I begged him to stay and cried into his mouth.

'So then what? Tell me everything then, what did he
say?'

'Nothing much.'

'Oh bollocks he didn't, come on, tell me, did he beg
you not to?'

'Well.'

'Did he cry? Oh tell me the child-snatching pervert
cried. I love it when they cry.'

Scarlett's delight in Tony's downfall is contagious.
For the rest of the afternoon we giggle about the look
on Tony's face. His disbelief and anguish. By the time
we are getting ready for work I am convinced that I am
both victim and victor. Tony abused me terribly, used
me throughout school and then kept me hanging on.
Lying to me and wasting my time. And now finally I
am free.

'We should go out on Friday, after the club, there's a
place called Club Velveteen. We'll dance, drink, get
drunk.' Scarlett is picking through my wardrobe

slinging clothes onto the floor. Finally choosing a violet satin slip she convinced me to buy a few days before. I've been looking at it with trepidation. I can't imagine ever wearing it. It clings to every curve.

'Absolutely... let's celebrate my freedom you mean?'

'Yah, Absoloooootly, darling.'

Scarlett has this pretend posh voice that she puts on from time to time. I never know if she's taking the piss out of me.

'Can I borrow that white dress of mine back?' I have no intention of wearing it, but she's annoying me.

'Oh sorry babes, the dry cleaners lost it.'

'Sketchley's? On the high street? They're normally really good.'

'Yeah, shocker isn't it darling, still I'm sure Daddy will buy you another one.'

I check her face for sarcasm or bitterness, there's nothing. In fact she's smiling openly at herself in my wardrobe mirror, her hands on her hips.

'Darling, I'm absolutely gorgeous,' she says in her pretend Sloane accent. 'I'd pay to fuck myself in this.'

At Valerios, the lights are set to seductive. Most of the girls have been booked two or three times already this evening. I love these summer nights; when the girls are happy, flushed with champagne and a good night's wage. The seediness that can hang over the club evaporates in the party atmosphere. When the club is full couples dance and laughter shrieks from the red booths. The noise levels rise as conversations flourish and all the men overspend. Caught up in the sensation that they are part of something.

Valerios can, at times, have the ambience of a drunken wedding reception. Groups of stag parties singing along to Dan's rendition of *New York, New*

York. The hostesses place their handbags in a pile on the dance floor and dance around them. It's much more of a collective experience than the hush of intimate conversations and embarrassed coughs on the slower nights.

Dan finishes his set with a rousing chorus of *Mack the Knife* and then announces a five minute break before, 'The sexiest woman alive. All the way from Sao Paulo. For your viewing pleasure. Viola Viola.'

He comes backstage. I tell him about Tony. That I felt it was time to call it a day.

'But you're alright though?'

'Yeah, I'm fine.'

'Oh. Right. Okay then. If that's how it is.'

'What?'

'It's just it always seemed, from what you said... well, I thought he seemed like he was very important to you. And yet you're sat here smiling like he meant nothing.'

And with one small shrug he switches my mood from up to down.

Just like that.

'Dan, stick the tape on, will you?'

My act is abysmal. I'm too angry to concentrate and too concentrated to smile. Dan doesn't know anything about Tony and me. It's like Scarlett says, Tony took advantage. He was using me and I'm better than that.

Mario is standing at the back of the club by the bar, his face under lit by the red table tamps. Casting shadows on his face, enlarging his teeth and eyebrows. Making him look like a Gaudi gargoyle. As I remove my top he yawns. The deliberate, exaggerated yawn of a small child or first year drama student.

200

Backstage he's waiting for me. From behind a haze of cigarette smoke and aftershave, he says, 'I think we need to talk.'

I follow him reluctantly up to the flat. I know exactly where this is going. I have a steady sense that I am taking another step further away from myself.

Scarlett taps on the toilet door. 'Hey Tiggy, what's with you and Mario?'

I'm sat on the cistern, my head in my hands. I'm arguing with myself about whether there is any moral difference between taking off my bra and taking off my knickers. That total nudity is not a shameful thing. Not one step closer to prostitution. A small anxious voice is gaining an increasing audience in my thoughts. She's saying that this has gone on long enough. That it is time to stop.

'Tiggy, I know it's you in there. What is it? Did he hurt you?'

'No... I'm... he-' I open the door and Scarlett squeezes herself in, closing the door, leaning back on it, saying 'What are you hiding in here for then?'

'Mario thinks that my act isn't titillating enough. That I should take off my knickers.'

'Oh?' Scarlett cocks her head. 'And I'm thinking that you don't want to do that?'

I shake my head.

'So don't. Simple.'

'Oh come on Scarlett, if I say *no* to Mario then I won't have a job.'

'So get another one. You shouldn't be here anyway.'

'Meaning?'

'Meaning that this is not a place for girls like you.'

'And what sort of girl is that?'

'Er, you know, nice, sweet. Oh you know what I mean, Tiggy. You're not exactly your normal stripper material are you?'

'Maybe not, but I like it here.'

'You know, Mario won't stop at you being naked. It'll be something else next, He'll want you to dance with another girl or use sex toys or something. That's the game we're playing.'

'I'm not playing a game.'

'Tiggy! We're not working in bloody Garfunkels! Don't you know anything about these clubs? It's all about which club is the most risky, dirty, classy, and as soon as one club does something new the next one will try and do something better. Mario's a proper bastard, but he's not stupid.'

'You think I should say no?'

She nods and then opens the cubicle door, 'Come on, we can't stay in here all night.' I follow her through to the washbasins trying to avoid my anxious reflection while Scarlett tops up her lipstick.

'There. I am practically perfect, he is so in the bag, can't keep his beady eyes off The Tits. This should give him something to think about.' She tugs the slip dress down a little further revealing another inch of cleavage. Reminding me that maybe Scarlett isn't the right person to ask about a moral crisis.

'Look I've got to get back. I've got a punter, so tell Mario you want a bit of time, he'll leave you alone for a week or so and you can have a proper think about what you're going to do. We'll chat later, yeah? Tomorrow or something.'

'I thought we were going out tonight?'

'Business Tiggy, can't say no. Sorry, I've got a target to reach. Laters.'

'But you said. What with Tony. And. You promised.'

'You know this clingy thing is really unattractive Tigs,' she says waving one hand in my face. I'm about to remind her that we discussed this earlier, that we had an agreement, but by the time I've got my hands on my hips and the words on my lips she's gone.

Dan has already packed up. He's changed out of his black suit and into jeans. When I find him, he's pulling a faded blue T-shirt over his head. His body is tanned and hairless. Tony had the start of a beer belly, a gentle pouch of middle-aged spread. I loved to lay my head on his stomach. I imagine my head laying on Dan's chest, his fingers in my hair.

Dan grins when he sees me, pushes his fringe out of his eyes with one hand and picks up his holdall with the other.

'Dan, are you busy? Do you... um... can we drive out to the coast tonight? No problem if you can't... if you're busy or something.'

He shakes his head. 'Sorry Tigs, got to get straight back tonight, can't even give you a lift. Rain check yeah? Perhaps meet at The Dive later this week for a pint?'

He kisses my cheek quickly, almost paternally and then he leaves.

I walk home, five long rainy miles. So that's that. No Tony, no Dan and Scarlett's off God knows where. I'm so bored of feeling so lonely. The streets are a thousand shades of grey. For the first time in ages I wonder whether leaving home was the right idea. At my father's there was always clean clothes, home cooked meals. Maybe over time we'd have found a way to talk to each other.

I don't sleep much. I sit up in bed smoking and

scrawling pages in my diary. I drink vodka and try not to think about my mother, or what Scarlett might be doing now, what deprivation Mario will expect from me next or whether Tony is feeling any of what I'm feeling.

Three vodkas later I roll myself a joint. It takes me three or four attempts and almost a whole packet of Rizzlas to create a papier-mâché patchwork spliff. I have to lay the whole thing out in front of me like a jigsaw and then piece it together. It still falls apart. If I had Copydex or some other latex adhesive then this would be the time to use it.

Two more vodkas and I hit on the perfect solution for my melancholy.

I know with total certainty that what is needed is a mood-based compilation tape: a TDK audio epitaph for my relationship with Tony. I will create a musical montage that will purge, soothe and release me from this gloom.

With the perfect tape I will finally be free.

I drag all my singles, cassettes and LPs out into the middle of the room. Then I work out the tracks for each side. I'm figuring 4.5 minutes per song which is a little over. I'll see what room is left at the end of the side.

The Jesus Jones, Neds Atomic Dustbin and The Wonder Stuff all get chucked to one side as I pull forward the hard stuff, Chicago, Abba and REO Speedwagon, Then guiltily I allow myself to savour the single malt whiskey of music *Ladies and Gentlemen I present the beautiful, the exquisite, Cliff Richard.*

I pick the cellophane off a new 90-minute cassette and with almost religious observance click it into position.

Side One. *Miss You Nights, A Heart Will Break, Please Don't Fall in Love,* I cry singing this. Enjoying myself so much that I play it again. Forgetting to stop the tape and having to rewind it back. Then comes *Ocean Deep*. A little known single, tragically overlooked, that speaks my life. I add in a few jazz ballads that Tony used to play. Chet Baker singing *Don't Get Around Much Anymore*, Ella Fitzgerald scatting *Just One of Those Things*. I know already that these are the songs I will fast forward through later. I rewind again and tape over them.

Oh and about now I play Charlene's *Never Been to Me*. Far too many times. Because, oh hell, because I suppose I'm horribly drunk and well it's fantastic.

More importantly, how has the writer of this major work been overlooked?

Later, convinced that Chicago are unrecognised geniuses, I conclude that *You're the Inspiration*, is the definitive love song of my generation. So good, that it needs to go on again. And surely there is no song more delicately realised than Kylie Minogue singing *Tears on my Pillow*.

Side Two, I've given in completely. After *Time after Time* and then *Stay with me 'till Dawn*, the remainder of the tape becomes *Tiggy's Best Cliff Love Songs* compilation. I lie back on the floor while the room spins and Cliff articulates my desperate hopeless abandonment.

But I need more. Just one more fix. Something a little stronger. I climb up the sofa and fall onto the LPs and then I find it. The Kids from *Fame* Soundtrack LP. The holy grail of heartbreak.

I gingerly drop the needle onto the track and press the pause button back off and start to record *It's Gonna be a Long Night*.

I sing, I drink and I smoke.

These are the three things I can trust.

There is nothing and no one else.

Then I play the tape back. It is perfect. A spiritual experience. I have reached a new stage of enlightenment.

I'm lying on the floor singing *Starmaker* when Scarlett comes home. Her face hovers in the air above me. Then she appears to be splitting, like I'm looking through a kaleidoscope at thousands of Scarletts.

'Hi,' I say with some effort. I am in a transcendental state and from here it's hard to commune with the humans.

The many Scarletts all say 'hi' back to me, then reach down and pull me up. I slump against the sofa and shake myself back to earth. My head feels weird.

'What happened?' Scarlett is staring at me like I should be sent to a nuthouse.

'Cliff and a spliff,' I say, which I find hilarious. So funny in fact that I laugh and laugh rolling around on the carpet.

'STOP!' Something bad happens to my cheek.

'Ow!' I rub my face. 'How did that happen?'

'I slapped you, now what's going on?'

'I loved him,' I say. 'I loved him so much.' My tongue is thick and my words come out lisped and groggy.

'You know, Tiggy. I believe you.' Her voice is crystal sharp. It makes my ears ring, she's being very loud. 'Now listen to me carefully.' Why is she shouting?

'Shhhhhh,' I whisper and my finger tries to tap, but misses, my mouth.

'I'm sure that whatever you're going through is some sort of fucked up life crisis. But there is no excuse for this music... Jesus.'

'But-'

'No.'

206

She picks up the Cliff Love Songs LP, 'And *this*,' she dangles my beloved Cliff album like a dead animal from her red fingernails. 'This is banned. No Cliff. From now on this flat is a Cliff-free-zone.'

'But-' She can't mean it. 'No. You don't understand.'

'Give me one good reason why *this* should be allowed to stay?'

'Cliff's my daddy,' I slur happily.

'Isn't everyone? Tiggy, how about you find yourself a man your own age and stop listening to this crap?'

Isn't everyone? What's that supposed to mean?

'No. My flat. Cliff stays with me.' I snap the LP from her hand and press the tape back on.

'Fucking hell, Tiggy. Do you practise being pathetic or something, coz this amount of it ain't normal!' And Scarlett slams her bedroom door closed behind her.

Chapter Thirty Eight
Tiggy

In the letter from my mother she says marrying so young was her mistake. She foolishly believed that marriage and motherhood had something to do with romance.

She puts it simply. There is no ambiguity. She got married because she was in love. Her whole childhood she had been waiting for this moment. The rich, handsome open-hearted man who would go down on bended knee and make her life complete.

But beautiful as she looked in her cream taffeta wedding dress she hadn't thought about life after that day. About the dragging repetition of being wife and mother.

My father was born in Sussex in 1945. The year the second world war ended. My mother was born in Hampshire five years later. The world was already different, although rationing and multiple bereavements were still a long way from forgotten.

They met in 1968, at a summer ball in a Georgian country house. The sixties might have been swinging in the metropolis. Flower power was drifting in around the corner. But for my parents, life was elsewhere. Life was planned and disciplined, comfortable and reassuring.

When I think of them meeting I imagine something along the lines of *Brideshead Revisited*. An ivy-clad mansion set in acres of landscaped lawns. The gravel crunching under the tyres of the silver Rolls Royce carrying my mother past the walled gardens, the lake and into the circular drive where her gloved hand is taken and kissed gently by the host, 'darling you look simply charming'.

She stays close to the wall, tugging on the sleeves of her green satin dress, fidgeting with the pins in her hair. Biting her nails, watching everyone laughing and dancing. Maybe remembering how at prep school she'd stood like this in the playground at breaks, watching the other children playing and fighting. Not knowing how to join in.

She watches shyly, innocent of the fact that she is the most alluring, enigmatic woman in the room.

Later there would be fireworks over the gardens. The terraces and balconies filled with rich beautiful people applauding the display, complimenting the host on his tasteful spectacle.

The band strikes up with, *That Old Black Magic*, the terrace empties as everyone goes back in to dance. My mother stays outside. The cool evening breeze on her skin. The scent of rhododendron, hydrangeas and camomile, perhaps chirruping crickets. She has a single pale white orchid in her blonde hair. She watches the evening turn to night, the grey and blue merging into black. She leans over the balcony, thinking about what might happen should she jump.

My father comes out onto the balcony, young and handsome in his black suit, his face a little flushed from all the dancing. He smiles at her, this beautiful lonely woman. He holds out his open hand and the band plays *Moon River* and under the starlit sky they dance silently. Fireflies circling their heads. Shooting stars fizzing into space.

They fall in love during that dance, as simply and easily as in stories. As though fairies sprinkle glittering love dust over the dancing couple.

All I know is that they met at a summer ball in 1968, that within weeks of meeting they were engaged to be married. That's how things were for them.

They married the following June, and within months of the marriage, my mother was pregnant. By the following April she was mother to a screaming child that refused to be comforted.

In her letter she says that she achieved all her ambitions by the age of 18. She married a rich, handsome man for love. She wondered why people made life look so difficult when it came so easily for her. She hadn't considered what would happen after the wedding, when my father having wooed and won her, returned to his work. The heady glow of first love cooled into comfort and certainty, her pre-determined future stretched remorselessly, inexorably ahead of her.

'I thought your father and I would be different, that we were the exceptions. When I realised that we weren't, I lost my balance.'

She says she should have left then. In the first year when she realised she had swallowed a lie. That happy ever after was just for stories, but of course by then she was pregnant.

She doesn't say that she blamed me. She doesn't need to.

Chapter Thirty Nine
Scarlett

Roberto's chimp-faced assistant is sat opposite me staring at The Tits, and asking me if there is anything I need. You to fuck off mate would be a good start. I've been waiting in the back room of Club Velveteen and other than me and Chimpface the place is empty. Without the lights and music it feels less like a Hollywood movie set and more like a smoke-filled snake pit. The walls are muddled with framed black and white photographs, all signed with what looks like the same black felt tip. They all say shit like 'Roberto, thanks for your wonderful hospitality – George.' Or 'I.O.U for a fabulous night.' I suppose I'm meant to recognise the faces and be like totally impressed by all Roberto's showbiz friends, but it's lost on me.

But I look at the pictures coz it beats thinking about how I'm alone down here alone with just Chimpface for company. Come on Roberto.

Chimpface was born to bully. He's got that pitbull build and is so muscle-bound that he can't cross his legs. Where his neck should be there is half an inch of solid block meat, a proper east end tough lad, and at least four times my bodyweight.

The estate bully where I grew up was a lad called Evil. He had some other name like Kevin or whatever but everyone knew him as 'Evil' and he was. From the age of eight he terrorised everyone. He pulled the wooden fences out of the gardens in the maisonettes and chucked them through the windows. He'd collect up the dog shit from the estate, and there was plenty of that, and pat it into balls, and then catapult it at the women pushing prams. The aim was to get the ball right into the pram and give the baby a face full. When he wasn't bullying the Indian kids he was forcing the girls to lift their skirts, asking eight year old girls whether they liked being fingered.

One of the girls, Sadie, told her mum, who told Evil's dad, who got right onto him. You could hear the screaming along the whole of the walkway along the outside of the block. Sadie's kitten went missing and was posted back to her paw by paw.

He was nice enough with me, it's like you've got to keep them on side, make them think you're not scared of them even when you are.

Roberto's sidekick isn't half the bastard that Evil grew up to be, but he's working on it. Roberto is the kind of gangster that Evil would call 'all fur coat and no knickers.' Roberto has always got his gang with him, a bunch of mental-looking blokes who sit about trying to look hard.

'You can go through now,' Chimpface grunts taking one last look at The Tits and then lumbers along to the back of the club and opens a back door that leads to a long dark corridor. He taps on the door and Roberto says to come in.

Roberto's sat in this giant office behind a big black desk, on a leather swivel chair. The room is musty, the air full of smoke and dodgy deals. Behind him are more black and white framed photos like in the hallway. But Roberto's in these ones, his arm around the shoulders of smug-faced film stars. A couple of his hangers-on are in the room. Roberto's obviously seen one too many gangster films because he's smoking this big fat cigar and wearing a pinstriped suit with a red shirt. The hangers-on are all like clones of Chimpface, not a knuckle above ankle level in the room. None of them speak. They stand there all posed and wooden like the blokes in Nina's mum's catalogues. You know, like, arms folded, arms in pocket, hands on hips is the extent of their repertoire.

I don't know why Roberto needs a tame set of deviants around him. Maybe it's an image thing. He thinks it looks cool or something, but to my mind, they look more like Bad Manners or Madness: all suited and booted and ready to break out into song. Mario works solo, which is about the only thing him and I agree on. Other people are excess baggage.

I try not to think about how all the exits are barred. I need to keep it together. Roberto has to see that I mean business. I'm wearing Tiggy's best black trouser suit with some flat black patent shoes. I wish now I'd worn heels, steel tipped stilettos that could take out an eye if needed.

What I need is a gun, a tiny pink pistol that I could keep in my clutch bag and stick into the mouth of anyone who touches me without permission.

'Good to see you again, Scarlett,' Roberto points at the chair opposite. I sit but I'm still thinking about that pistol.

'Thanks for meeting me,' I reply nice as pie, cute and respectful, the way these big bully boys like their girls.

'I've been looking forward to it.' Yeah, I bet you have mate.

That evening when Lola and I came here Roberto asked me how much *to own me*. He sent one of his boys over to invite us to his table and when Lola was in the bathroom he asked me my name and then said, 'How much to own you?' I told him I wasn't for sale, because right then Mario and I had an understanding and you don't switch teams when you're doing alright, do you? But that was before. Now Mario and me, we're playing a different game.

Roberto leans forward, elbows on the desk and clicks

his fingers together, snap, snap, snap. 'You say you have an offer? Tell me Scarlett, what are you offering?'

This is the bit that I've been practising. And good old Roberto, it's like he's read the script.

'Something way too good to refuse, Roberto.' I say, then wait for him to feed me my next line.

Chapter Forty
Tiggy

I wonder if it is at all possible to obsess yourself to death.

Every song on the radio is 'our song'. Even the Bryan Adams monstrosity seems written for me. I've started having conversations with an imaginary Tony. I tell him stuff and create his answers.

It's been two weeks and I still can't concentrate on reading anything. I've lost count of the number of times I've bumped into things. My diary is overflowing with desperate sentences.

I blame myself. I shouldn't have forced things; I should have been more patient. I keep thinking about that bit from the bible that they always used to read in school chapel about how love is patient and kind. How it endures everything. How life is all about faith, hope and love.

I have none of the big three.

I even look forward to the September meeting with my father. Anything to distract me from Tony. He leaves a message cancelling our restaurant arrangements and suggesting that I come to the house instead. When I arrive he's not there. I don't know why I'm surprised.

'He'll be here in an hour or so,' Margaret lets me in. She's wearing brown culottes, a red faded linen smock and green wellies. She has chunky striped gardening gloves in her hands. If my mother was a hologram then Margaret is entirely solid, entirely real. The sort of person you'd want next to you in the trenches.

'I'm in the garden, come on out. Lovely day isn't it? You wouldn't think that it was autumn already. Time just seems to rush past.'

I sit on the white iron furniture in my father's patio garden, watching Margaret fiddling on with the pots. Margaret is so practical, so efficient, her face concentrated on cutting and pruning. I wouldn't have the heart to cull the plants, would let them kill themselves through my desire to keep them safe.

I have to prevent myself yelling at her to stop every time she snaps another forlorn looking flower from its stem.

Her gloved hands are holding onto a bundle of brown deadheads. She picks up some shears and starts cutting back and snipping, tugging away at leaves, chucking them without compassion into the basket at her feet. Then she stands back with her hands on her hips and smiles at the pile of plant debris. 'There, that's better.'

I have deadheaded myself. I am a desolate bundle of debris. I am compost.

I do not feel that I am overreacting, not at all.

'You okay there?' She's pulling her gloves off and wiping away the perspiration from her forehead, squinting at me, the sun in her eyes.

'I'm fine.'

'Is this about your mother and her letter?'

'No.'

'Because you can talk to me, if you wanted.' She says this casually but we both know that I've never confided in Margaret. I'm not sure why.

I guess I always had Tony.

'Thanks, but I'm alright really.' Margaret nods and takes her basket and efficiency off to the other end of the garden. A few moments later she goes back into the house.

There's nothing in my diaries around the time my mother left, nothing about how I felt then. I try and find emotion in the scrawled words, try and get a sense of the girl I used to be. It's as though she's not there. Like I got up, went to breakfast, had room inspections, chapel, lessons and then prep, then bed and over and over again. I have maybe nine or ten distinct memories of the five years I spent there. Then everything merges. I wonder where I went when I wasn't writing my diary. How I filled my days.

Only Tony is in sharp focus, the fixed point. The one person who I felt could see me, understand me; the one person I've tried to hold on to.

Like the moment my mother set sail for her new life, I anchored myself to Tony.

The last night at school he met me at the end of the lane near the phone box. We drove half an hour away and stopped at a pub. Sat across the table from each other holding hands.

'So. This is it. You're a free woman now.' I tried to smile at him but my face wouldn't move. I thought I'd be happy to leave school. I'd held my breath every day for years waiting for the moment when I could exhale, when I could be free.

'So, come on then, what are your plans?'

You, I thought, You're my plan.

I shrugged. The juke box was playing this old Dolly Parton song about a girl always loving a boy. A red-headed barmaid was singing along even though she was patently tone deaf.

'Travel? Work? Now you're free of the dreggoids the

world will be your oyster.'

'I just want to be with you.'

'Here you are.' Margaret comes out with a jug of Pimm's, overloaded with mint, cucumber and ice. She looks at her watch.

'I'd say the sun was over the yardarm.' She pours us both a large tumbler.

'Thanks, is Daddy definitely coming back then?'

'He's on his way.'

'Yeah, I bet he's rushing to see me,' I mumble grumpily.

'It's like that, is it?'

'Well, you know what he's like.'

'No. You tell me,' Margaret sips at her Pimm's, watching me closely.

'Well, we're not exactly close are we?' I say. 'Not that it matters, right?'

'Hmmm, and why do you think that is?' Margaret takes another long slow sip of her drink.

'What?'

'Well, you're not exactly easy to get close to, are you?'

'Oh it's all my fault, is it?'

'No... no... of course not, look-' she pauses, placing her glass down on the patio. 'It's not my place to say anything.'

Then she gets back up, slipping her gloves back on and starts fussing with the plants, leaving me feeling accused of something, but unsure what.

Margaret is so equipped. She made the step from single woman to stepmother overnight, like there was nothing in it. She made it look so simple, so obvious. The first time we met I was still in school, anxious, angry and resolved to hate this new woman who wasn't

218

my mother.

But I liked her straight away, not that I let her know. I didn't want to give my father the satisfaction. But, despite her tendency to dress exactly like a garden ornament, I think she's great. She has some essential component of resilience that seems to have bypassed me.

What does she mean? Not easy to get close to?

'Margaret?'

She doesn't turn around, 'Yes dear.'

'Do you really think it's my fault? Am I really that awful?'

She stops, cocks her hand on her hips and smiles. 'No, no. It's not all your fault. But you know there are two of you, Tiggy.'

'Meaning?'

'Meaning that your father is not a mind reader, nor am I for that matter. How are we supposed to help you if you don't let us?'

'I don't need any help,' I say petulantly. I don't. I'm fine. But Margaret ignores me and carries on.

'Now, I'm not for one moment suggesting that your father is the most emotionally accessible person in the world, but you're not exactly, well sometimes you're like a little tin god.'

'What? What does that mean?'

'Look, I believe in plain speaking, and know that you had a hard time of it. And maybe I don't know what I'm talking about, but seems to me that blaming everybody, from soup to nuts, isn't making you very happy now is it?'

Soup to nuts?

'Margaret, you're right. You don't know what you're talking about.'

'I know that your father worries.'

'Yeah right. Like he cares so much.'

'Tiggy, enough is enough.'

I say nothing, staring straight ahead instead. Who does she think she is?

'Your father is not the heartless brute you make him out to be.'

Oh shut up Margaret.

'Oh and now I suppose you're angry with me too. Great, that's wonderful, Tiggy. That's fine, hate me if you must.'

'I'm not angry with you or anyone actually, Margaret. And I don't need any help, I'm fine.'

'Of course you are.'

'I am,' I say and glare at her. She's supposed to wither under my vicious gaze but instead she smiles.

'Good, well then you can stop wearing those martyr clothes then can't you?'

'Oh, what do you know about anything anyway?' I say grabbing my bag. 'Tell Daddy I was here. His daughter. Tiggy. In case he's forgotten.'

Out on the street I burst into tears. I don't act like a martyr. I don't.

Chapter Forty One
Scarlett

I tell Roberto everything. About how Mario is going to be moving on from Valerios sometime soon and how I was thinking that maybe Roberto was interested in buying the club. That I might be able to help him.

'I have my own people.'

'I would be your people.'

'Why should I trust you?'

'Let's just say that if I can fuck Mario over then I'm there.'

'I like you Scarlett and I appreciate you coming here to talk to me, but the thing is, I don't think Mario is planning on selling.' He goes on about how he's not interested in Valerios, which I know is a lie, and how Mario's plans don't interest him; another lie. That he doesn't need me. Wrong again. He says he's got his own people who can get him whatever information he needs, and he's not heard anything about Mario moving on. And I figure he means Lola, which I was expecting, but I have something else.

'Besides,' he says, 'Mario and I have other scores to settle. We go back a long way you know. And anyway, what is it you want? What's in this for you?'

'I want a share in the club. I want to run Valerios,' I say seriously, imagining that pink pistol shoved deep in the back of his open throat. 'I have cash, I can give you £50,000 up front.'

He laughs really hard now so I say, 'Well, okay if you're not interested. But I have ideas, I can make a fortune for you.'

'Money isn't everything. That was Mario's problem, too greedy.'

'Mario isn't going to be a problem,' I reply quickly, adding, 'I'm not Mario, I'm not talking new money here, I'm talking a class act, a decent establishment, something you'll be proud to put your name to.'

'What about all Mario's clientele?'

'What about them?'

'If he is moving on, as you seem so convinced, then he'll be taking his client list with him.'

I laugh. 'I hope so. Most of them will have to whistle if they think they're getting into my club.'

'You, Scarlett, are quite an enigma.'

'You, Roberto, are looking at the woman who can make your dreams come true.'

'You're serious aren't you?'

'Deadly.'

'You say that you can guarantee that Mario won't be a problem?'

'Mario isn't going to be a problem for anyone soon,' I say with just the right amount of venom so he knows that I mean what I'm saying.

'I see.'

'But, if you're not interested...' I get up to go, because I know enough about catching punters and who will or won't pay and how and when to push and pull. Roberto thinks he's hard with all his chimps, but he's wriggling on my line.

'Wait Scarlett.'

You see... hooked. I got a big old Italian fish swinging on my wire.

'Sit down, let's talk business.'

I sit back down and nod, my back feeling clammy against the leather chair. I lean forward and put my feet together and remind myself that I have waited and worked for this moment. I'm not going to fuck it up.

'Scarlett, suppose I wanted Mario gone. What makes you think that that I wouldn't have done that ages ago. I have contacts. I have people.'

I have, of course, thought about that, and now I begin to relax because this is the conversation that I have been rehearsing. I pause a bit, like I'm thinking on my feet here and say, 'You're the first person the police would suspect. They'd be down here asking you questions, fingerprinting the whole place and they'd stitch you up for something, and Mario's mates would see to it that you got some kind of punishment. But I know someone who will do it. He'll do the time, he'll confess. The police won't bother you.'

I am a total genius. Roberto isn't looking at The Tits, now he's leaning in listening to me. He presses his fist against his mouth looking at my face. His big furry beard making his mouth look like a rodent's arse.

'Okay, this is more interesting. But why Valerios? You could buy a share in any club. Fifty grand is a decent amount of money. You could do a lot with that.'

'Sure, but I want Valerios and I want 50% of the profits.'

'Why Valerios?'

'Because it's Mario's. And because removing Mario is my little treat to myself for being such a good girl.'

He smiles, pauses, considers and then says, '10%' And I smile back because if we're talking figures then I know that he's properly interested.

'Why me?'

'That's easy. I need a backer, someone for protection. I'm still a little girl in a big man's world, so I need you to take care of me.' I bat my eyelashes as I bullshit him, then go for what I'm hoping will reel him in. 'Because you have class Roberto, and I admire that. I want to be your protégé, your very grateful protégé and we won't let any riff raff in our clubs, they will be properly exclusive.'

We settle on 35%, which is more than I'd bargained for. 35% on condition that there is no come back on Roberto.

'If the police so much as ask me for the time then the deal is off and you Scarlett, had better be prepared for the consequences.'

I'm so glad to be out of the dungeon that I take a huge gulp of London air as I walk along the street, then hack it back up as I inhale a mouthful of bus fumes.

I find a payphone and make the call to Evil who practically orgasms when I tell him what I need and what's in it for him. Straining at the leash to get started, trying to add in a few of his own psychotic ideas.

'Stick to the plan Evil. This is important.'

I feel a bit weird when I put down the phone because it's not every day you sort out that kind of business, so I make another call to cheer myself up.

True to form the child-snatching perverts, wife answers.

I slip into my almost perfect Tiggy impression, I'm like Tiggy with bells on, like I said, I'm good at faking things and drama was the only lesson I ever went to. Taught me all I needed to know.

'It's me, Tiggy,' I say. 'Did you ask him yet?'

Chapter Forty Two
Tiggy

I fume the whole tube journey home, glaring at anyone who dares to sit opposite me. Shifting angrily in my seat whenever someone sits down. How dare she talk to me like that. She's not my mother. She doesn't know what I've gone through.

Back at the flat I can't settle.

I tap my fingers on the coffee table. I pull back the curtains and empty the ashtrays. I wash every item in the sink, towel dry it and place it back into the cupboards. I pour Jif onto all the work surfaces and scrub away with scouring pads until the kitchen reaches new heights of cleanliness.

I pace the front room searching for a distraction, for something to slow my ticking brain. I rummage back through the bins and pull out the spliff buts and line them up in front of me.

I'm smoking my 16th butt and finishing off the end of the Vodka when Scarlett comes in. She looks at her watch, shakes her head and says, 'Good day, was it? Fuck. That's really disgusting, Tiggy.'

I don't respond, instead I watch as she unzips her bomber jacket and removes handfuls of jewellery from the inside pockets in thick tangled metallic clumps.

'Alright Fagin,' she says in her best cockney. 'You'll be proud of your little Scarlett Dodger today. I have had a very productive day... very productive indeed.'

'You are kidding?'

'Course I am, this lots from Top Shop and er,' she checks the price tags, 'Dorothy Perkins... nice, eh?'

'You'll get caught one of these days.'

'Well, everything's just that bit sweeter with a spoonful of risk eh, Tiggy?'

'Hmmm.' I pour out the final shot of Vodka.

'Come on then, spill it, what's the problem?'

'Why does everyone think there's a problem?'

'It's six in the afternoon and you're pissed, you're smoking second-hand spliff, you look like shit and you've cleaned the kitchen, which is a total giveaway. So come on,' she sits down next to me. 'Tell me, and you can have this.' She dangles a pink diamonte necklace in front of my eyes, swinging it from side to side. 'Come on, you're under my spell.'

I half smile, she is funny.

'Margaret, my dad's bitch of a wife, said that I act like the martyr, that I blame everyone else for everything.'

'And?'

'And nothing, that's it.'

The necklace stops its dance, then disappears as Scarlett swoops it into her hand.

'Jesus, Tiggy, you serious? You're not getting the necklace. You know what, here's a question. How the fuck would you cope if you actually had a real problem?'

The question must have been rhetorical, because she walks out of the room before I have a chance to answer her.

Saturday morning and I wake up groggy and pick the sleep from my eyes.

Primal Scream's *Come Together* is blaring so loudly that the walls are shaking. Scarlett has a certain quality, which means that when she is awake everyone in the building is awake.

My bedroom floor is cluttered with more balled up letters to my mother. I step over them on my way to the kitchen. One of them sticks to my foot. I pull it off, read a few lines then blush. I need to move on. This whole unsent letter thing has to end. The letters are full of self pity and vitriol. This isn't what I really feel, not sober anyway. I bunch it into the wastepaper basket with the others.

Her leaving was cowardly. However poetically she states her case in her letter You can't buy back six years with a little lyrical prose. You can't walk in and out of people's lives and expect everything to be okay.

But I can't carry on like this.

I tip the contents of my wastepaper basket into a plastic sack, and then collect up my bitter ramblings from my bedroom floor.

I intend to take control. This is my chance for a fresh start.

I empty the contents of my shoebox into a pile on the sitting room floor. I put to one side all things Tony. The letters, the pictures and the compilation tapes. Including the one I've been listening to on repeat for the last ten days. I pull out a green striped shirt he gave me to sleep in when we were at school.

I throw it into the sack.

Cross-legged, on my bedroom floor I read through his letters for the last time. Then slowly and deliberately rip each one into pieces. I use a Bic biro to pick out the tape from our compilation cassettes. Pulling out reel after reel, scrunching up the brown tape. I consider adding in all the books he has bought me over the years, but settle on pulling out only the title page where he has written 'For Tiggy with love.' Or 'You'll love this... x.'

I am dry eyed and determined. Each time I find

another arty card. Rothko, Klee or Rousseau, I know before I turn them over what they say, where I was when he sent them to me.

I tear everything into strips and push them into the sack. I am erasing so much of myself, but this is the right thing.

Finally, I remove the framed photo of Tony from my bedside, placing it into the bag, pulling the ties together in a yellow bow. I dump the sack in the hallway.

The music from the sitting room changes to Brand New Heavies and now Scarlett is singing. She loves Acid Jazz and garage music, the volume hitches up a notch.

I owe Scarlett an apology.

Scarlett's painting her nails a luminous orange, watching a team of vogueing dancers on *Going Live*.

She's customised one of my denim skirts into five inches of frayed material, leaving a wide gap of flesh before the start of her thigh-high striped stockings. Her hair is in plaits. Like a soft porn Pippi Longstocking. Perched on the coffee table; beside her is an open copy of *Cosmopolitan*. The article is called 'How to seduce your man.'

I cough. 'Scarlett. Look, I'm sorry. I've been awful company haven't I? The whole drunken vodka self-pitying stuff... you're right. I'm sorry.'

She doesn't look up, her nail polish brush poised in the air.

'Scarlett... come on. I promise not to play the tape anymore. In fact I've destroyed it. Look.' I drag the sack back from the hallway and into the sitting room. 'The old Tiggy has gone. No more moping. I'm a whole new improved me.'

'Really?' She makes controlled even strokes across her toenails. 'Okay then,' she nods towards the magazine. 'You won't want to know how to get your guy?'

'No. Not interested in men. I've given them up as a bad lot.'

'Is that right? Thank God, coz you were doing my head in a bit back there.' Her eyes glimmer liquid lavender.

'Absolutely, I've been a real pain I know. But no more, I promise. I am a strong independent, single female.'

'Uh huh. Well we're wasting our time here then.' She throws the magazine onto the floor. 'You like?' She waggles her florescent nails at me.

'Um, very daring. So shall we do something later? You know go swimming or something. If you like?'

'Oh, I've been running already, but come out with me tomorrow. It'll be cool. I'll go easy on you. Promise.'

'Oh, running, I don't know.'

'I've told you, no pain, no gain, Tiggy. Besides it's good to try something new from time to time. You know, stretch yourself a little.'

'Well of course. A spoonful of risk, right?' Scarlett claps her hands together and smiles like I've handed her a gift wrapped box from Tiffany's.

'Oh yeah, now my girl. Tiggy's getting it.'

Chapter Forty Three
Scarlett

The first time Ed touches me I flinch. But I remind myself that this is the last week. Five more nights and then no bloke touches me ever again. I close my eyes grit my teeth and force myself to keep it together.

The hotel room is all that crappy fake wood and floral walls, somewhere round the back of Marble Arch. He places the 'Do not Disturb' sign on the door and then comes back into the room, tugging at his tie, pulling his shirt out of his trousers. I wish I'd drunk more champagne. I look around for a mini bar, hoping that he's bought a bottle of whiskey but there's no sign of anything and he's tapping the bed and beckoning me to come over to him. I think he's trying to look sexy, but he makes me think about those leeches from olden days. Like he wants to burrow into my skin and suck out my blood.

Ed says he's a furniture salesman, divorced with three kids; three little girls. Loves them to death, would do anything for them. He took the photos out of his wallet in the club and told me all about Shelly, Susie and Sonia. And I'm like thinking how someone actually had sex with him through choice and that is just plain wrong. He talks about them like no one in the world ever had children before. How their births were like watching a miracle. That no one can explain how that moment changes you. Yeah, yeah, break my heart with your meaningful story, Ed.

'My whole life changed in the second I saw Shelly for the first time.' His eyes filled with tears and he rolled his fat, fag-stained fingers over the photo. They're standing in front of a green Vauxhall Viva, making gap toothed grinny faces. The eldest has a face loaded with spots and braces, the middle one is a total porker and the youngest has these mutated squinty eyes.

'They're adorable Ed. You must be very proud.'

'I miss them so much.'

'How often do you see them then?'

'I don't,' he says and starts to cry. God, save me from crying men.

It turns out that Ed's wife left him. She took the three lovely girls with her and set up home with some other bloke somewhere in Brighton. He gives me the whole back-story of how they met in what feels like real time. How he proposed, the wedding day, the presents, how she caught him with his cock in the nanny's mouth, how it wasn't his fault, because, like, after the kids she just went off shagging totally and what the hell was he supposed to do.

'It's totally unfair that because of one, one minor indiscretion – once in ten years I make a bloody mistake – and she gets half the house, the kids, everything, because of one tiny mistake. I'm so lonely.'

His eyes are red and puffy so I pat his hand and say, 'It must be hard for you.'

But obviously shagging a hooker will make it all better. Just call me Florence Nightingale.

We're here in this Marble Arch dump with no fucking mini bar and the Leechman sat on the bed. I undress and grab a condom from my purse placing it on the bedside table, then start to kiss his chest.

'Don't,' he says, 'just lie next to me.' He switches the light out, puts his arms around me, pushes his face into my hair and inhales. 'You smell like her,' he whispers, his arms clutching around me, holding me too tight. I can feel his heart beating, his breath changing into small sobs. Oh please, if he's going to get like this over the smell of Coconut Alberto Balsam, then I'm in for a long night.

I hear him fiddling for the condom and thank God, because that means there's a chance I can get out of here sometime before dawn. He climbs onto me and silently fucks me, his hand over my mouth, his eyes closed. Within seconds he orgasms, calling out her name.

We lie side by side in the dark. There's like, loads of noise in the corridor, the soundproofing is so cheap that you can practically hear the cockroaches and rats thinking about their tea. And there's shed-loads of traffic outside, shouts from the street, sirens blaring. The sheets are some low life form of plastic.

'That was wonderful. Thank you,' he says and starts crying again.

I try not to move although my whole body is shaking with his, he's practically fucking epileptic, writhing and moaning and holding onto me saying, 'I just want them back, I just want my babies back.' Normally this would make me giggle, but I'm not in the mood tonight. Finally, he falls asleep and I lift his arm from my body and peel myself off the sheets and him.

You can tell a lot about a bloke by the way he fucks you. Some of them just want it over with as quickly as possible and that kind of confuses me because you'd think that they'd want to get their money's worth. They will all tell you they are there for different reasons but it boils down to the same thing, the idea of sex, the idea of getting something that other men can't get. Mostly they want to impress themselves.

Mum once tried to give me that whole 'sex is when a man and a woman love each other very much' lecture. Even at five or however old I was when we had that crappy conversation I thought well that doesn't make sense does it? I laughed because it was ridiculous. 'You'll understand one day,' she said. I don't think I will. I don't think I'll ever understand mean what loving someone has got to do with getting naked and contorting into strange positions.

I don't get what all the fuss is about, why people spend their whole lives fixated on this one thing, this dumb act that means naff all to anyone really.

They come back for more, not because what they got the first time satisfied them but because it didn't. Because they had this idea that they could walk into the club and find some girl and ask her for everything they ever wanted, but it's all in their heads, because once they have you there, naked and ready in front of them, most of them just go silent and fuck you dead quickly. Or they want to talk and cry. Like crying is too shameful to do in front of anyone you're not paying.

There's nothing worth nicking in the room so I flick through his briefcase and look at the pictures of chairs, tables and wardrobes. It's all that posh pine and mahogany stuff and there are little wood samples stuck to slips of plastic with daft names like *Suffolk Country Pine* and *Lakeside Beech*, they all look the same to me. Ed isn't selling the Mangy Melamine he's surrounded by in this room. Under the paperwork, the spreadsheet and order forms there's a sticky-paged copy of *Teen Tramps*. I push the briefcase away. Ugh. What is it with men?

The nice ones, the ones who want to think they're good blokes. They're the ones who piss me off the most. They treat it like it's a date. Like, 'So how are you?' Like it's important that I get pleasure. I mean, imagine... that's just desperate!

The first few times I went along with it, moaning and

233

faking, then I figured that maybe I could move it along a little so I said, 'What I really want, what I get off on, is for you to treat me like a tart. That's why I do this job, because it's what I like.'

Their eyes pop open with delight, because now they can forget all that stuff they've been reading in their wives magazines. Now they can go for what they wanted in the first place, they just needed permission, the nice ones always do.

Ed rolls over on the bed and starts blubbing again. Sobs are filling the room, bubbling around me. But he doesn't move, I peer over him and his eyes are tight shut. The daft geezer's crying in his sleep, like a fucking baby.

I look again at the picture of his girls. They're ugly and awkward and probably still young and stupid enough to think their father is God, not some bloke who pays hookers to have sex with him in cheap hotel rooms and has porn in his briefcase.

I'm not saying he doesn't love them. I'm not saying that he's not crying for real. It's just that I don't care. He lost them because he couldn't keep his trousers on, and that's his fault.

Men like him come to the club because they're lonely, because they are hoping for a bit of comfort and nothing that happens in this room will change that or make it better.

You get what you pay for, sex with a stranger. Whatever your reason to be here, decent bloke or dodgy geezer, the service is the same, although for a few extra quid I can pretend that I give a shit.

If you ask them what they want they say 'pleasure,' which is a lie. Sure they get aroused and they orgasm and that. But that's just a bonus. The sex is really about power, revenge, shame, hating themselves. It's about the kid who bullied them at school, the women who hurt them, and having too much money or not having enough.

I put the photograph back in his wallet, steal a few extra tenners and then let myself out of the room. As soon as I'm out on the street I start to feel safer. I think I'm getting that syndrome soldiers get in battle or when they come home and they can't stop shaking and hallucinating. I've seen too many shitty hotel rooms, too many shitty men and lately sometimes when I look at the punters I hate them so much that it's hard to breathe.

I get a lot of time to think about why these blokes come to the club. In the end I figure that they are here for the same reason as the girls, it all comes down to a photo they keep in their wallet.

Chapter Forty Four
Tiggy

Sunday morning we go running. I'm looking good, I think, in my grey sweatshirt and sweatpants that my father gave me last Christmas when returned from a trip to America.

Scarlett raises an eyebrow at the red letters spelling Virgin across my chest, but says nothing. She's wearing hot pants, a tiny sports bra and her hair in high bunches. We both have Nike trainers, although hers are those trendy ones with proper airbags in the sole.

It must be the lack of airbags that hold me up because all I can see is Scarlett's white soles disappearing into the distance. I get across the road and into the park, where I collapse on the grass. 'I... I... I... Shit. I can't.'

Scarlett turns and runs back, jogging on the spot.

'Tiggy, the first ten minutes are always the worst, you have to keep going. Come on you're twenty-one, not forty-one, this should be easy.'

'I... I... I,' can't speak apparently, my lungs feel like they're burning and then I start coughing up nicotine flavoured brown phlegm.

'You're a classy girl, Tiggy,' I wave her away. 'I'll be back for you in half an hour.' She sprints off across the park as though she's being chased by wolves. Other people are running but Scarlett's leaving them all behind her, focussing on each runner ahead and systematically disposing of them one by one.

After my bath, and Scarlett's shower, I try to find the

grace to laugh at myself.

'Perhaps if you slowed down on the fags and the vodka?'

'Yeah right, give up the cigarettes and this time next year I'll be racing Linford Christie in Barcelona.'

'You know what I mean.'

'You smoke and drink, you're hardly in a position of moral superiority.'

'I take care of myself Tiggy, No fags 'till the evenings and I eat fruit. I look after my body... you-'

'I what?'

'Don't. It's true. You're skinny coz you never eat anything. Fags and vodka are not a proper diet.'

'I do eat. I had a slice of toast this morning.'

'Well, what about the child-snatching pervert? That was hardly a good idea was it?'

'Don't call him that.'

'Okay, but I have a question. Why the old geezers? What's the Cliff being my daddy thing about? Why not pick someone your own age?

'I don't know. Because I never meet anyone?'

'Oh behave, we're always meeting blokes.'

'*You're* always meeting blokes Scarlett.'

'Well, what's with you and Dan Dan the Piano Man then? Bit of a spark there isn't there. Why haven't you two hooked up?'

'Dan? He's not my own age, he's like ten years older than me, and besides he's with Jackie.'

'Ahhhh. *He's with Jackie*, but you like him right?'

'No... anyway, he's not available.'

'Didn't bother you with the child-snatching pervert.'

'He wasn't. It wasn't... don't-'

'It was *different*. You loved him. I know.'

'Besides... Dan doesn't like me like that.'

'Course he does.'

'You think he likes me?'

'*You think he likes me?* Listen to you. What happened to the whole "I'm not interested in men" thing. That lasted a long time.'

'What?'

'Girls like you, you'll never last a second without a bloke to mope over.'

'Seriously Scarlett. We're friends.'

'*Friends,*' she says as though describing a venereal disease.

'But, say I did like him, or any man for that matter. I mean, if you like a man then what do you? I mean how would you? You know... do?'

She pushes her tongue into her cheek like I'm a moron.

'How would you, you know do? Good question.'

'You know what I mean.'

'This is the new independent Tiggy, is it?' Scarlett grins widely. 'Are you asking what I would do to get my man?'

'Yes, I guess I am.'

'Okay, what I would do is whatever it took. But, if I was you and I was making this much fuss about a tosspot bloke from *sarf* London then... well... I'd probably have to top myself, Tiggy.' She yanks on an invisible noose, makes a choking noise and then lets her head drop listless and drooling from her neck.

She chucks the latest issue of *Cosmo* at me. 'Here you go, have a read of this and see if it tells you how to *get your man.*'

Then she's off out on business, apparently. I don't ask. I'd rather not know.

I pick up the magazine.

Cosmo recommend that I don't smell like toilet duck. If I brush my teeth and toy with my mouth, I'm halfway there. That and *In the Air Tonight*, which can apparently hypnotise any man into a trance like state. Oh, and finally, it's important that I be confident. They slip it in at the end like it's as simple as wearing Chanel No. 19.

It's always best in these things to be yourself, isn't it? Well unless the someone you happen to be feels sick at the thought of someone not liking me that way.

Nothing is more attractive to men than a confident woman.

So that's me buggered then. Why can't anxiety and low self-esteem be an aphrodisiac?

In my bedroom mirror I itemise the faults of my naked body. There is nothing erotic about my flesh and bone, nothing so clandestine about the fuzz that Mario thinks men want to see. If they used their imaginations then surely they could work it out.

I tell myself that on holidays people walk about in next to nothing, that naturists see the naked body as beautiful, that in some cultures wearing clothes is an insult.

That it will be three seconds and I don't know the men.

But Scarlett's words have nudged something in me. I do know Dan.

And I don't want him to see me differently.

Is there a difference between dancing topless and stripping totally?

Does it take me from one place to another, make me a different person?

I don't know.

But I need to work it out because Mario isn't going to wait much longer for an answer.

Chapter Forty Five
Scarlett

Tiggy makes Bambi look like the Yorkshire Ripper. She must have grown up in a world full of cartoon singing woodland animals. Someone should shoot her mother that would wise her up, give her something decent to cry about.

And she's soppier than a pervert's wet dream, she whines on at me in that cotton wool voice of hers. It's like 'Did you replace the vodka Scarlett? Do you think you could take the rubbish out for once? Um do you think you could pick up the wet towels from the bathroom floor Scarlett?' Like I'm her kid or something.

This place was like a dump site when I moved in, and now because she wants to have some kind of life change, we've all got to live by Tiggy's new standards, like there's nothing else going on in the world.

This morning I'm trying to get a lie in. I'm sort of awake but pretending that I'm asleep, hoping to squeeze out a few more winks when Tiggy's knocking on my bedroom door and moaning on about milk. I'm like, 'enough is enough'. So I get up and go to the door and say, 'What now?'

'There's no milk.' She's holding an empty milk carton, her evidence of the crime. Tiggy, the Milk Detective.

'Not my problem.'

'I bought two pints yesterday and now there's none left.'

'So, get some more.'

'Why do I always have to buy everything?'

'I bought cigarettes yesterday.'

'Because you'd stolen a packet from me the day before.'

'Borrowed, Tiggy. I just borrowed some. What is it? Do you want some money or something?'

'No, it's not about the money.'

'Then laters Tiggy, I'm trying to get some shut eye here.'

'It's half eleven. You should be awake.'

'What? Is there a getting up time now?'

'No, I, well I thought you'd be awake... and well the thing is, that I love having you here I really do, but it was only supposed to be for a few days. And it's been a month now. And... it's just if you are going to stay then... well you can't go about stealing other people's stuff... it's not on.'

She's obviously been working herself up for this conversation because when she's finished her little speech she sort of relaxes like that's her done. Which is good because she was in danger of boring The Tits off me. And that would be a tragic loss to society. I'm about to tell her to get a life when the buzzer goes so I run for the intercom and answer it before Tiggy can continue nagging. I have to laugh, because her timing couldn't be better.

'Sandra's on her way up for you.'

'Sandra? I don't know anyone called Sandra.'

'Well, she knows you and she's on her way up.'

'You're sure it was Sandra?'

'Yep. Definitely. She said, "Antigone. It's Sandra, can I come in?" Sounded a bit posh actually.'

If she was bouncing off the walls before, now Tiggy looks like she's been spun up to the ceiling and smashed back down on the carpet.

'Sandra? Oh fuck. Scarlett, help me.' She's dead upset and scared. I feel sorry for her for a nanosecond. Then I figure that she got herself into this mess when she started shagging the child-snatching pervert. So I give her a pat on the back and then kick open the door to my room.

'You're on your own babes, this ain't nothing to do with me. Not my business, is it?' She's actually gone white and her hands are shaking like a proper lunatic.

'Please Scarlett, what should I do?'

'Don't go round taking other people's stuff?' I suggest helpfully and then slam the door.

On the estate there were always bitch fights when some slapper had got herself knocked up by someone else's bloke. We all used to hang over the sides of the balconies and gangways, clapping and yelling, 'Fight. Fight. Fight. Fight.'

They were brilliant, because when the blokes got violent they beat the crap out of each other, but the women when they got started, it was like all the verbal shit as well. They'd be tugging at each other's hair, spitting and scratching and yelling, 'You stinking dirty slag.' Telling each other stuff like, 'I hope your tits rot and drop off.' Or, 'When you suck his cock, remember that's me you're tasting.'

It was like this whole performance. Usually it ended in a few bruises, that was all. The women would be back to being best mates a few weeks later, when the bloke started screwing someone else on the estate and the whole thing happened again. The blokes always took it too far with knives or bottles and by the time they sobered up they were missing an ear or a finger or something.

There was only one time that I know of when it got out of hand. None of us kids saw it, but we all heard about it. One of the women from the maisonettes,

Chrissie, this women who made this big fuss over her hair and her nails, thought she was better than everyone else got into a fight with Mad Julie. The women in the flats called her a stuck up bitch because she had a job behind the Lancôme counter in Selfridges. Plus, she pissed everyone off by refusing to buy their Avon stuff, saying that she wouldn't put any of that cheap muck on her face.

Anyhow back to Chrissie's fight with Mad Julie from the flats. Mad Julie was a total nutter, she had like a million children in every colour of the rainbow and was the estate bike. She'd shagged most of the blokes in the flats. A few months before, she'd been slapping Dawn about for flirting with her Darren. Darren and Julie were like Scott and Charlene on *Neighbours*, always splitting up, but they always got back together. Considering every time they split up, Julie got pregnant by some other bloke, and Darren seemed to take it all pretty well.

You never saw Julie without a bottle of Thunderbird in her hand and she was always leaving her kids outside Ladbrokes so mostly we just avoided her.

Anyway, Julie got it into her head that Chrissie had been getting off with her Darren or something and apparently she punched Darren's lights out, and then, Thunderbird bottle in hand, went over to The Crown to pull Chrissie outside. Only Chrissie refused to go out and fight her. She said that there was nothing going on and that perhaps if Julie was worried about Darren putting it about, she should put him on a leash.

And Julie was pretty pissed up and furious and hated Chrissie anyhow, so when Chrissie added, 'Although what with you being a dog perhaps you should be the one with a collar and lead.' Julie went ballistic. She slammed the Thunderbird bottle down on the bar and then pushed the shattered edges right into Chrissie's face. With one jab she fucked that woman's face for life, right in front of half the estate.

Someone called an ambulance and the coppers turned up, but that's the thing with The Crown. There ain't no grass on the estate. So no one had seen anything. The coppers think they have informers and that, but it isn't like it looks on *The Bill*. Everybody knew what had happened including the police, but they couldn't do anything because there were like, a hundred people who said that Julie had been with them that evening. Chrissie didn't press charges, there wasn't any point. She lost her job at Selfridges, no one wants to buy make up from Frankestein's monster. For a while, whenever she walked past the flats the lads used to yell, 'Five... Four... Three... Two... One... Thunderbirds are go.'

So I prepare myself for a good old-fashioned mudslinging bitch fight. I grab the pillow from my bed and shove it up against my door and then light a fag.

But these women are like nothing I've ever known before.

Right there in that room is why marriage is a rubbish idea, and why people shouldn't trust anyone ever.

And lord knows someone needs to teach these posh women how to fight. It's all chat chat chat. Boring.

I fall asleep with my head resting on the inside of the door.

Chapter Forty Six
Tiggy

Sandra is on her way up.

I have no idea what Sandra is doing here.

I light a cigarette then put it out in case she tells me off.

My palms are melting.

I have fantasised about meeting her so many times over the years. Dreamt about it. We would meet in a cafe somewhere. I am looking beautiful and tragic. She is weeping silently behind dark glasses. Her inferior beauty obvious. Over coffee I apologise sweetly, showing genuine remorse. All the while she is acknowledging that I am the better woman. She can understand why Tony chose me over her. As she leaves she will stop at the door and then turn to me and sadly say that she wishes that she could have made Tony as happy as I do. I will supportively nod and we will exchange an eye lock of mutual understanding

But Scarlett's right. I am a complete moron.

The moment Sandra steps into the flat. The moment that she is in front of me, I realise that whatever childish fantasy I had of our meeting is about to be blown out of the water.

Firstly, my jeans are filthy, my hair is unwashed and scrunched back off my face, which is sporting last night's make up and a few enthusiastic-looking spots. It would be a very large stretch of the imagination to see me as a black and white film noir Ingrid Bergman beauty.

I think about washing my face, brushing my hair or

picking up some of the LPs and newspapers from the floor. I think about all sorts of things but when Sandra taps on the door I am still stood freeze framed in the middle of the living room.

Sandra looks as confused to be in my flat as I am to have her there. After a few inconvenient and stuttered out niceties, 'Would you like to to to come in? Would you like a c... c... cup of tea?' and a few clashes of overlapping questions, she agrees to sit in the living room while I make us both a cup of tea.

I haven't seen Sandra for three years and jealousy has distorted my memories. I have created her as a boisterous, heavy weight around Tony's neck. Now that she's here I'm reminded how slight she is, her a long straight nose, her scissor straight blonde bob, her pale green eyes. The girls at school called her The Governess. Sandra's clothes always seemed so wrong. While other teachers were following high street fashions, wearing suits with shoulder pads like Crystal Carrington or crazy patterned bat wing jumpers, Sandra wore A-line skirts, tiny silk camisoles, cashmere cardigans and always *always* Clarks sensible shoes. There was something eternally uncomfortable about her. Even in my school uniform I felt more fashionable than her. Another secretly claimed victory. Now sat shaking in her co-ordinated pastels on my crappy worn out sofa I can't help but notice that she looks lovely, actually. Feminine and fragile.

And I am worse than shit.

I bring the tea through. For inexplicable reasons, I am using a sugar bowl and milk jug, as though Sandra were a royal visitor. The afternoon sunshine magnifies the smears and fingerprints on the inside of the windows. Everything in my flat seems in that instant to be shabby and cheap. The curtains hang drab and crinkled. For the first time it occurs to me that curtains should probably be washed from time to time. I tug on my T-shirt and try to pick the dried toothpaste from my jeans. I am embarrassed that Sandra can see where I live, ashamed that I have not made more of my life.

Sandra takes the cup of tea with a quiet, 'Thank you.'

Then we sit in silence for a while, both assiduously studying our cups of tea.

I'm regretting not offering her vodka. I'm regretting all kinds of things.

Sandra finally places her cup of tea on the table.

'I haven't come to fight,' she says slowly, her voice a little shaky.

I place my cup down too and nod.

'Can I tell you something?' She looks directly at me. I catch a glimpse of pale green pleading eyes before I look away.

I nod again. I seem unable to speak.

'It's okay, Antigone. I'm not here for a row, or a showdown, and I will not be stopping long. But I want to get a few things straight. Is that okay with you?'

I nod.

'Good. This doesn't have to be any more messy than it already is, so hear me out.'

I swallow and force myself to look at her and nod again.

'God. You're so young. Look at you. I don't know what he was thinking. Must be some sort of midlife crisis. And there I was thinking it was me. So embarrassing. I thought I am so insecure that I even doubt my own husband. But look at you? How old are you now? Twenty? Twenty-one? Right. What do you see in him? Seriously Antigone, he's hardly a dream catch. I mean God, what do you talk about?'

I don't answer. I have no idea what to say and so after a short silence Sandra continues. 'I went to a doctor because I thought maybe I was depressed. I had everything going for me. A job I loved. A husband I loved. Good sex life.' She coughs a little and we both feel the knowledge of that statement. 'Money in the bank' she continues, 'my family and friends were all well and healthy... but somehow I felt... like nothing... and as though my life wasn't substantial somehow, that it was some sort of a charade. Am I making any sense?'

'Like a hologram?' I say quietly and then I try to hold her gaze, to concentrate on what she is saying, but I'm thinking about the 'good sex life' comment and how her hands, mouth and body have experienced so many shared things.

We have invaded each other's privacy.

'A little. Like I was going through the motions, cooking dinner, making love, making plans... we even discussed children.' She looks incredulously at me. 'And the doctor said, "Welcome to married life. Get used to it." I felt so foolish. Silly old me. I've been living for some ridiculous idealised version of existence. So I knuckled down and got on with it. I did as the doctor said.'

I try to think of something to say, but fail. I'm thinking of her body under Tony's. Him smiling over at her from the adjacent pillow. He will have looked at her the way he looked at me.

I reach for my cigarettes. I feel sick.

'Is it okay if I smoke?'

'It's your flat. But they're not good for you, you know.'

I light the cigarette with shaky fingers and then realise that I haven't bought an ashtray through, but

Sandra is talking again and I'm scared to move.

'So, for the last six years I have kept on. I have told myself that this is life. I have told myself not to demand anything more. But the doctor was right you know, because as it turns out it was married life after all. Or being married to Tony. Because finding out about you was a gift.' She sniffs a laugh. 'Of course, at first, I thought I was devastated. I cried and I shouted and I said all the things you're supposed to say. But then I realised that was just pride, the idea of the embarrassment of being cheated on, especially with someone so very young. Because actually I felt something else underneath. I felt relieved.'

Her finger nails are perfectly French manicured. She's wearing a simple gold wedding band.

I have a memory; Tony and I lying in a hotel room, him trying to leave, me clinging on for a few extra minutes, minutes that by right should have been hers.

'I'm sorry,' I say pointlessly.

'Don't be,' Sandra looks a little surprised herself. 'I'm free. I don't have to worry about why Tony's not as interested in me as he used to be, or where he's going at strange times of the day, or why he seems distracted when we are together. It's not my problem anymore.'

'It's over between us.'

'Don't lie to me, Tiggy. I'm tired of being lied to.'

'But it really is over, it has been for a while. I swear.'

'Okay, okay.' She waves my comment away then points at the Marlboro Lights. 'Can I have one of those?'

I push the packet towards her, 'Sure.'

'I've given up... five years ago now, but this feels like

a good time to start again. Is there an ashtray or do you always use the floor?'

In the kitchen I hold on tight to the worktop. Whoever this woman is in my front room she is not The Governess, she isn't my version of Sandra the wife. I grab a half full bottle of Vodka from the freezer and slug down an inch before searching for two ashtrays.

'I don't suppose you have anything stronger than tea do you?'

'Vodka?'

'That'll be great. Is there any orange juice or tonic? I don't think I could cope with it straight.'

There's some Happy Shopper orange juice in the fridge drawer. I bring that and the vodka bottle through. Then return to the kitchen to look for clean glasses. Settling for two tumblers that in a previous incarnation were tubs of chocolate spread. Sandra pours us both large measures of vodka and orange while I wait nervously for her to continue.

'And an ashtray?'

'Sorry.' I stumble back through to the kitchen and return with two ashtrays.

'Thank you, Tiggy.'

'S'okay.'

'You're turning into a beautiful young woman aren't you? God, you make me feel so old.'

I sit fidgeting with my cigarettes and my nails. In the cafe fantasy I am on the stronger ground. In reality I am seriously considering hurling myself from the window. I hope she isn't planning on making a day of it.

Sandra sits up and takes a deep breath and looks around the flat. I wish that I had taken down the Billie Holliday poster, the Louis Armstrong picture. So much of the flat was my vain attempt to fill the walls and spaces with things that Tony might approve of. When she turns to look at me she holds my gaze and I notice that far from being strong and together that her eyes have red veins through them from crying. Her makeup is covering over dark sleepless rings.

'You must hate me,' I say.

'No not really...'

'Oh.'

'Disappointed? You want me to fight you for him? Is that what the calls were for?'

'No. No. I'm just... I'm sorry.'

'I'm not your rival, Tiggy.'

'But-'

'Please let me finish. Things are going to be hard enough at school without you making them worse.'

'I wouldn't ever try and deliberately make things worse for you... or Tony.'

Sandra looks at me with an expression I can't explain, 'No? Okay. Maybe you've changed your mind or I'm mistaken. I'm hoping that you of all people might appreciate what school life is going to be like for me once it gets out. I know full well that the girls all think I'm ridiculous, and don't understand how poor old Tony could be stuck with The Governess. And well, I accept that they are going to be over the moon. There won't be a girl in the sixth form who isn't rushing to take my place... or your place now I suppose.'

She's right. The teachers are the mini celebrities at school, and their sex lives a source of endless rumour and suspicion. Sandra will have several weeks of giggles and nudges to contend with.

'I'm not planning on telling anyone anything.'

'It's being at the same school. A mistake in hindsight. And I can just about cope with the sniggering, but when they discover that it was because of a former pupil... well.' She lifts her hands in submission. 'Those girls can be... well, you know.'

I do know. If the new intake of pupils is anything like the girls in my year then they can sniff out a tragedy and spear it with spite in seconds.

'They won't find out. I've told you. Tony and I are over.'

'It's bad enough that my husband is having an affair. But with an ex-pupil?'

'They won't find out,' I repeat.

'Of course they will. You said you wanted them too.'

'I used to. I used to think it would show them something. But, Sandra I'm not seeing Tony and I'm not going to tell anyone anything about it, ever. I promise.'

'That's such a relief. You know, once you'd called and he told me, everything made sense. I've been so busy trying to make him happy, to get his attention somehow. And then those calls and-'

'I only called to-' Sandra waves my words away and starts to sob. I feel like the most stupid, selfish girl in the world and I realise that I am crying too.

Sandra smiles at me through her tears. 'Well, maybe I'd have done the same at your age, maybe we're both fools. Poor old Tony. And he ends up with neither of us.' Then we both laugh and cry and for a moment when she's laughing she doesn't look like The Governess at all and I can understand why Tony fell in love with her, and why he didn't leave her.

'I really am very sorry, Sandra.'

She looks at me almost maternally, 'Well, it wasn't only you was it? I think Tony has played the bigger part in deceiving me. Still... maybe I let him, oh who knows.' She takes a sachet of tissues from her handbag and wipes her face. 'Before I go, there was one other thing that I need to ask. Promise me you'll tell me the truth.'

'Anything,' I reply.

'Tony says that you and him, well it started long after you left school. I want to believe him, but he's lied to me for so long, and... well... I wanted to check... with you... it did start after you finished school... didn't it?'

She's not asking me a question, she's pleading with me not to tell her what she can't bear to hear.

'I'd rather know the truth though, whatever the consequences,' she says firmly.

'I was nineteen before anything happened.' I lie. 'It was after I'd left school. When I'd come back from travelling.' Because I might be immoral and naive but I'm not so dumb that I can't tell when the truth isn't what is needed.

'Thank God,' she says and her shoulders drop with relief. 'Right. I'll get going.'

'Okay,' I say and I apologise again.

'What's done is done,' she says. 'I'm hoping maybe we can all move on quickly... me... you and Tony.'

'There is no me and Tony,' I say again.

'Fine. Well, what a mess we've made between the three of us.'

'I know.'

'Talking of mess. What is it with you public school girls anyway? Tony says you're working as a stripper.' She sounds disbelieving. 'Why on earth would you choose to do that? I remember you as a quiet, bookish type.' She looks at me again as if searching for the younger Tiggy. 'I used to worry about you sometimes, when your mother left. Those marks on your arms.' She looks again around the room and shakes her head. 'But you know, your father paid a fortune for you to have a decent education, and then?' She raises her hands, 'Maybe this is what you want, but stripping? Is that really what you are planning on making of your life?"

After she leaves I look again at my flat and my life, then I reach for my diary and make a thousand new resolutions to change.

Chapter Forty Seven
Scarlett

Y ou know, it's like, the smarter the suit, the smuttier the bloke.

It's just as well there are hookers, because if some of the punters asked their wives for the stuff they ask us, then there would be whole lot of women running from their Hampstead mansions screaming.

I shouldn't even be here, normally I wouldn't be anywhere near this kind of a punter but Mario's not giving me any of the decent payers at the club. He must be saying something at the door because no one's booked me at all the last two nights, and some of them won't even look at me.

So I get to see what it's like to be Lola or Georgia, sat at the bar all night drinking soda water and watching while other people make decent cash.

Whatever Mario's telling them it obviously didn't bother Percy.

So here I am in another shit hole hotel in Pimlico, another flea-filled mattress, another set of miniature soaps and shampoos, another twatty concierge on the door looking at me like I'm vermin.

Percy has all his own kit. He opened out his suitcase and there was like an entire S&M store in there. Handcuffs, whips and vibrators, the whole caboodle. So now he's handcuffed to the bed, face down which really isn't a good look for him. His back is scarred with whiplines and bruised with tiny heel marks. He must be getting his kicks in other clubs, other cities, because I've not seen him before. He's got me wearing a rubber basque, high heels and cracking a whip against the floor.

Lola and Georgia have this whole deal going with the fetish punters. They have regulars, men that they've been working with for years. They come in same day, same time each week or each month. The girls act like they're really pleased, like, 'Oh Simon, you're my favourite client, with you it's not like working.'

Fetish is supposedly where the big money is. Fetish and group sex with Arabs. It's all bollocks because I've made almost enough money to retire and I don't do regulars, and I don't do groups sex. And I've not keen on the fetish thing. Guo put me right off men who like their own blood. And now I'm here I remember why. It's not all it's cracked up to be.

'Tell me I'm a bad boy,' Percy says.

You're a freaking pervert mate.

'You're a bad boy.' With a giant hairy arse.

'A very bad boy.'

'A very bad boy.'

'I disgust you, don't I?'

It's an easy question to answer so I tell him the truth, or the almost truth. 'Yes, you're disgusting. You Percy, are the most disgusting man I have ever met.'

Percy groans with pleasure. I figure that Lola and Georgia have it worked out. This is easy money if you have the stomach for it.

'Walk on my back.'

'You what?'

'I want to feel your stilettos.'

I climb up onto the bed and as I step on him, he shudders.

'You okay?'

'Ahhhhh... harder.' Yep, he's okay.

Percy offered me £1,000 to do anything he asked. When I

256

said no, that I didn't do fetish he doubled his offer. I don't know whether it's the Mario thing, the *dinner party* at Greens or what. But I want the money and then I want out of these hotel rooms.

'Well, what kind of thing would you do to me?' I asked. I'm keen to make the cash but that Guo stuff has really put me off blood and cutters, the mad ones are more likely to be the obsessives.

'I won't do anything to you. I want you to do things to me,' he said and his eyes went black. I bet just talking about it was making him hard.

'I don't know,' I said.

'£2,500? And we leave now.'

'And I don't get hurt?'

'Promise.'

'Done.'

These shoes are definitely piercing his skin. I'm wincing at the thought and Percy's writhing around with pleasure, his back soaked in sweat. I figure if he's not bothered then I shouldn't be, so I step it up a little, trying not to slip over. He sighs with relief.

'Does it hurt?'

'Yes, Mistress?'

'Do you want me to stop?'

'No, Mistress. Please fuck me.'

So this is Percy's thing is it. Okay. I step down off his back and reach for his vibrator. He must be joking. The vibrator is massive. I hesitate. On what planet is this pleasurable for him?

'I'm in charge,' I say, then add, 'I decide what happens to you.' I kind of don't know if I want to laugh or throw up because this is not a pretty sight. I mean, how do people work out that this is what they like?

'Please, Mistress.'

I start feeling really strange, my skins feels itchy, I'm sweating and I have this sensation that I'm on the other side of the room watching myself. I look over my shoulder to where I think the other me is standing but there's nothing there. I pinch my skin hard. I've got to focus on this job.

Percy has blood and sweat oozing from his back, a harness on his face his fat hairy arse staring at me, his balls dragging against bed covers.

I don't want to look at the vibrator or think about where it's been.

Even without the fact that I'm feeling like a jellyfish on acid, this is like Lola territory. My punters hardly ever ask me for this stuff. I think coz I'm young. Most of them know that's taking it a bit too far. But Percy doesn't give a shit about my personal welfare, or whether he is going to shock me all the way to Peckham and back. I mean this bloke walked into the club in four grand's worth of Armani, and he's not bad looking, with his clothes on. No doubt someone's father, definitely he has a wife, and he's naked and begging me to. No way.

The vibrator has to be twelve inches long and three inches wide. I might as well be using one of the hotel fire extinguishers from the corridor. It's not rocket science to figure out that any insertion into any orifice is going to be pretty painful.

'Please, Mistress?'

He turns to look at me, adjusting his muzzle and licking his lips. I'm thinking about Hannibal Lecter and of how he likes to wash down flesh with a nice Chianti.

I switch the vibrator on and Percy groans at the gentle mechanic whirring.

'Are you teasing me Mistress?'

He lifts his arse up towards the vibrator, there's blood dribbling onto his arse cheeks. I taste vomit in the back of my mouth. I gag, and then from nowhere I start thinking that Wills and his mates must have been looking at me like this. Blood dribbling down my back, my arse in the air; though fuck knows my arse is cuter than Percy's. I turn to vibrator back off. I can't do this.

'Percy, look,' I say, and I try to push up The Tits, to distract him a little. But Percy isn't interested in The Tits.

'I beg you, Mistress.' I shake my head.

'I can't. Honestly.' I'm shaking like a park bench meths drinker. I don't know what's happening to me. My head spinning like the waltzers. I step over to the other side of the room.

'I'll make it £3,000.' Percy stares up at me like a dog wanting a walk, and I look at him all pathetic and trussed in his chains and I think 'why not, right?'

Three grand's enough to bring me home and dry, well almost.

Percy's smile is wider than Georgia's arse when I nod, but as I walk towards him I think again about William Clarke Price, and his Sloane boy bullies and their sick little party games. My legs buckle and quicker than I can stop it. I'm on the floor and I'm shaking and my chest hurts and it's like there's this alien trying to get out. Then there's a blood-freezing scream. I don't know what's causing it or where it's coming from, but I know I have to lie down.

By the time the scream is gone so is Percy, taking his cash, his gadgets and all his perversions with him. I lie on the hotel carpet sobbing and sobbing until the duty manager lets himself in and tells me to put some clothes on and get out.

Out on the street the air is heavy and moist, the breeze smells like summer storms. I stumble along the pavement like an old drunk then sit in a shop doorway and count the beats in my head as they slow and calm. This must be what it feels like to be Tiggy. The Sloane reject is rubbing off on me.

It's 5am and I didn't earn a fucking penny tonight. I'm in danger of turning into a Jason.

But I'm so close, I'm not going down like this.

I hail a taxi.

The driver rambles on and I stare silently out of the windows at the shit grey air.

Turning on the back light of the taxi I snap open my handheld mirror and start to re-apply my makeup. I'm still gorgeous. I'm still young and I will beat Mario. Mario is going to be so sorry that he ever met me. Stroke by stroke I start to feel better. By the time the taxi pulls in to the curb I am reformed and remade.

I hammer on the door of Club Velveteen louder than the coppers on a dawn drug raid.

Chapter Forty Eight
Tiggy

September starts to merge into October. The stalls around the high street start closing up at 2pm. Daylight only seems to last a few hours of each day. The flower stall switches from summer flowers to yellows, burnt oranges and deep reds. Maybe it's the weather, the claustrophobic constant drizzle. Maybe it's the disappointed faces of the shoppers in Shepherd's Bush shopping centre, but I miss Tony. I've wished away so many summers desperate to return to school and into his arms. Waiting for him constantly felt insufferable. But now knowing that I'll never see him again seems to hurt a little more day every day. A sort of cumulative grief.

Of course, I haven't spoken to him since Sandra came to visit. And I know Tony and I are never going to be together. But he's been my ballast keeping me from capsizing, without him I feel exposed. Out of habit I store thoughts and moments to share with him, but the keeping of them for no purpose, fills me with emptiness.

I can't talk to Scarlett about how I feel. The very mention of Tony's name and she goes off on a rant about child-snatching perverts and how girls like me are 'all about the bloke'. I can't work out whether she is a fervent feminist or a misogynist.

But Sandra was right. My life has been a mess while I've been waiting for Tony. And if I am no longer waiting for him, then what am I waiting for?

Outside the Oxford Street branch of Office Sirens I

straighten my skirt and button up my jacket. Then I tie my hair back neatly into a ponytail. In my Top Shop outfit I could almost fit in to the London office world. I press the buzzer and a crackly robotic voice tells me to push the door and come on up.

I'm greeted in the corridor by a woman called Janice. Janice's make-up looks suspiciously as though she has been colouring in her face, but she seems blissfully unaware. She's wearing clickety patent court shoes and a nylon blouse that was made for a woman a few sizes smaller. Her skirt is skin tight and pleats over her middle-aged spread. Scarlett would have a field day. One of her favourite pastimes is screeching with laughter at 'normal' people in the TV. My novel reading is frequently disturbed by her gleefully yelling, 'Oi, Tiggy. There's a troll in a dress on the TV!' or 'Fucking hell, he's shaved his arse and now he's talking through it.'

Janice hands me an Office Sirens clip board with an Office Sirens pen attached by a red plastic cord.

'This is for you.' She over annunciates her consonants, like she's learned English from a cassette. 'There's a short questionnaire which we ask all applicants to fill in, and there's an extra sheet of paper if you need it. Let me know when you're ready.' Her smile is slightly glazed and vacant.

I thank her and look at the form.

I do well on the address and education but then there is a gap where my work experience should be, other than the three weeks of reception work I have nothing. Three whole years of nothing at all.

'I've been travelling,' I say apologetically as I hand her back the form.'So there might be a few gaps.'

'That's okay.' The vacant smile still holding for the time being. 'Lots of people take gap years these days don't they? It's completely normal.' But her voice tails off as she looks more closely at my form and sees quite how limited my experience is.

'Um, I was away for three years after Boarding School... on and off,' I say adding 'sorry.' Because I can see the smile slipping from her face as she pushes the clip board back at me.

'Well, any work at all will do, even if it was fruit picking or waitressing that's fine. It all counts. So fill in any of your travelling jobs, because then employers will get an impression of what kind of young woman you are.'

'But I, I didn't do anything like that.' I feel an embarrassed flush moving from my neck through to my cheeks, 'I was travelling, not working.'

'Nice for some.' She snaps the clip board from my hands. 'Well, wait there and Sally will be through to take you to the typing test.' Janice is very clearly trying to maintain some kind of professional demeanour but her eyes are no longer vacuous pools. Now they are flashing a dark glint of annoyance.

'Great,' I say as charmingly as I can. 'Thanks Janice, you've been very helpful.' But it's too late for me to make amends now. It's obvious that Janice has concluded that I have been silver spoon fed doses of happiness and privilege from birth.

I meet Dan at The Dive Bar in the basement of the King's Head pub in Chinatown. I arrive early and order us two pints of lager. The place is deserted so Terry, the barman quips, 'You're starting early. Are you sure you can handle both of those?' He's chatty with me until Dan arrives and then his attention is entirely and unashamedly focussed on him. He practically drools into Dan's pint as he places it on the bar.

I grab an end booth down one of the two exposed brick tunnels that count as seating areas in The Dive. 4pm is the best time of day to be here. This is a smoker's paradise, and fills up quickly as the local offices empty, so by sixish the air is simply circulating other people's exhaled cigarettes. And the toilets are filthy and so small that you have to squeeze yourself against the wall the close the cubicle door. But they play Nina Simone, Billie Holliday and Herb Albert. And the main source of light is wine bottles stuffed with candles. Dan thinks he's in jazz basement bar heaven.

I talk him through the dreaded temp agency visit.

'She hated me because she thought my family was rich. No more than hated, she despised me.'

'Why does that surprise you, Tiggy?'

'It's prejudiced, isn't it? If I went around slating everyone whose parents didn't have money I'd be called a snob. But people like Janice can do it back to me and everyone thinks it's fine.'

I watch the candle drip wax down along the wine bottle on our table. Or rather I watch the wax drip along last night's wax.

'Oh hold on. I see you wince when you hear Sloaney accents. Half the reason you're at Valerios is to avoid your Violas and the like.'

'I don't talk like that though.'

Dan holds his thumb and forefinger up together, indicating that perhaps I do sound like that a little bit.

'I'm not one of those girls!'

'The woman from Office Sirens wasn't to know that was she?'

'I suppose not.'

'People have their reasons, and besides, you can't worry too much about what other people think.'

'If only it was that easy.'

'Anyway, you haven't heard about my latest Mario trauma.' Dan arches his eyebrows mischievously.

'Has he asked you to play naked?'

'Worse,' he says.

'Go on.'

'He wants me to cover that Bryan Adams song.' It's clear Dan thinks this is asking the unaskable. 'I said, "Mario, I think everyone who needs to hear that song has heard it often enough to last a lifetime," but you know Mario.'

Dan just glinted his teeth at me and said, 'Well, maybe I should get someone else to play it then.'

His impression of Mario is so bad it is almost good.

'He's got some power thing going on at the moment,' I suggest. 'He seems to be threatening everyone. And he's definitely in Scarlett's bad books. Whenever I mention his name she yells 'bastard' at the top of her voice.'

'Well, I hate to agree with her, but she may be right. Anyway, I told him I'd think about it to keep him happy. But what's worse is that I did. I actually thought about it. Last night I started working out the first few chords and then I-'

'What?'

'I thought, What the fuck am I doing? Who am I becoming?'

'It's only one song, Dan.'

'No it's not. My point is that I came into the job thinking it was one thing. I thought that at least I was being paid to be a musician. But if I start playing music that I hate, well, I'm selling my soul, aren't I?'

'Well... not quite.'

'It makes me no better, no different to your mate Scarlett. I, young Antigone, am a whore.'

'Hardly, and besides we've all got to pay the rent somehow, Dan.'

'This is true. But every man has his limits. And Bryan Adams is mine.' He nods at my empty pint glass 'Another? Here, have this.' He hands me his cigarette and then heads along the tunnel back to the bar to fetch our drinks.

I watch him chatting with Terry, their easy conversation, Dan's complete oblivion to Terry's crush and his comfort in his own masculinity. I toy with his rollie in my hands. My half-crush is in danger of filling out. Watching him I realise that I do love the way his fringe falls forward. In fact I love everything about him; his faded jeans, the way his T-shirts hang on him, the leather band around his wrist. But what I love best is that he has no idea how very gorgeous he is, and how decent he is. What if Scarlett is right and he does fancy me and I'm being moronic?

'What?' Dan says handing me my second beer. I decide to put my cards on the table. Well, near the table anyway.

'I was, I was... wondering what Jackie thinks of you working at the club?' I try to say this nonchalantly.

'In what way?'

'Oh come on, it's full of women. Some of whom are very attractive. It's full of sex... and... strippers.' I'm grateful the bar is too dark for Dan to notice my deepening blush.

'Well, Jackie's very attractive. What are you saying? That I'm like the men who go to the club?'

'No, just that if I was your girlfriend then I would be jealous, I think. I'd be worried.'

'I'm not sure why you're bringing this up now, but Jackie knows that not only am I a fabulous and talented musician, but I am also one hundred percent faithful to her. Not every bloke in the world is like the men who come to the club or-'

'I didn't mean-'

'It's okay, Tiggy. I know what you mean. This is about Tony, isn't it? And you trying to make sense of things?'

I nod. Dan seems satisfied and so continues, 'Well, it's a choice, I think. Because there are always going to be girls or women that I meet and I have a moment where I wonder what it would be like... and I expect Jackie has the same thing... but-'

'But?'

'But, I'm not that guy. I learned the hard way already. Rachel really hurt me, and I would *never* do that to someone, least of all someone I love. I couldn't live with myself.'

'Okay.'

I think I might be a little bit more in love with him than I was a few minutes ago.

'Does that help?'

'Yeah.'

'Don't worry, not all men are like Tony.'

'No,' I say. 'Thanks, Dan.'

Well that certainly answers that question for me. I can't wait to tell Scarlett that she was wrong about him. There are still a few good men left.

'Anyway, enough about you, let's talk about me again. And my ideas for life after Valerios.'

'One song is not worth losing your job for.'

'Tiggy, don't let me down here. Cliff's bad enough, but Bryan Adams has always recorded middle of the road turgid crap. Well that *Summer of 69* one was okay, but-'

'Okay, save me the lecture and at least you have some skills. I can't even pass a basic typing test. And who the fuck knows how to use a telex? I'm doomed to spend the rest of my life as a stripper.'

Which is when Dan shakes his finger at me and winks. 'Ahah... Or maybe not. The whole *Adamsgate* scenario has forced me to have rethink. Because Jackie and I have been talking and I think we may have found the tunnel that's big enough for all of us to escape.'

Chapter Forty Nine
Scarlett

Delilah Goodings in the sixth form always got the leads in the school plays. In the First Year I thought she was the most beautiful, talented girl in the world. If she passed me in the playground or outside one of the classes I would breathe right in and puff myself out, hoping that she might notice me. All I wanted when I was 11 was for Delilah Goodings to look at me twice.

Delilah Goodings was prettier than Madonna and a better singer. She wore over twenty rubber arm bands and had a blonde streak in the front of her hair. She was almost never on her own. She was the most popular girl I ever knew. Her and her mates spent breaks in the music rooms singing songs and rehearsing for the new school musical or whatever. I'd watch them from outside, my hands freezing through the holes in the orange nylon of my parker pockets. They would laugh and sing and once I even saw Delilah snogging Jonathan Tyler. She kissed like they do in the movies.

In the Third Year Delilah Goodings wasn't at school anymore, she'd done her A-Levels and moved on. It was my chance to step into her shoes. The posters went up for the auditions of *Guys and Dolls* and I practised and practised and practised. I sung into my Fisher Price tape player and then played it back over and over until I was pitch perfect. I stormed the audition. I ran home clutching my school bag and waited for the phone to ring. I was going to be Sarah Brown. The phone didn't ring. Stephanie Simpson was chosen instead of me. Stephanie Simpson who made faces like someone was sticking pokers up her arse when she was singing; Stephanie Simpson who sounded like nails being dragged down a blackboard; Stephanie Simpson whose mother was a governor and who everyone knew had given the head master a *lift home* after the Governors Christmas night out.

I'm trying out my new Boots home manicure set when Tiggy comes bounding in like a badly trained Labrador wanting to lick and sniff at everything. Like every smell and corner of the room is interesting and must be explored.

'You're cheery,' I say, because it's like Tiggy has two settings. Miserable and mopey or Bambi/Labrador puppy.

'Oh Scarlett, guess what. It's like totally brilliant. Looks like Dan and I are going to set up a business together.'

'Thrilling,' I say so sarcastically that paint must peel from the walls, but Tiggy ain't noticing.

'Isn't it? It's just fantastic. He's met with this small business advisor and they've approved him some financing to buy this rehearsal and recording studio in Lambeth. He says he's getting a really good deal and that he's going to develop new talent and invest in new voices and-'

'Dan's the new Richard Branson now is he?'

'No, well, not exactly, but maybe, you never know what could happen.'

'Yeah, I think we do, Tiggy. He'll be filing for bankruptcy by the end of the year.'

'Oh come on, Scarlett. Be happy for me.'

'I am, Tiggy. Although you haven't explained why a rehearsal space needs a stripper yet.'

'I won't be stripping, silly. I'm going to be helping with bookings and answering phones on the front desk. Meet and greet.'

'Sounds almost too exciting... answering phones.'

'Isn't it though?'

'And what does Jackie make of this?'

'It was her idea to ask me, apparently.'

'Dan Dan the Piano Man's invisible fiancé is as mental as him. She's never even met you.'

'She trusts Dan's judgement.'

'Mental and stupid... unless... maybe they want you as their own private sex slave.'

'Scarlett, be serious. I want you to be happy for me.'

'I just worry for you. Why would a couple choose to employ their very own stripper?'

'I'm not a stripper... not really... it's just something I'm doing at the moment... it's not who I am... I've got A-Levels.'

'Answering phones in a shed in Lambeth is one step away from world domination. It's entirely you, isn't it?'

'It's not a shed... and at least it's reputable... something I can tell my father about.'

'Oh, it's about Daddy is it?'

'No, but, it will be nice not to be lying to him.'

'Since when have you wanted to tell him the truth? I thought lying to Daddy was something you enjoyed.'

'Well it isn't. I want my life to be more open, less secretive. Maybe it's to do with the letter from my mother, or because of Sandra. Or maybe it's because I went for a job interview and found that I was alienating myself from the real world. I think it's time now, time to go back. Time to get my life on track.'

'Any place for me in this new life then?'

'Of course... is that why you look so moody blue?'

I don't know if it's the way that she says 'moody blue'. Or the way she says it's time for her to 'go back'. Like the whole Valerios thing has been some kind of poverty tourism and now it's time to pack up her glass slippers and head back to Sloaneland before her chariot turns into a pumpkin.

'I really happy for you, Cinderella,' I say sweet as a sherbet dip.

When Roberto talks about 'the establishment' he looks the way I felt about Delilah Goodings. Roberto thinks that people with money and voices like royalty are extraordinary, shining special and superior. He thinks you can tell the quality of a man by where he spends his holidays, who his tailor is and whether he drinks single malt whiskey. But these people ain't better, their lives are easier from day one. They always have a safety net, whether it's a mother on the governing board, a rich daddy or a mate who'll parachute you out when you get bored of slumming it.

'You sure Scarlett? You looked a bit funny. Have I upset you?'

'Me upset? Crikey, no Tigs. How could you ever upset me?'

'Coz, nothing's going to happen overnight or anything, and you're still welcome to stay until you find your own place... or as long as you like... we'll always be friends.'

'That's really kind, Tiggy. I'm sorry if I was being strange. I'm probably a little jealous or something. But, well done. I really hope it works out for you.'

'Ah thanks,' Tiggy says. 'Come on, give me a hug.'

Tiggy puts her arms around me. Her long hair falls like an auburn glossy curtain over both our shoulders.

'Friends forever?' she says holding out her little finger like a mutant five year old, so I link my little finger with hers and we shake on it. Then she hugs me again, behind the smell of cigarettes, close up she smells like fresh linen and summer flowers. Because girls like her always do.

Stephanie Simpson's mum paid for her to go to a drama school somewhere in the West End and is probably giving *lifts home* to every producer this side of Broadway to get leading roles for her little girl. Delilah Goodings got pregnant by her uncle and had four kids by three different blokes by the time she was 22. When she's not monged out on Peach Scnapps she's dragging prams up and down the walkways of the maisonettes looking like a proper shambolic track suit wearing lunatic. Before I moved out of Clare's I passed her in one of the stairwells and I pretended that I didn't recognise her.

Chapter Fifty
Tiggy

The studios and rehearsal space are located behind a black door and take up three railway arches.

'It doesn't look like much, I know,' Dan says ruefully as he unlocks the three oversized padlocks, 'but wait till you get inside.'

The rain is drizzling down and I try not to look to anxious as Dan fumbles with the keys. It's not the most glamorous of locations. The arch next door is advertising 'cheap bodykits and fast resprays.' 'MOT's WHILE YOU WATE!!!' has been painted onto the brickwork.

'Ahah... we're in.' Dan shoves a handful of padlocks into his pockets and then pushes open the creaking door

He clicks on a series of lights on the wall, swearing under his breath as he endeavours to discover which combination will light the studios. He clicks some more and then there is light.

'Oh my God!' I say and jump up and down on the spot. 'It's like a proper studio, like in the *Feed The World v*ideo.'

Dan grins, 'Tiggy, that's just a sound booth. Now come on, let me show you around.'

I've never seen Dan so animated, but as he leads me through the arches he's chattering on with such passion.

'Jackie and I have been talking and we figure that between us, we can probably manage. She knows this great sound engineer who she thinks she can convince into helping us out, and with you doing the bookings

274

and helping out front, it might mean making teas and coffees and things-' he tails off a little embarrassed. 'If you don't mind.'

'I don't at all. I have to start somewhere right.'

'And the bank have approved the mortgage and the business plan and they've given us an extra £5000 for marketing. We're going to need T-shirts and flyers and well, I was thinking maybe that might be something you wanted to have a hand in, you know thinking of designs, ideas, anything that will attract in new bands and new talent.'

'I would love to do something like that.'

'Excellent, then your first task is to choose your job title.'

'Oooh.'

'And you'll need to help come up with a company name and a company logo. Something sensible that won't make me wince whenever I say it.'

'I'm on it, boss.'

'Boss. Sounds a bit strange.'

'This is so exciting. I can't believe it.'

'Well, you'd better start, because, hopefully in a few weeks we'll be in here, paintbrushes in hand, you me and Jackie getting this place exactly as we want it... well maybe less of the painting for Jackie. We might have to do her share for a bit.'

'Yeah, where is she? I thought you said she'd be here today?'

'Well,' Dan flicks his fringe from his face. 'She's gone to see her Mum. We've got some *news*.'

The way his face lights up with amazement as he says the word news can only mean one thing. I can feel dimples digging into my cheek and my face reflecting back his grin.

'She's not! You're not?'

'I most certainly am.'

'Oh my God. Dan that's amazing!'

'Yep. I'm gonna be a dad... and you are going to be Aunty Tiggy.'

'A dad, Dan... crikey.'

'Yep. A dad.'

'Does it change anything here?' I look around the studio, I'm already in love with it. But if Jackie's pregnant then-

'It makes us even more determined to make it work,' he says. 'Now come on, let's get a pint, celebrate and work out what we are going to call ourselves.

After a couple of pints at The Dive Bar, the new Director of Marketing/Office Manager/Administrator or whatever I am to be called for Burnhams' Recording and Rehearsal Studios decides that someone in her corporate position needs an equally swanky city centre pad.

I negotiate the heaving pavements of Tottenham Court Road and let my credit card get a little more worn down in Habitat.

After three hours I am so burdened with bags that I have to hail a taxi to take me home.

After a further three hours my flat is transformed. The shabby brown sofa sports a new crimson throw. The Tony memorabilia has been removed from the walls and instead I have replaced them with tasteful art prints. Magazines are organised into racks on the shelves. My LPs are in their new wooden containers.

I've Hoovered the carpet so thoroughly that it is almost a shade lighter. And have a new rug under the coffee table that matches the new cream curtains. The old curtains are folded up in the corner ready to take to a charity shop, because I'm not convinced they'll survive my washing machine.

I don't know why I didn't do this sooner.

I face myself in the new full length oak framed mirror in the corridor. It catches the light from the sitting room and makes the whole flat seem larger.

'Hi, I'm Antigone,' I practise. 'I'm the Director of Marketing.'

'Hi, I'm Tiggy, welcome to Burnhams' Recording Studio.'

'Hello. Welcome to Burnhams', I'm Tiggy. Office Manager.'

I haven't smoked all afternoon and I don't seem to mind. I look at my smiling face and think that maybe I am a little pretty after all. Maybe my body isn't so bad. Maybe my father will be proud of me now. Maybe my mother will look at me and wonder how she could have left. I look at myself a little closer and I see a glimpse of some of my mother's beauty looking back out at me.

I wonder whether she will notice it if she meets me.

I want to read her letter again. Even though I know it word perfect. I go to my room and pull the shoebox out from under my bed, rummaging for her envelope. Then I go through the contents again, slower this time.

I feel ill.

When was the last time I read it?

What if was mixed up with all of Tony's letters? What if I've thrown it out with the rubbish? There's a chance then that the sack could still be in the bin store. I run from the flat leaving the door wide open. Bashing at the lift button which refuses to move. The damn thing is out of order again. I run down the steps, all one hundred and forty of them. My head is flooded with forgotten memories.

As I run I think about my mother, and her blue grey eyes, about when she made me apple pie and I said I hated it. How I'd climb onto my father's lap to see if she would be jealous.

At the tenth floor I pause for breath, techno tracks are blaring from behind the doors, like the entire floor is a daytime rave.

I think playing at her dressing table, patting powder from a velvet puff onto my face, drawing her lipstick onto my mouth and the lipstick snapped.

Down past the sixth floor where a group of children are huddled on the landing, lighting matches, and smoking cigarette butts. They have a small turret of other people's dog ends in front of them.

I hated myself, because I thought she hated me. This beautiful woman must know what a naughty horrible daughter she had.

I crash my way into the bin store and almost retch on the smell. Steeling myself, I open up the bags, one by one, ripping at the black plastic, choking back the acrid stink, my eyes stinging from ammonia and mould and the visions of other people's rubbish. One sack is entirely full of used toilet roll, a whole sack of shitty tissue scraps, another nappies and beer bottles, curries, clothes, vomit, there seems to be a sack for everything. But not a single one has a scrap of yellow paper.

Unless, of course, unless we didn't take the sack out and have put it in the kitchen or somewhere else instead.

I take the stairs in twos, propelling myself forward on the handrail, panting and sweating. And then I am back in the flat.

It's not there. I try to be strong, try to remember

that this is a whole new me. But I'm reduced to my knees. Clutching at my side. I have a stitch, my body aches and I have lost it. The letter I waited six years for. The letter that shows that she exists, that perhaps on some level she does care.

It doesn't matter. It's only a letter. It doesn't matter. It's only a letter. It doesn't matter.

I remind myself that I am soon to be working with Dan. That I have so much to look forward to. But everything seems meaningless and empty.

All I want is the letter from my mother, who I have wished for so desperately and waited for so impatiently.

It doesn't matter. It's only a letter.

I collapse onto my bed and sob large greedy tears, swallowing back mouthfuls of tears and mucus.

Chapter Fifty One
Tiggy

S omeone has sprayed red paint over the sign
outside Valerios. The neon bars have been pulled
from the wall and shattered glass swept into a pile
away from the door. Mario is barking orders at contrac-
tors, 'I want this sign to be cleaned and replaced for
yesterday... you understand.'

It's a gorgeously warm autumn evening and Scarlett
and I have walked to the club together. Scarlett stiffens
when she sees Mario. He kisses his teeth in her
direction.

'Oh dear, someone's vandalised his neon penis sub-
stitute,' Scarlett says loudly. Mario ignores her and
clicks his fingers at me saying, 'You, me... we need to
talk.'

'I'll see you indoors.' I unlink my arm from Scarlett's. She kisses me on the cheek and says, 'Laters.'

'Come, come.' Mario pushes me into the club, his
hand on my back, pressuring me inside. Mario always
has this vague smell of stale Kouros and damp tobacco.

'Tiggy, that girl is bad news. She's no good for you.'

'She's my flatmate, my best friend.'

'Okay.' he looks annoyed. 'Then I'm calling time on
your decision. Tonight is your lucky night. Tonight you
are going to be a proper stripper. I've been too soft on
you. My mistake. You up for it?'

'Mario... I... um... you see.'

He grips my chin tightly, 'Are you saying no?'

'No... no... I'm just... could I have a few more

weeks? Days then?'

'Maybe it's better if you say no. Maybe you're not the right profile for this kind of work. Maybe you should leave.'

Profile? What, am I too fat and ugly? I try to hold Mario's gaze. To adopt a Scarlett pose. I don't know if it's Mario's aftershave which is dripping from his skin or my normal nausea. But if he doesn't move soon then I am going to up chuck all over his black satin shirt. I notice its cheap stitching with plastic buttons. My father would faint at the thought.

'So leave. I'm a fair man. I will pay you what I owe you right now.' He reaches for his back pocket.

'You don't need to, Mario,' I say quickly. 'I'm doing it.'

He looks mildly surprised and then waves me away, saying 'Okay.'

I scurry along the corridor. I know I am heading in the wrong direction. I know that I should turn back, but I can't. I'm stuck in some slow motion sequence where all I can do is watch myself make another mistake. It occurs to me that I should have asked Mario to increase my money.

Scarlett has already changed and gone through to the club, so I pull my clothes from my hold all and then sit semi-naked in the toilets wondering whether to wear the Basque or the silk French knickers and bra. Eventually, I'm dressed and I stuff my jeans and T-shirt back into the bag. It's probably time to go through.

But I don't leave the toilets.

I don't know why I'm making such a big deal about this.

I resist the urge to run.

I check my watch, hoping for some last minute

intervention, for Mario to relent and tell me he has changed his mind; for Dan to tell me not to do it; for someone else to make my decision for me.

The doors open and my heart lifts with promise.

'Blimey, it's hot in there tonight. Full of bloody drunken stag parties.' Scarlett wipes a foam make up pad across her forehead. 'You alright? Shouldn't you be inside?'

'In a minute. I just needed some thinking time.'

'Practising your moves?'

'Something like that.'

'So, which one are you doing?'

'The *At Seventeen* one,' I say. 'With purple wig and boots, for a change. But Mario says that tonight is the *big night.*'

'You going to give him what he wants?'

I nod. 'I think so. I need to keep working for a few more weeks. It's only until I start working with Dan. Not for much longer anyway.'

'It's a bad idea, Tiggy. Don't give in to him. He's a bully, and you shouldn't let people push you around.'

'I'm not. I'm fine about it.'

'This isn't right for you, you know.'

'Oh and you know what's best for me now, do you?'

'You're the one who's been fretting over it. You're the one who's been moping round the flat worrying your hair flat.'

'What would you do?'

'That's a pointless question.'

'Why?'

'Coz I'm not you, Tiggy. I don't turn every tiny little thing into a major international anxiety crisis. I don't even understand why you're making such a big deal about it anyway.'

Scarlett is looking at me with the same expression

as Janice from Office Sirens, like I'm a dumb Sloane who can't do anything.

'Well, actually,' I tell her proudly, 'I've told him I'm doing it.'

'Your funeral,' she says. 'But I wouldn't if I were you. You know you'll regret it.' Her face softens and she kisses my cheek. 'Good luck, though. Not that you'll need it.' She pushes a length of fake purple hair from my face and tucks it behind my ears. Maybe I've misunderstood her, maybe she really is trying to look out for me. 'You're too good for this place you know... really... but what the hell. Your life, your choices right?'

'Right,' I say firmly, although I'm not sure that this is a choice.

Mario taps his watch as I walk back into the club, saying, 'Tick tock, Tiggy,' as I pass him. I stick my chin in the air and don't say a word.

Chapter Fifty Two
Tiggy

'You're on in five,' Dan says through the curtain. A scenario so familiar that it usually makes me calmer, makes me feel confident enough to walk onto the stage.

I'm sitting on the dirty floorboards backstage, scratching at my wrists. Fiddling with the elastic on my French knickers.

I should have practised this. Stilletos and silk could be a humiliating combination. What if I trip stepping out of them?

I position my handmirror so that I can't see my eyes. I'm sure they must have all the seductive allure of a rabid dog.

I pull my wig down tighter and try to stand.

My knees buckle and shake.

The last few notes of Dan's final song filter through the curtain. I lift my chin and exhale.

The crowd are applauding. Dan announces me. I don't move.

He calls again. 'Viola Viola.'

I'm going to throw up.

He says, 'One moment, please.'

Dan comes backstage. 'You okay?' I shake my head.

'Mario says that it's tonight or I'm sacked.'

'I'm guessing by the way that you're shaking that you're not up for it.'

I nod.

'Then don't. Get out there, do your thing but don't strip. He can't do anything once you're on stage.'

'But he'll sack me.'

'So what. You know, Tiggy, it's your body, what you do with it is up to you. You can stick ping pong balls up your fanny for all I care. But we'll be set up soon.'

'Ping pong?' I laugh, although it's probably on Mario's list.

'Or do you want me to wear that costume and pretend I'm Viola Viola.'

He flips his hand under my chin. 'Do what you want to do Tiggy, not what other people tell you. You'll be okay?'

'Okay, okay. Oh fuck it. What's the big deal. I'll go on, give me two seconds.'

Taking a deep breath and remind myself that I love what I do, that there is nowhere else I would rather be. I love it so much I'd do it for free. I am sexy, strong, sensual.

I am going to be sick.

I nod to Dan and he pushes the cassette into the machine and the music starts.

I step out through the curtains, Mario moves forward from the back of the bar and takes his private booth right up at the front of the stage. He lights a cigarette and taps his fingers on the table in front of him, his gaze focussed on mine.

I try to ignore him.

I spot Scarlett coming back through the doors, customer on arm, making her way down the front booths. Then the lights switch from red to pink on full glare in my face and I can't see the crowd. But I can hear them. Scarlett's right. Tonight is a raucous night. Lately Mario seems to be letting in anyone with a bit of cash.

I dance through the routine with all the grace of a

baby deer on roller-skates. I clear my head of everything, tuning out the yells from a large group of young men, the wolf-whistles, the yells of, 'show us your tits darling'.

There is only me and this stage.

I pull back my blouse. I turn my back to the audience and the lights glow sulphurous around me.

I try to forget myself. Try to imagine I am alone.

I've forgotten the steps.

Someone yells, 'Get 'em off!' I stop.

Mario frowns at me.

I close my eyes and focus on my routine.

I wave my long purple hair over my shoulders and lift my hands behind my back, unclipping my bikini top, slipping it slowly down one arm, off the other and then tossing it over my shoulder. Men are whooping from the corner table. I turn around to face the crowd, my hands still over my breasts.

There are only ten seconds of the song left and normally I would tease by turning back round again, suggesting that I might remove my underwear, then turn around again, showing my bare back, the silky French knickers.

I slip my hands into the knicker elastic, letting my fingers tease a little.

Dan is watching me from the wings. He looks concerned, for some reason this fills me with fury.

I am tired of being pitied. Sick of people thinking that I'm not strong enough, not brave enough, that I can't make my own decisions. Scarlett's right, I can be a right Jason sometimes. I can take off my knickers for a second. It's not as though worlds will collide or wars will start. This time I will take control, I will make my choice, I will not be a victim.

I'm strong and capable and in control, I love what I

do.

I'm wearing a wig, I'm wearing four inch stilettos.

I am Viola Viola.

Antigone Arnold is no longer in the building. And maybe this is a mistake, but I've made so many already, who really cares.

Let them yell and whistle.

I am not chicken shit. I am not scared.

I am the new liberated me.

I am unashamed.

A rush of adrenaline shoots through me and I stare out at my audience.

They are all here for me. So, I will give them what they have paid for.

Fuck it, in for a penny. I step out of my knickers. There's a gasp, mainly from the waitresses and hostesses who know that this is new for me.

I feel great. Like there's not a man in the room who doesn't wish that he was with me. I flip the wig back and turn around. Mario is smiling. The lights flicker round behind me resting on members of the caterwauling crowd. Scarlett is staring at me almost shocked. I can't see Dan. Mario gets up from his seat and makes his way towards the door, slow clapping me, his object achieved.

I stand completely naked in front of Scarlett and face her with a challenge like, 'See... I'm just as tough as you.'

Her hands are over her face.

Then I notice Scarlett's customer and realise that for the first time in my life I have my father's full attention.

I run.

Chapter Fifty Three
Tiggy

Dan catches up with me in the back alley. He has my clothes with him. 'Come on. Put these on before you freeze.'

I'm naked, other than my stilettos, bent over towards the wall, one arm holding me up, the other clutching my freshly emptied stomach.

'Hey, Tiggy, you okay?'

I don't want him to see me like this.

'Come on. What is this? So what, so you took off your clothes-'

'Dan, it's got nothing to do with that... honestly.'

'Look, we both know-'

I never find out what we both know because right then I throw up again. Dan pulls my hair back behind my head stroking my back.

'Wow. I think there's a shopping trolley in there somewhere.'

'Shut up, Dan.'

'No, seriously if they made vomiting an Olympic sport then you'd be set.'

'Oh God.'

Finally I stop and pull on my jeans and T-shirt. I can only see my father's face. I can't believe that I will ever get past this feeling. I am pretty certain that in 50 years time – when I am sat at the window of some residential common room, a patchwork rug over my knees, wheelchair rocking back and forth – when I think of that moment I will still blush and feel regret.

I will unpack my list of a lifetimes worth of embarrassments, my own personal catalogue of humiliations. And I bet it will still be in the top five.

Why tonight of all the nights?

'Apparently, some men get sexually aroused by women vomiting during sex. It could be your unique selling point, Viola Viola the Vomiting Stripper.'

'Dan. It's not funny.'

'Tell me?'

'My father is in there.'

'Your father?'

'He's in the club... he saw... well everything. I am never going to be able to face him again.'

'What do you mean, he's in there?'

'Exactly that. My father is in the club. He saw my act... Oh God, I'm going to have to kill myself.'

'What was he doing?'

'I don't know. Looking for women I suppose. I thought he was really happy with Margaret, but then he's not going to tell me if he goes to Hostess Clubs is he? I mean... oh shit Dan... he's going to kill me. No. *I'm* going to kill me.'

'Who was he with?'

'Scarlett. How embarrassing. She said not to do it... shit.'

'Doesn't that seem a little bit too much of a coincidence, you know. Of all the clubs in all the world he had to walk into yours and then book Scarlett.'

'I don't know, Dan.' But I do, his words have a tone to them, a certain sound.

It rings out like the truth.

We look at each other for a long time, both searching for an explanation.

'I bet she set it up,' his face is thunderous; 'I'm going

to kill that little bitch.'

'Dan, don't do anything stupid. Please. Leave it.'

'Like hell I will.'

'Dan, please, let's just go back to mine, maybe it wasn't her. Look we're both upset. Maybe there's an explanation.'

'No, you go home, don't look so scared. I'll be along in a bit, I've got another set to do and... well, I just need to sort a few things out.'

He pushes my bag into my hands, kisses me on the cheek and then runs across the street back into the club.

I pace the floor.

I chain smoke.

I check the machine for messages.

Dan doesn't call, doesn't turn up.

I try not to think about my father's face, because each time I do my stomach lurches like someone has chucked it across the wall. I can never go back to Valerios.

Scarlett wouldn't do this to me. Why would she?

I try vodka, but am scared to drink more than one glass. I am not sure I would ever stop.

I tidy the flat frantically scrubbing and scouring. I bleach the toilet. I clean the taps with an old toothbrush. I get on my hands and knees and scrub behind the washbasin plinth. I find an old scrunchy, a ring I'd forgotten about and what looks like a decomposed mouse or vole.

I'm putting it all together as I scrub.

She has no reason not to like me. I have been good to Scarlett. Scarlett is my friend. Or at least I thought she was my friend.

What is it about me that makes people act this way?

Every five seconds, I look out of the window for Dan's car.

The buzzer goes and I dash across the room to answer it, someone is holding it down. My stomach flips over, but not with nausea, with some kind of premonition, trepidation, something. I pick up the intercom with shaking hands.

I don't know what I know, but this feels wrong.

'Tiggy, let me in. I've got no keys.'

I buzz her in. Realising that even if she didn't invite my father to the club I don't want her in the room anymore. I want her out of the flat. The lift clunks down from my level, making for the ground floor. I open the door to the flat, determined, this time, to stand up for myself.

I'm sure that Scarlett has something to do with this.

I wait, hands on hips, watching the light flash as the lift passes through the floor. I don't care, I can't possibly be anymore sick. She has to go.

The lift doors open. Scarlett falls out in front of me onto the floor, her face pulped, blood pouring from her mouth. Her voice just a whimper.

'Tiggy... help me.'

She reaches her arm up towards me, as though maybe I can save her.

'Fuck, Scarlett. Hold on.'

I call an ambulance.

I kneel on the filthy lino outside the lift, Scarlett's head on my lap. I tell her that everything is going to be all right. I stroke her hair and find my hands covered in her blood.

I remember something about not moving people. I have no idea how she got herself home, maybe her sheer determination. She's moaning agonisingly. I've offered her water but she pushed it away.

They always have water on telly don't they? I should have listened a bit more that time St John's Ambulance came to the school. The only thing I can think of is the recovery position, except that they also say that you're not supposed to move someone with injuries.

I wish Dan would turn up. He'd know what to do.

Finally, I hear the sirens pulling into the forecourt and the lift doors close as they call it down. 'Scarlett, they're on their way okay, just hold on.' She gulps out air then drags in breath. Maybe a lung is punctured or something, because she kind of rattles when she breathes in and she's been coughing up blood.

'What happened here then?' Two scarily competent and calm paramedics arrive in their green overalls, making this scene feel almost mundane.

'One... Two... Three... lift... there you go luv... you'll be sorted in minutes don't you worry.... you her friend? What happened?'

'I don't know... she just came home like this.'

'Hey luv, do you know who did this to you?' The tallest one leans over Scarlett, who even with a battered face still looks beautiful. She makes a tiny mew, and I wince.

'Is she going to be okay?'

'Let's hope so luv... though looks like someone's given her a proper going over... there are some bastards out there... young girl like this.'

I don't know if I should mention the club. They might leave her here to die if they think she's a hooker.

I stand hopelessly, watching them strap her onto a

stretcher, swab her, attach some kind of fluid then wheel her into the lift.

They keep talking to Scarlett, telling her everything will be fine, even though she's not responding. Maybe it's to keep her conscious or because they need to know for their forms. They ask over and over who did this to you, and do I have any idea? I don't know. I say that maybe it was muggers, still unsure what I should or shouldn't say. Scarlett leans her head up and says very quietly, in a crackly blood-soaked voice just loud enough so that we can all hear.

'Dan Burnham did it.'

It takes me a few seconds to realise that she means Dan – my Dan.

Chapter Fifty Four
Tiggy

Everything moves like I'm in a dream.

I drink endless cups of black coffee from plastic mugs. In the hospital waiting room I read posters about the dangers of smoking. I learn the number for the National Drugs Helpline off by heart. I flick through leaflets on dementia, urinary tract infections and the Peri-natal Implications of Maternal Hypertension.

It seems that my current anxiety is caused by some sort of pre-eclampsia in my mother's womb, months before I was born. My neuroses were determined while I was still an embryo, which is reassuring.

Perhaps there are some more pressing external factors that might be raising my blood pressure, but what do I know.

Nurses, doctors and police come out at talk in hushed tones. Scarlett has three fractured bones, she's needed 38 stitches.

I sit on the plastic chair.

I develop a loathing for powdered coffee.

I fidget at Scarlett's bedside while she sleeps. There are tubes and wires coming out all over the place. She looks like an underground map.

I am disturbingly grateful when someone leaves their copy of *The Sun* in the waiting room, at last something new to read. After two minutes I go back to the National Drugs Helpline poster and try adding the numbers up. It's too easy.

I cannot feel anything, my head hisses with white

noise.

The police have questions for me.

'How long have you known Scarlett?'

'Just a few months.'

'What is the nature of your friendship?'

'We're flatmates.'

'What do you know about Dan Burnham?'

'That he wouldn't do it.'

They write everything down without much interest.

'You're sure about that?'

I nod vigorously, 'Absolutely. There's no way that he would hurt anyone. I don't know why she's saying it was Dan.'

'Do you know where we can find him?'

'Yes, but there's no way that he would do it.'

'And Scarlett, who is she exactly?'

It's not until the police and the hospital staff start asking me for more information that I realise I know nothing about Scarlett. That her name is Charlene, that she thinks her mother is a bitch and she doesn't know who her father is, that she grew up somewhere in North London.

No, I don't know her full name, or her birthday. No, maybe I don't know her that well considering we live together. No I am not withholding information.

Carol, the policewoman who's been asking me all these questions tells me to calm down, not to worry, that finding out about people is what they're good at, that I must be in shock. Carol looks as though she has been squashed. She's 5ft tall and 3ft wide, with seemingly no curves. She looks like the pictures of people I used to draw as a child.

We've been sat here over an hour and I need more

coffee.

'I'm going to get a drink.' I move to stand, I nearly stumble, my right leg has gone dead.

'Let me,' she says baring her teeth. I think she's trying to smile.

I walk up and down the corridor wondering if you can get thrombosis from waiting.

'Thanks, Carol. Just black, no sugar.'

Her shoes squeak on the lino. Her calves are larger than her thighs.

Carol's right. I know suspiciously little about Scarlett. And what I do know doesn't seem relevant. How will it help if I tell Carol that Scarlett likes fruit and running? That she shoplifts. She has a penchant for bizarre outfits or that she works as hostess. That she's not scared of anything or anyone.

Carol clumps back along the corridor, a plastic cup in each hand, dribbling small trails of coffee. She hands me a cup, I sip at the luke warm water, swallowing congealed lumps of coffee.

'Well, they picked up Dan Burnham. They're taking him to Swallow Street Station, to ask him a few questions.'

'Scarlett must have made a mistake. There is no way Dan would hurt anyone.'

Carol's postbox mouth stays long and straight.

'So how do you two know Dan Burnham?'

'We work with him.'

'Okay. Where's that then?'

I don't want to say but I know I have to, and it's not like I've done anything illegal. 'We work at Valerios, it's a club, and um... Dan's the pianist, Scarlett, she's a hostess.'

'And you? You're a hostess as well?'

'Oh no. Gosh no. No... I... I'm... um... well. I'm a dancer.'

'A dancer?' She says this with just enough judgement to show me that she knows exactly what kind of a euphemism *dancer* might be.

I hesitate, not because of Carol, by now I've stopped caring about her opinion, but because I have just remembered by father's face.

'Yes, I'm a stripper,' I say without a shred of pride.

She moves a few inches from me, 'I see.'

My opinion has been diminished. I am no longer a reliable witness. I am no longer a nice middle-class girl whose friend has been a victim of random violence. I am the club soiled, stripping friend of a hooker. I know that Carol has ripped my integrity from her notebook.

Carol tells me to wait where I am, not to go anywhere. They might want to talk to me some more. They want to know when I last saw Scarlett, if I can think of any reason that Dan might have to be angry with her.

When she returns, over an hour later, she is carrying a larger pad and pen. 'You wouldn't mind giving us a full statement now, would you?'

I nod my head.

After another hour of explaining about the club and how I know Dan and how Scarlett and I live together, Carol reads me back my statement.

'And you're saying that you know of no reason why Dan might be angry with Scarlett.'

I say 'no.' shaking in my trainers, lying to the quadrilateral policewoman.

'Interestingly, I've been given a copy of his statement and he says that the last time he saw you he told you he was going to kill her.'

'Oh... oh.'

297

'Antigone, you do understand that this is very serious, and it seems that Dan Burnham, well, this isn't the first time. There was a G.B.H allegation a few years back. He got cautioned. So, maybe you don't know him as well as you think you do?' Carol is delighted with herself, a gloating smile playing on her face. 'Seems that he knows how to throw a punch if needed.'

I think perhaps punching *her* might make me feel better.

'So,' she says pulling the pages from the pad, 'shall we start again? So, you've known Dan Burnham for how long?'

Scarlett finally wakes. 'Hi... ow.' She places her hand on her cheek and looks with curiosity at the tube attached to the back of her hand.

'It looks worse than it is. Well, the nurses say it does.'

'How bad does it look?'

Her eyelids are puffed and blue, her bottom lip swollen and split, her earlobes torn where someone has ripped out her earrings.

'Not good. But it's nothing permanent. It'll all heal. They say it's mainly superficial.'

She shifts on the pillows and lifts herself up gingerly, wincing with each movement.

'Well, I guess my hostess days are over, eh?' She tries to smile, but her face contorts with sudden pain. 'Thanks for coming, Tigs.'

'S'okay, look, Scarlett, why did you say it was Dan?'

Scarlett stares at me tight lipped, her face unforgiving. 'You think I'm lying?'

'Oh come on Scarlett, Dan wouldn't do this, you know that.'

298

'You weren't there Tiggy. Besides he's done it before hasn't he? That drummer in his shitty band?'

She closes her eyes, moves slowly onto her side, and then rolls away, turning her back to me. How does she know about Dan and Mickey? I have so many questions for Scarlett, not least about why she was sitting with my father. But the only thing that matters now is Dan.

'Scarlett, I'm sorry you got hurt, maybe you're confused, because it wasn't Dan. Dan wouldn't have done this to you. Please stop saying he did.'

'I thought you'd be on my side, Tiggy,' she says, her voice so cold that I shiver.

I leave the room. Carol is waiting in the corridor.

'We're going to talk to her again later. Dan insists that it wasn't him, but then they always do, don't they? Besides, why would she say it was Dan, if it wasn't?

Exactly.

'Go home, take a shower and get some rest. Come back in the morning, we'll know more then. Oh and it might be an idea to pick up a change of clothes for your friend.'

Chapter Fifty Five
Tiggy

I go home.
I don't shower or rest, instead heading straight into Scarlett's room.

Her room is clinically tidy. The duvet pulled flat and straight, the chest of drawers empty. There are no photos, no posters. Her green suitcase is zipped and placed by the door. Packed. Ready to go. I place the case on the bed. It's locked. I sit beside it for ten or twenty minutes, contemplating the two miniature padlocks.

I take a sharp knife from the kitchen and pushing back feelings of self-reproach, I cut through the cardboard, turning the case upside down.

Her belongings spill out onto the bed. Her gold lame dress, her red low cut baby doll, velvet miniskirts, running shoes, strappy stilettos, shorts, vest tops a walkman, knickers, bras, at least twenty Polaroid snaps of Scarlett in my Viola Viola costumes. Oh and a couple of my 12 inch singles and a pair of my jeans. I put the stuff that belongs to me to one side and then open a neatly tied plastic bag. Picking through the contents. It's mainly hotel matches and business cards. There's a child's dummy, the rubber teat stiff and cracked.

Think, Tiggy. Think.

I lay out her jeans, a T-shirt and a change of underwear to take back to her.

I take a shower and while warm soapy water flows over

me, I'm chilled by the thought of her room. It looks uninhabited, like she was never really there, never intended to stay long. Like she doesn't exist. She's an apparition, a demon.

Carol's question rings in my ears, 'And Scarlett, who is she exactly?'

I'm towel drying my hair when something my father used to say tracks across my mind like a code.

'Where your treasure is, there will your heart be also.'

And treasure is often hidden right? I go back into the room and this time I'm a woman on a mission.

The chest of drawers, and the bedside cabinet are all empty. I pull the furniture away from the walls. Sellotaped to the back of the chest of drawers is a cardboard backed envelope. Inside is a passport, bankbook and photograph envelope.

I open out the photo envelope and skim through the pictures, just a couple of photos, mainly of Scarlett. One of a woman who might be her mother. My letter is in there, of course, the lost letter from my mother.

The complete bitch!

I carry on searching. This time without any guilt or shame. I don't know what I'm looking for. A clue? An explanation, perhaps a motive? Under her bed I find the black bin liner. I know before I tug it out into the room that it is full of yellow paper, of Tony's letters and my scrunched up unsent letters to my mother.

I rip it open.

In the bottom of the bag, squashed in amongst the letters and Tony's shirt, is my white silk dress, the one Scarlett said that Sketchleys had lost.

It's splattered in blood, the bodice ripped.

I open up the bankbook.

Tracey Ford has £95,000 in her account. I open the hard blue passport cover and the photo of a stranger glares back at me. It's in the same name, Tracey Ford. The year of birth 1974. Four years after mine. This girl is only 17. The photo is a couple of years old. Tracey's bleach blonde hair pulled into a clump, sprouting like a pineapple from the top of her head. Her face clogged in makeup. Glitter blue eye shadow and pale pink lipstick. A few angry looking spots on her greasy chin. She looks exactly like every teenage girl on the back seat of every London bus. Deliberately talking too loudly, swearing and smoking, desperate to shock.

I look closer. I wouldn't have recognised her, except for the eyes, that inscrutable violet.

I hear her saying, 'Tiggy, I'm whatever you want me to be.'

The phone rings and I answer in a daze.

'Tiggy?' Dan sounds tired, anxious. 'She wants money.'

'What?' I still have her bankbook in my hand. 'She can't. Dan she's got £95,000 in her bank account.'

'Fucking hell. Well, apparently that's not enough. She wants another £5,000 from me. Going for the full 100k.'

'Like hell she is, the thieving little cow. Is she out of hospital then? I mean how did you speak to her, I mean where is-'

'Shhh, calm down. It's okay. I've been bailed, I'm home. I called the hospital, said I was her brother, that I was worried. They got a phone to her. Anyway, she's still there.'

'Dan, you shouldn't have spoken to her. It'll look like you're trying to scare her or something.'

'I don't care what it looks like. I had to know what

she was doing.'

'And?'

'And she wants money. £5,000 by tomorrow.'

'Why... Why Dan... why is she doing this?'

My knuckles are white around the handset. If I'd doubted it, I am now certain that Scarlett had something to do with my father being at the club.

'Why do people do anything? Look, I'll have to use the money for the studio.'

'No Dan. You said yourself that without decent marketing we'll get nowhere.'

'With me in prison we'll hardly be making our fortunes will we?'

'No. I guess not. Oh, Dan this is my fault.'

'It isn't.'

'It is. I told her all about the studio idea, the marketing.' Over the last few weeks I have trusted Scarlett with everything.

'It's not your fault. But you do know-'

'That you didn't do it, Dan?'

'Yeah, I guess?'

'Of course I do. I never thought you did. Not for a moment, but I don't understand any of this. She doesn't need the money, and why you?'

'I'm not sure Scarlett needs a reason.'

'Still... '

'Is she badly hurt?'

I picture Scarlett's battered perfect face, the blood on the lift floor. Her cold voice, her back turned away from me. The clinical emptiness of her room. Scarlett has been living in this flat for weeks and everything she arrived with is ready to go. She was obviously planning to leave within seconds. And I thought we were friends. She must have seen me coming.

'Dan, you know what, I have a feeling that Scarlett

won't be scarred for life.'

'Well, that's something I suppose. Look, anyway, I'm meeting her tomorrow at 4pm. I'll give her the cash, get this over with. I don't want Jackie worried. Call me at home if you have any bright ideas that might help.' He tells me again word for word the conversation and the arrangements.

After I hang up, I stare at the passport and the bank book, tapping them on my hands, thinking and thinking. There's no way that she can get away with this. I trusted her, I confided in her.

I take a bus to the hospital with Scarlett's clothes. I don't even bother to look surprised when the nurse tells me that she has checked herself out. 'Don't worry though; she took a taxi home about an hour ago. You can get home and look after her.'

Her suitcase and boom box are gone. Her key is on the sitting room table.

The sun shines into the flat, smoke rising from the warm butt of a cigarette, with just a trace of lipstick. Like a scene from a film noir. As though the suspect was here a second ago and other than this, she hasn't left a trace. She has clicked her Scarlett shoes together and vanished.

Chapter Fifty Six
Tiggy

On the escalator up from Sloane Square tube I realise that I have no idea what I am going to say.

Margaretta Terrace looks peaceful in the October sunshine. A tree-lined terrace of three-storey, grade two listed town houses. Secluded from the bustle of the King's Road. It is all so elegant, so ordered. So terribly white and clean. Even though the summer has been scorching and by rights all the hanging baskets should be full of dried out remnants of summer, the hanging baskets are overflowing on every porch.

Watered, manicured, perfect. Like nothing bad could ever happen here.

My stomach hurls itself over and over as I lift the white iron door knocker of my father's house.

Margaret greets me with a kiss on both cheeks and a rueful smile. I blush.

'Is he in?'

'He's in his study. Go on through. I'll get him.'

I wait in the front room. Looking over the deserted street streaked blonde by the sunshine.

Margaret seems to be taking an age to find my father.

I pace the floorboards.

I watch for the door to open and practice an opening line.

'Daddy, I know you must be angry with me.'

'Daddy, I'm sorry.'

'Daddy, please listen to me.'

None of them seem right somehow.

I look at the black and white photographs galleried throughout the room. Shots of bow tied men bracing themselves against the attack of the camera, looking mistrustful in their silk knee length frock coats. They have comb over Brylcreemed hair and ludicrous moustaches. They're standing in a garden, against a wall of trailers and blooming plants.

It must have been a picture of immense and beautiful colour. Stern-faced women are seated, bustled and starched, on straight backed chairs in front of their men. One holding a perplexed looking Jack Russell. Beside her a flat capped boy stands in his Boy's Brigade uniform, his even younger sister dressed like Alice in Wonderland, all drapery and frills. These are ancient family members that I have never met and know nothing about.

The Arnolds, going back decades.

They make me feel ashamed.

These fusty-faced people fought in wars so that I could use all that privilege to drink vodka and smoke dope.

So that I could air my laundry, so publicly.

Margaret comes back into the room.

'Will he see me?'

She nods. 'Yes. Go through to his study. Will you be okay?'

I shrug. I have no idea.

In the study I wait for my father, tracing my finger along the sides of his solid mahogany writing desk. Pushing down the spongy green leather inlay, like I used to as a child.

I rarely come in here. Everything looks the same as ten years ago, preserved almost. My father has a nostalgic sentimental penchant for fountain pens and giant bottles of ink. These are things that he loves, books, letters, fountain pens, the blotting pad under his wrists, where he doodles while making phone calls from his black dial-up phone, the moist sponge pad where he dips stamps before pressing them onto thick ivory linen envelopes. The floor to ceiling sash windows looking out over the terrace.

I hear him come into the room, feel him, feel the weight of my guilt, my embarrassment and need for forgiveness.

I turn to face him.

We look at each other in silence.

Some silences are punctuated by thought, by longing and urgency. Some are beautiful; the orange of a sunset against a deep blue of a night causing witnesses to pause, to slow and stop. Some linger threateningly waiting for the next spill of anger and retribution. Some are so full of emotion that there is no room for words.

My father's shoulders are tight, his face implacable. He bites his upper lip and then coughs, clearing his throat. He removes his reading glasses and I try to step across the distance between us.

'Daddy, I...'

I try again.

'Look, I...'

And again.

'Daddy, I know you must be...'

I give up and look at him, my eyes pleading.

His return gaze is brittle. I think of those family portraits and I see the resemblance. The Arnolds excel at stiff, straight and sanitised

'Daddy. I didn't mean to hurt you. I'm sorry.'

'I don't think *sorry* really covers it, do you, Tiggy?'

He replaces his glasses and gestures me to sit down, taking his seat behind his desk. I sit, the leather is worn and tattered. I rub my hand along the rough arms.

'You used to climb up onto that seat... when you were little.'

'I remember.'

'Of course, you would wriggle away, and I'd pretend not to notice.'

'I loved being in here.'

'I suppose that this is my fault is it?'

I shake my head, I try not to cry, 'No, Daddy.'

'Because I don't know what it is that I did that would lead you to...'

'It's not your fault.'

'Are you on drugs? Is that it?'

'No.'

'Then for God's sake, why girl?'

'I don't know.' He looks away, out of the window at Margaret pretending to water a hydrangea.

I really don't know.

We are silent for a while longer.

My father looks back at me. 'How long?'

'Daddy, it's not important.'

'How long have you been lying to me?'

I can't answer him. I stare at my feet.

'Fine.'

'Look, I don't expect you to forgive me-'

'That's just as well.'

I know my father well enough to know that trying to talk to him now is hopeless. Only I have no choice.

I take a breath and prepare to try again.

'Daddy... I-'

My skeleton almost leaves my skin as his hand slams on the desk.

'SHUT UP! I don't want to hear another word. I have NEVER been so humiliated in all my life, NEVER. You understand? I have given you everything. Holidays, ballet lessons, that damn pony, piano lessons, the best education that money can buy. Contacts that you refuse. Job offers that you sneer at. I've tried to give you time to work out what you want. But you have consistently rejected every opportunity I to make something of yourself.'

'Daddy, that's not-'

'HOW DARE YOU!' He comes round from the desk and stands above me. So close that I can see the saliva jetting from his mouth.

'You are *determined* to throw your life away, *determined* to reject every value and every opportunity that I have given you. Well, enough.'

'I'm not... It's not like that... but you've never exactly-'

'Your mother, I understand. Sending her hateful vicious letters. You want to throw your life away then we can't stop you. But what is it exactly that I have done to you Antigone?'

My mother?

'I've spoiled you. I've given you money, let you make a fool of me. Probably laughing at me the whole time-'

My mother?

I feel ill.

He sits back on his side of the desk and takes a bottle of whisky from the bottom drawer of his filing cabinet. He pours himself a large measure, he doesn't offer me one.

'Mother?'

'Lord knows you have good reason to be angry with her, but me? What have I ever done? I have tried my best. But you have no respect for me. For yourself. For anyone.'

'What did you mean about letters?'

He knocks back a dose of whisky and then pulls out an envelope from his blazer pocket.

I recognise the paper immediately.

The letter is written on yellow paper. In my handwriting.

It is one of my more drunken, more vitriolic, unashamedly self-pitying letters.

It should never have seen the light of day.

'Daddy, how did you, how do you have this?'

And then I realise that I already know the answer.

'Your mother asked me to try and talk to you, but that was... before.'

Oh, the fun Scarlett's had at my expense.

'I didn't write this. I mean, I did but I didn't send it.'

'I don't want to hear any more lies.'

'I'm not lying.'

'It's your handwriting.'

'Yes, but Daddy-'

'Give me one good reason not to throw you out of my house?' His face is flat with anger and I stand, trying to think of a reason, but he's right. I have lied to him my whole life.

There are words at the back of my throat, but I can't salvage them, can't seem to spit them out.

I can't believe that my mother has read this letter.

That she thinks this is what I think of her.

I wasn't myself when I wrote it.

This letter is from an angry drunken girl who feels completely betrayed.

It's not how I feel.

Who am I kidding. It's exactly how I feel.

'Antigone, can you explain anything at all to me?'

I shake my head. I have nothing to say. I can't tell

him, I can't.

'Oh, just go. I don't want to look at you anymore.'

I run from the room, from the house. The sun is shining too brightly. Neatly tailored flowers blossom cheerily from window boxes, birdsong fills the air.

I have always felt wrong here. All this beauty and perfection. Me in the middle, messing up everything.

I run along the street, nearly tripping over a miniature dachshund attached by a diamante leash to a stick skinny Sloane. Approaching the tube the green metal grids are being pulled across and crowds of commuters are trying to squeeze themselves onto buses. Both The Royal Court and Oriels are three people deep at the bar. I take a seat in the green and put my head in my hands.

There's nowhere left to run.

Chapter Fifty Seven
Scarlett

Dan had the nerve to accuse me of messing Tiggy about.

I was like, 'Hold on a sec mate, you're the one who's been flirting with her, leading her on.'

Tiggy's Dad had left the club all bundled up with rage. All like, 'I have never been so disgraced, never.' Pushing me out of his way and storming off. Well, how was I supposed to know that she'd choose to rip off her knickers and show the world her pubes? She's got terrible timing, Tiggy. And that song's a shit song.

Dan says, 'Leading her on? That's ridiculous, Tiggy and I are friends, not that you'd understand the concept.' He came storming into Valerios, dragging me backstage and getting all in my face about how could I upset Tiggy? I mean how dare I? Like she's some precious, delicate thing that has to be protected. I mean, call me a bitch, but I wasn't the one taking my clothes off on stage was I?

'Friends yeah? Course you are. Now why don't you go play some crap tunes to your non-existent fan base, mate? Let me get back to work.'

I turned to go, but he grabbed my arm. 'Not so fast. How did you get him here?'

'Who?' I said, all wide eyed. He was like, 'Don't play the innocent with me Scarlett. You were with her dad and you know it.'

So I said 'Her dad?' with my best surprised face. 'What do you mean her dad?' And Dan clearly figured I was lying, so I gave up the surprise, and instead said. 'Oh dear, you don't mean that my punter was her Daddy? Oh dear, did Daddy see poor little Tiggy?' And he gripped my arm real tight, his fingernails digging into my skin, trying to give it some of that sarf London hard boy stuff.

'What the fuck has Tiggy ever done to you, eh?'

'I don't know what you're talking about?'

'Come on Scarlett, she gave you somewhere to stay, she sticks up for you all the time, she thinks you're her friend and you throw it all back in her face.'

Dan's pinkie ring is pinching the skin on my upper arm, his eyebrows are wriggling away all excitedly. His eyes black with anger and I'm thinking he's loving all this: Tiggy's great protector, her rescuer. He's a big old knight on a shining horse is Dan. Except of course he's got some other tart knocked up on the other side of town.

'What's your problem anyway, Dan? What's it got to do with you?'

'She's my friend.'

'Really? Oh right, so what would your fiancé think then? Sniffing around her, trying to get into her pants? What is it? Jackie not putting out?'

'You are a poisonous, vicious bitch.'

He raised his arm, like he was going to hit me, so I stuck out my chin saying, 'Go on then, mate.' And he clenched his hand into a fist and pushed me away from him saying, 'Nah, you're not worth it.' Coz he's such a nice bloke right. Dan Dan the Piano Man, the big hero.

The club was half empty by the time Dan got himself back up on stage to do his final set. He banged out number after number like he didn't give a shit.

In the toilets I sorted out my make-up, straightened up my dress, spraying a little extra perfume between The Tits. When I walked back into the club Dan was halfway through *Thorn in my Side*, and staring right at me. Like

313

I'm gonna be bothered. Oh break my heart with your relevant Eurythmics lyrics Dan.

I went to the bar to get a drink and the other girls were all staring at me and whispering. Lola gave me look like I was worse than shit and Georgia hissed and then turned her back on me.

So I'm sat there with the other girls making snide faces and Dan thinking he's big and clever, not bothering with his jazz stuff and instead deliberately singing all these pop songs that he thinks are going to make me feel bad. When he started singing *Devil Woman* I thought, 'Oh fuck this mate. I've heard enough Cliff Richard to last a lifetime'.

I gave him the finger and I went outside for some fresh air.

That shitheap blue fiesta of Dan's was parked round the back, so I tried slashing the tyres with a broken bottle the way the estate boys used to, but it wasn't working. Even after I undid the valves and let the air out it was like totally unsatisfying and I could hear Dan's god-awful voice singing out from inside the club, so I snapped off a wing mirror for good measure.

Then I lit a fag. I stood in the back alley, looking at Dan's shitmobile and tried to focus on the last £5k.

Mario was standing at the back door, his gold teeth glinting under the street lamps.

'What,' I said, 'are you fucking looking at?'

He pissed off back into the club, I stubbed out my fag and I went back in too. Dan was finishing his song as I walked in, and all the girls stopped talking so there was this silence. I mean you could have cut up the hate in that room and handed it out in slices.

When Dan started singing again, I was almost thankful. He's there banging on about how *The Bitch is Back*

and I'm like do your worst Piano Man, do your worst.

Chapter Fifty Eight
Tiggy

I'm dreading going home. Dreading having to call Dan and tell him that I've come up with nothing. I pace the pavements slowly. Coming towards Daffodil Towers I am nearly knocked to the floor by a group of skater boys who obliviously continue, shrieking and yelling.

Scarlett has dismantled my life like a child with a toy, pulling out the sticks one by one until all the tentatively balanced balls have come flooding down. I drag my feet along the walkway, scanning the paving stones for something sharp. I pick up an aluminium ring pull and flick it against my fingers. I curl it into my palm and squeeze until I feel the sharp edges. I open out my hand and there's a hint of blood.

I chuck the ring pull down.

Scarlett is not going to win this. There has to be something.

Outside Daffodil House, Tony is sitting on the bench in front of the mural, holding a bouquet of red roses, a bottle of Moet Chandon by his side. I watch him for a few moments. This is the scenario that I have dreamed of every night since moving into this flat. Tony is single, and he is here on my doorstep. I have missed him more than I can express, his smell, his touch, but mostly his reassurance. He looks a little tired. He has a few extra flecks of grey hair. But he is still the man I have loved my whole life.

His timing is perfect and terrible at the same time.

He must feel me watching him because he looks up and turns in my direction. Standing up he straightens down his trousers and searches my face for something, permission maybe. The yearning in my eyes collides with his and he holds out his arms. I burst into tears as I run towards him.

I feel certain I could stay burrowed in his coat forever.

'You haven't forgotten me then?'

I push my head back inside his coat. Maybe if I stay here all the bad monsters will go away.

'Come on. Come on. I'm here now. Let's go in.'

Tony takes in the changes to the flat.

'Looks like you did a good job of eradicating any signs of me.'

'You're still everywhere, really.'

'Glad to hear it,' he laughs. 'Though this is better, more you.'

'I'm still working out who that is. The new Tiggy.'

'I always liked the old one. I loved her actually, still do. I bought her these.' He holds up the roses and champagne.

I don't respond. My emotions are in freefall. He is my sun on a rainy day, my candle in the window, my everything. And he is sitting in the chair that Sandra chose to sit in. I have to stop making the same mistakes. I can't continue to use Tony as a getaway car, however tempting.

'Tony. I can't. I'm sorry.'

'Okay.' He puts the flowers and champagne down. 'It was always going to be a long shot, just coffee then? And maybe you can tell me what's going on. You look terrible.'

'Thanks.'

'Come on Tiggy. It's me you're talking to and if this sad face isn't from missing me, then I want to know what's causing it.'

So, I explain everything, the letters, the accusation against Dan, my father coming to the club. Even as I am telling him I'm struggling to believe my stupidity, how gullible I have been. I wait for Tony to remind me that he warned me, but he doesn't. I show him the Polariods I took of her stuff, the strange dummy, the bank book and her passport. I wanted to show Dan, because I couldn't quite believe it all myself.

'This is some weird stuff here, Tiggy. What's with the dummy?'

'I've no idea, but I just feel so useless though, Tony. Poor Dan.'

'So, what can I do to help?'

'Nothing.'

'I'm not so sure. I can give you the money.'

'No. I couldn't, it's my fault, all of it.'

'Tiggy. Please let me help. I have savings.'

I shake my head.

'Or we could always go through to the bedroom and make each other feel much better?' He smiles weakly.

'But we won't,' I say sadly.

'Even more reason to let me help you.'

'I don't know.'

'Look, I love you. I worry about you, and it would make me feel better knowing that I have been able to do something practical at least.'

'But five thousand pounds, Tony'

'Oh come on, Tigs, I've quit my job and Sandra is going to take me to the cleaners in this divorce, so take it while it's there. Besides, if she deserves half of everything for being married to me for ten years then you can have a little bit of the spoils for being the girl I've loved for most of my marriage.'

'I never wanted the spoils,' I say. 'I wanted you.'

'And now you don't even want my help.' His eyes are so dark and mournful that I have to turn away. 'We could call it a loan?'

I grip my hand into a small fist and use what little resolve I have left.

'Still no Tony, it has to be no.'

'Okay, well then Little Miss Independent, you can at least share this with me, say goodbye in style?'

'Okay.'

We drink the champagne with all the joy of a couple at their own funeral. Tony holds my hand and we scrutinise each others' faces. It's like we know we might never meet again and we're trying to squeeze out every last drop.

'I have one last question for you, Tiggy.'

'Anything.'

'The stripping. Was that about me? Was that to get my attention?'

I shake my head. 'No, I think when it all boils down, it was all about my father somehow, or my mother. Maybe everything was.'

'Ouch,' Tony winces. 'But you're probably right.' He admits reluctantly. 'But he'll come round. He will. He's a fool if he doesn't.'

'Thanks,' I tell him. 'For the champagne, for everything.'

'For being a child-snatching pervert?' He raises an eyebrow.

'For all the times you made me laugh when I'd had a horrible day, for getting me through school. I wouldn't have survived without you.'

319

'Yes you would. You're tougher than you think.'

'Hmmm.'

'So what are you going to do?'

'I don't know.'

Tony empties his glass and then picks up Scarlett's passport and laughs to himself.

'What?'

'I was thinking it's a shame your dad isn't talking to you.'

'Don't remind me.'

'No, it's that he's an influential man. He's probably got a pal in the police who could stitch her up for illegal earnings.'

'The Chief of Metropolitan Police, no less,' I laugh. 'They're golfing buddies, but I don't think my father is going to be calling in any favours for me for a while.'

'But...' he says and we both have huge grins spreading across our faces.

'Scarlett doesn't know that does she?' We say in unison.

'Tony... you are a genius. I could kiss you.'

'Oh, I think I deserve more than a kiss, don't you?'

'Tony!'

'Sorry, we're off limits. Forgot.'

Eventually we can't ignore it anymore. It is time to say goodbye.

We part for the last time and it all feels surreal because I can't imagine loving anyone the way I loved him. What we did was wrong, I know. But it is part of who I am now and so I can't regret it.

I still have so many tears left to cry for Tony.

I will want to call him twenty times a day.

I will want to write and know how he is.

I can't imagine not sharing my triumphs and

misfortunes with him. But this will be the last time. I promise myself that from now on I will find a new place to go for my comfort. I am no longer his mess to clear up.

And he was never truly mine.

Chapter Fifty Nine
Scarlett

I'm stopping at the Ritz. I need to lie low, and I figure after all my hard work I need a little comfort.

The desk clerk was a right arsehole at first, like scrutinizing my passport, and with my face being messed up and everything, I looked a right state. But then I whispered to him that my manager would be here soon, and I'd be so very grateful if he could keep my real name under his hat and slipped him £50.

I'd switched the green cardboard case for a knock off Louis Vuitton, and bought these giant Dior, Jackie O sunglasses, so that I was another rich bitch Sloane girl taking some time away from the Chelsea gossips to get over their plastic surgery.

As soon as the porter closes the door I throw myself on the bed. Then regret it coz all my ribs are still really painful.

I'm in a junior suite. This room is like your proper princess room. The furniture is straight out of the Barbie house. I sit at the white and gold dressing table and have a good look at the bruises and scratches on my face.

The truth is I have no idea who beat me up. I'm thinking maybe that Guo, or that Max bastard we robbed, but my money is on Mario. If I say it was him to the coppers then they are going to start sniffing around the club and wanting to interview all the girls, and Mario might do a runner. I need to know where Mario is every fucking second of the day.

Either way, I'm left five grand short of my target and

there's no way of earning it while my face looks like this. So Dan had better come up with goods. It's not like I need the money. I just want it, and a girl should get what she wants.

I lie on the bed in my complimentary bathrobe and stare at the gold chandeliers. The curtains go from ceiling to floor and are bunched with gold tassels. I untie them and let them fall to the floor. Then I sneak behind them and look out over Green Park. I want to call Mum and tell her where I am. She'd never believe me. You know the people who tell you that money's not important are talking such shit.

I roll over on the bed and find the lunchtime episode of Neighbours on the TV. Mrs Mangel's having a right old moan at Joe and Jim about something. She's a manky old bitch her. I smoke rainbow coloured cocktail cigarettes, flicking the ash into Ritz bone china.

At eleven I ring Roberto and Chimpface tells me that we're game on.

I'm due to meet Dan at 4pm, so I have to get down the estate early.

I meet Evil in The Crown and explain what is needed. He's wearing some sort of shiny suit, like a Burtons reject or something from the Mr Byrite clearance rack.

'You look different,' he says.

'Yeah, you too.' He looks like shit. He always had a face like a pit bull chewing ten wasps, but Evil hasn't been taking care of himself.

'I wouldn't have recognised you.'

'I dyed my hair.'

'I can see, looks great.' He puts his hand on my knee. 'Still got great tits though,' he squeezes The Tits with a giant clumpy hand.

'Everyone thought you were dead or something.' He

lets go of The Tits and sticks a finger straight up his nostril.

'Well, I'm not.'

'No.' He pulls out a large bogey and wipes it onto the underside of the table.

I decide to get this over with as quickly as possible. I explain slowly but he still needs me to go over it with him again and again. He is such a thick bastard.

'Evil, it needs to look like a race crime alright?'

'But I'm white, innit?'

'No Evil. Him, he's not.'

'Is the geezer a fucking pakki? I hate fucking pakki scum.'

'Evil do you even know what pakki means? Anyway, he's Italian or something.'

'I fucking hate them too.'

'Evil, concentrate. Here's what you need to do.'

I tell him for like the zillionth time, and I make sure he understands that he only gets the money after, after he's done it, and after he's done the time or whatever. That if anything goes wrong then he isn't getting anything. And Evil is like, 'Yeah, whatever.' But you know the way he's looking forward to it, I get the feeling he's not doing it for the money, he just wants to know what it's like to kill someone for real.

Before I leave he leans forward and says, 'We could have something you know Trace, you and me, we could have a whole thing going on.'

'That's nice that is Evil,' I say.

And he's like, 'I do have a real name. No one ever calls me Kevin anymore.' And he looks all sorry for himself.

'Get this sorted and maybe we'll chat about us, Kev.' His face is this giant love heart.

'Really?' he says.

And I say, 'Sure. Course. Why not? But you need to get this right first, then maybe.'

I tell him again from front to back, and this time he listens really carefully.

I've got just enough units left on my card to call Chimp-face again and tell him it's sorted. The phone cards this month have pictures of flowers on them, sunflowers, daisies, poppies, bright and summery. Mine is these cute blue cornflowers and when I chuck it on the floor with the others it is like this phone box carpet. All the plain green floral cards mingling amongst the plain green ones, it's like a proper garden is growing inside the phone box. I think how if I was Mayor of London like Dick Whittington, then maybe I would have all the red phone boxes painted as different flowers, so on the street corners there were these giant bouquets, and maybe I'd have the buses painted like rainbows. I think the place would be a whole lot cheerier.

I walk along Charing Cross Road, picturing a different colour for every bus that passes. I'm whistling to myself and feeling like a genius. I climb onto a half empty Route Master winking at the conductor, feeling like a proper princess. Then swing up to the top deck, lighting a fag.

Whoever beat me up did me a favour. As of now I am no longer a hostess. No more Mario, no more Lola, Georgia or any slimy punters and their god-awful boring stories. I don't have to listen to any bloke ever again. And as for Evil and me being a couple? Do I look like a total retard mentalist?

On my way to meet Dan Dan the Piano Man, I check out my reflection in the shop windows. My face is still a bit mucked up, but I still look aces. I've let myself spend a couple of grand. Flashing your cash at some envious stuck-up shop assistant turns out to be more fun than nicking stuff.

I'm loving this gangster thing, this boss lady business, I was born for this. I'm thinking that anytime soon I am going to be like Roberto with my own bodyguards and posse. I'm going to get the girls to come up and give them a whole initiation test like Mario, but different. I'm going to teach them everything I know and then some.

My plans are total genius. Mario had it all wrong. He had this whole idea that blokes want girls to be available. But Roberto's the one with the smart ideas. If all the blokes want is a quick shag then they can get that round the back of Kings Cross. There are tons of cards in phone boxes with girls promising to do any kind of perversion. You only have to walk down Soho and look at the junkie skanky girls in the doorways to know that they would eat their own shit for a tenner.

I'm not going to be employing any skanky girls. All my girls will be gorgeous. I'm going to get them an education, proper stuff like walking and talking really proper. When I'm done, all my girls will speak like Tiggy. The men who come to my club will know that these are the most beautiful women in London. But here's the other thing. My girls will tease, flirt, and perhaps even let the men believe that they give a shit. But, there will be absolutely no sex. My girls will be untouchable. I catch any of them making private arrangements with a punter and they're gone. The more they say no the more the blokes will keep coming back, the more they will spend. Because what Mario never worked out, is that it's what you can't have that you crave. My girls and me, we're going to make a fortune.

Chapter Sixty
Scarlett

The New Piccadilly Café in Denman Street is half empty. It's kind of dark inside, even though it's dead sunny outside, coz the windows are so dirty. The smell of fried food makes my tummy rumble. I sit on a wooden bench at a red formica table. I make sure that I'm facing the door. All this being a psychopath has given me an appetite, so I order egg and chips. The piped music is playing, '*Everything I do – I do it for You.*' Jesus Christ, how much longer do we have to deal with that? I'm thinking maybe once Evil has sorted Mario perhaps I could send him over to Canada to sort out that crater-faced mutant Bryan Adams.

Dan's late, which pisses me off. Maybe I'll take the money and not drop the charges. Maybe I'll ask him for more. I could do with a car, now I think of it. A pink sports car, leopard print interior. I'll be like Grace-fucking-Kelly.

I'd forgotten how wet the piano-playing mutant is. He comes in with this expression on him like he's trying to be dead hard. I'm like, 'Oh come on, you couldn't even punch out your own shadow'.

'I wish I could say it was nice to see you Scarlett.' He sits down. Ouch, cut me with that razor sharp tongue of yours, Dan.

I don't say anything, instead I eat my lunch. Mushing my chips in my mouth. Perfect, fat crunchy fingers, none of that fast food potato free fries. These are the proper deal and Dan is not going to rush me. No sarf London geezer interrupts me.

After Bryan Adams, maybe Evil could start taking out South London, brick by brick, street by street.

Dan watches me for a bit and is obviously waiting for me to say something. But I don't, because I don't have to, because this is my time, right? This is my moment and he is the one in trouble. He's like this wet rag of an excuse for a bloke. He's one of those that think they're a 'really good listener'. Here's something for free – men only listen to women when they know that their dick is going to be a disappointment. I hate those blokes more than anyone, the ones in chinos and tank tops and little horn rimmed glasses. Who sit in sawdust-floored pubs and talk about the brilliance of art galleries and books. I mean, what the fuck sort of bloke plays chess and wears chinos? Tiggy has this totally awful taste in men. Dan Dan the Piano Man makes Harold Bishop look attractive.

Then he speaks. All pretend nice, but adding a little more cockney than normal.

'Scarlett. I want to give you a chance to stop this.'

'Yeah yeah, whatever Dan. Did you get the money?'

'Scarlett, drop the charges, you know I didn't do any-thing.'

I ain't confessing anything, I've seen *Bergerac* and *The Bill*, I know about people wearing wires. Like Scooby Doo or James Bond, when the villain can't help but spill all the beans just before the end, and ends up giving away their evil plan or whatever. I'm no fool and I'm not being set up by anybody.

'You nearly killed me, Dan Burnham,' I say loudly for the wire.

Dan says, 'Fine, if that's how you want to play it.' He gets up from the table.

'Oi. Wait up,' I say.

'Just a sec, Scarlett,' he smiles like a smug toad. 'I've got someone here who would like a word.'

And then of course Tiggy comes in, what a surprise! Dan looks like he reckons he's got the upper hand, but I yawn and pat my mouth.

'I haven't got time for reunions folks, just give me the cash.'

Tiggy really needs to work on her entrance. She comes in wearing these baggy jeans with a thick leather belt and this Inspiral Carpets T-shirt saying *'Cool as F**k'* on it. Her face is made up perfectly, her hair straightened and feathered making her lips look bigger, her cheekbones higher and acting like she's your proper North London cool girl. She looks the whole indie deal, but it's totally bogus because she can have her hair cut at the coolest salon in town and wear Camden market jeans, but we both know that she'd be happier in a Cliff Richard T-shirt banging a tambourine at some hippy festival.

'Tracey, how are you darling?' she says in a voice so much posher than she normally uses, then she grabs my shoulders and air kisses me on both cheeks. 'Mwah! Darling, you simply must tell me what you've been up to. Gosh, you look very well, although I do hope those nasty scratches don't leave a scar. Would be terrible if you lost both your lovely faces. You'd be ruined.'

'BOO!' I say, and laugh as she jumps. It's too easy. 'Behave Tiggy, I'm trying to talk to Dan here. Business.'

'Yes look, Dan's explained all about your blackmailing. I'm sure you think it's very funny, but it's not going to happen.' She takes a chip from my plate and dips it into my egg yolk then pops it into her mouth.

Tiggy's stepped it up a notch. Good for her.

If she'D been more like this when we lived together then I might have had a bit more time for her.

'I'll leave you to it,' Dan says like the big man that he is.

'I'll be right outside Tigs, if you need me.' What a hero.

Tiggy's looking really pleased with herself, but I haven't even got started yet. Okay then Antigone, you think you're smart and sassy in that getup, but your mate's in big trouble here.

'Get lost, Tiggy,' I say.

Tiggy doesn't move, instead she takes a pack of cigarettes from her pocket and taps them on the table, so that one flies up above the others. She pulls it out of the packet with her mouth and then lights it, blowing the smoke out in rings. I'm half getting impatient and half getting into her performance. Maybe Mario was right to hire her after all, she's definitely watchable, though God knows why. I'm trying to work it out when she blows a lungful of smoke in my face.

'I think you're the one in trouble. Dan didn't do anything wrong, did he?'

Ah, the wire again.

'Yes he did, he hurt me,' I say adding, 'and he's going to pay for it.' Then Tiggy is across the table, her face right up in mine, her fist curled around my top, her knuckles against my neck. Her face is all crazy, yet sort of calm too. She says, 'Cut the crap, Scarlett. Call the police and drop the charges.'

Wowie. She means business. But I can match that move and raise it.

'Get your fucking hands off me, you stuck up bitch,' I spit in her face. She lets me go.

'Is that what this is about?'

'You what?'

'Why are you doing this to me?'

'Doing what?'

'Do you hate me because my father has money?'

'No, I don't hate you, don't flatter yourself. I was just helping you out, because-'

'Because what, Scarlett?'

'Look at you, Little Miss Fancy, all moping and sorry for yourself, like your childhood was so much harder than everyone else's, and you acted like your whole life was about the bloke. It pissed me off is all.'

'I've never said that my childhood was harder than yours.'

'No?'

'No.'

'I don't know what you're complaining for anyhow. I only did what you were too scared to.'

'You were doing me a favour?'

'Yeah. I'm your fairy godmother.'

She stares at me and then raises her hands, saying all sarcastically, 'I'm sorry, Scarlett, could you remind me about the extortion bit in Cinderella? I seem to have overlooked it.'

Then she's on about how she knows it was me that made those calls to Sandra, and what was that for and I'm like, 'Oh please that was ages ago and the child-snatching pervert needed to be made to pay for what he'd done. If I'd gone to the police he'd have been in a whole lot more trouble.'

'Okay, but why steal the letters, why send them to my mother?'

'Because I care about the fucking rainforest, Tiggy. And all those unsent letters were a waste of fucking trees. You wrote them, you must have wanted her to read them on some level.'

'Oh, you're a psychoanalyst now are you? Well you're not as clever as you think, trying to get me to make a move on Dan, telling me he fancied me.'

'Right that was all me wasn't it? Coz, you're so inno-cent that it never crossed your mind. Like you could last a second without some bloke to hide behind.'

'You don't know anything about me.'

'Oh behave, Tiggy. One look at you and I knew you were a sad basket case.'

'You were wrong.'

'Really, so, if you're such a loner then what are you doing here protecting him? I mean, what is really going on with you two?'

'The idea that we're friends is a little too much for you.'

'Where's the invisible fiancé?'

'What does it matter to you?'

'Doesn't actually.'

'Okay, so how did you get my father to the club?'

'Hah. Funny thing that, Tiggy. You know how you go on about him not giving a shit? All it took was one phone call. He was there in a flash, like fucking superman or something.'

And she stops and stares at me. She's such a soft sap.

'Really? What did you say to him?'

'That his baby girl was in trouble.'

'And he came straight away?' She looks kind of surprised by that, and when she says 'really?' again, I think oh fuck this, because I'm not here to play happy endings and happy families.

'Left just as quickly though, didn't he? Once he saw what you were really like.' Which is when she slaps me, pretty hard actually for a posh girl. But I've been hit harder, had worse. I'm not scared of her.

'You're going to regret that.'

'I don't think so, Scarlett. No. In fact, I'm sure I won't.'

'I'm going,' I say. 'I got stuff to do,' although actually I fancy that £5,000, but hey, Dan can go to prison instead. I don't give a shit.

I get up to go, but Tiggy puts her hand on my forearm, saying quietly in her normal voice.

'I copied your bank book.'

I pull my arm away, 'You never.'

'Useful things, Polariods.'

'So you got a couple of snapshots of my loot, so what.'

'So a friend of my Daddy's is very senior in the Metro-politan Police and he was really intrigued about how a young girl like you could have made such an awful lot of money in such a short space of time. He seemed to think that maybe some of those earnings weren't entirely legal.'

The stupid Sloane.

'I earned that money. It's mine. I worked fucking hard for that.'

'I'm sure you did. I'm sure you have strongest jaw muscles in Mayfair, but prostitution isn't legal, is it?'

'You stupid bitch,' I say because she is, and I really want to slap her right now.

'No, I'm a clever bitch.' She holds up a copy of my bank book and smiles like she is so clever, like a cat in a vat of cream or something.

I clap, because this is a bit more like it, and because I feel kind of proud, like my little girl is all grown up now. I sit back down and figure I had better talk to her, try and reason with her. I sort of go to take a fag from her pack and then half way through remember that we're not mates anymore. Tiggy pushes the pack towards me.

'Oh just have one, Scarlett.' And she sounds almost tender, friendly like when we were living together. I can feel something in my chest, same as that time when Nina got taken away by the police. Same as when she waved at me from the back seat of the car and I felt my eyes burn. I swallow the feeling down in one. I've used up everything I have to get here, to this café, this chance around the corner. I have done things that I swore I'd never do. I am not losing this one to some posh bitch who's had everything handed to her on a plate.

She sits there doe-eyed and patient, watching me smoke. I decide to wait, let her speak, see what she wants.

'Just tell me why?' she says finally, and I'm about to say something glib, something cheeky, but I'm just knackered right now. I tell her the best truth that I can manage.

'You know Tiggy, your life was bullshit and you know it. You should be thanking me. You were making a right mess of everything.'

She shakes her head slowly, 'No, not true. I would have got myself sorted out eventually.'

She grinds a cigarette into the bottom of the ashtray. 'Well, I certainly didn't need a cheap little bitch like you interfering.' She looks at me with almost a sneer, like I'm less than nothing. An image of Percy comes back to me. I look away.

'Fuck you.'

'Fine then. Drop the charges, or I get Daddy's friend to take back everything, and you're right back at square one, Tracey.'

Chapter Sixty One
Scarlett

I make the call to the police from the payphone in the café. I've come too far to go back. Tiggy stands next to me listening to every word. I'm thinking she'd make a pretty good gangster, except when I'm done she runs out of the door, yelling out 'we did it!' Dan's waiting and I watch them hugging happily. It's like if I had to sum up Tiggy in three words it would be Jason, Jason, Jason.

I go over to the table and pick up my bag and coat. I guess you can't win every time, can you? Then Tiggy comes back in, holding an envelope.

'There's a thousand pounds in there, and I want you to have it.'

'But... why?'

'Call it dignity, call it a bribe, you take the money and never ever come near me or my friends again. Okay. Leave us alone, yeah?'

'Okay,' I say, a little confused. I was going to leave them alone anyhow. I've had enough of Tiggy and her traumas.

'You know Scarlett, if you need money that badly, badly enough to betray me and hurt me when all I ever did was try and help you out; if money means that much to you, then have some.'

Oh, she's trying to make me feel bad isn't she? That's the trouble with Tiggy, she might look all cool and gangster on the surface, but underneath it's all Hollywood movie, sentimental romantic shit. She's convinced that deep down everyone wants to be loved, that there's always a happy fucking ending.

'Someone told me that if everything else fails then you can at least hold on to your dignity.'

Dignified? Moronic more like. Like even in the middle of all this crap Tiggy's worried about getting her manners wrong.

'Sure, okay then.' Then, coz it costs nothing I add, 'You're a really great person.' I make a pretend apologetic face, like she's humbled me with those words, like now I've seen the error of my ways and how shallow I've been. There's a grand in cash. I want to whoop but instead I pretend to look sad. I go to take the envelope. She pulls it away from me.

'I do have a couple of questions.'

Oh for God's sake, this is the trouble with the shy ones. The moment you give them a voice they don't shut up.

'Doesn't it worry you that if you carry on this way, people aren't going to like you?'

Tiggy says this clutching at her heart. Oh please!

I give her what she wants.

'Yes,' I say, tears in my eyes. 'I realise now what a fool I've been, and I'm going to try harder to be a better person, to make my life meaningful.'

She hands me the envelope.

'You know Scarlett, if you're not careful you are going to end up all on your own, with just big piles of money for company.'

'Oh dear, that would be so awful,' I say, crossing my fingers behind my back praying that she's right.

I step out into the sunshine, whistling as I walk past the homeless lads huddled in the theatre doorway and through to Piccadilly Circus and along Regents Street to Roberto's.

I've got money, I've got the club and I'm gonna get

Mario back.
  I am fucking magic I am!

Chapter Sixty Two
Tiggy

So this is really how it ends.

I write to my mother. I explain that although I wrote those letters, that I didn't ever mean for her to have them. I ask her to be patient. That I will want to see her soon. That I think we have a great deal to say to each other. That I hope she is happy.

I write to my father. I write that I love him. That I think we still have time to try again, to make a fresh start. If he wants to. Whether my father is able or prepared to try is up to him.

Finally, after 16 long weeks at the top of the charts, Bryan Adams gets knocked off the number one slot. Households all over the country feel able to turn their radios back on without trepidation.

Bonfire Night, Dan and I meet at The Dive Bar. We talk about our plans for the studio. The paperwork is all finalised and next week we are having our first ever team meeting. I'll finally be meeting Jackie.

Dan rattles on for a bit about Robert Maxell, a multimillionaire and renowned bully, who has been found dead, drowned falling from his boat. People think it might be murder, suicide or whatever. Couldn't have happened to a nicer bloke.

Which leads us on to Mario.

The papers have been full of stories about him.

Apparently Mario went into some pub called The Crown, somewhere in Islington or Tottenham, and got into a fight. He was having a go at this black kid, calling him names and threatening him. Mario had a knife and went to attack the kid. So this man from the estate, Kevin something or other, tried to separate them and in the struggle the knife accidentally landed in Mario's body twenty five times.

It would sound absurd except that everyone in the pub saw the whole thing and swears that this is exactly how it happened. Kevin was protecting the lad and himself – he's a hero.

The one detail that the police couldn't understand was how later in the mortuary the pathologist found that someone had written 'Tosser' in lipstick on Mario's naked bottom.

'You know Dan, I bet Scarlett has something to do with it. You know that she's running Valerios now? She's changed the name to *Scarlett Dreams...* I mean, come on, it has to have been her.'

'You think?' says Dan.

I think about the state of my white dress and her falling out of the lift and that child's dummy. I know that I don't know the whole story and that maybe I don't want to.

I'm feeling a little drunk and emotional when we leave the pub and head for the underground.

We're taking different lines, so Dan waits with me on my platform. The tube comes while we're still in mid conversation.

'So,' I say hurriedly, '10am next Monday then?'

I've never been any good at goodbyes. Even temporary ones. I'm a little scared that when we're working together our friendship might change.

'Well, you know Tigs, if you're not doing anything this weekend then how about coming over? We'll take a walk out later. There are fireworks in Battersea Park. It'll be good. Jackie's really looking forward to meeting you.'

But what if she doesn't like me?

What if I don't like her?

What if she thinks I'm. Actually. I stop myself.

'Yes. Thanks. I'd like that Dan.'

'Mind you,' he adds, 'it does mean going south of the river. You okay with that?'

'I think I can probably cope.'

I squash onto the tube clicking my headphones into my walkman, pressing the tape to play, my hands thrust deep into the pockets of my dirty Levis. Joni Mitchell serenades me as the train rumbles me home to Shepherd's Bush.

I may not know what I want, but I know what I don't. I may not have a boyfriend, but I have friends and I have plans. Things at Burnham Studios might not work out, but I wouldn't swap my uncertain future with my old life for the whole world.

The phone is ringing from inside my flat. I drop my keys outside the door and then my bag strap breaks, spilling my makeup, pens and matches across the floor. I gather the contents back up swearing loudly, and open the flat door, running into the sitting room in time to hear my father's voice click off.

I throw the bags down.

I pick up the answer phone and take it over to the sofa.

I sit down and press rewind.

I've been running, hiding, waiting, and complaining so loudly.

And all I ever wanted was for him to love me.

Please, please, please, please, please.

I press play.

I light a cigarette and I listen to my father's message over and over.

Acknowledgements

Author's thanks go to:

The Tonto Boys – Stuart Wheatman and Paul Brown for the opportunity.

The inspirational Carol Clewlow and the multi-talented Carol McGuigan for all their encouragement at the start when I most needed it, and for their continued support.

Thanks to Claire Malcolm at New Writing North. Adam Maxwell for creating me a gorgeous website. Anna South and Caroline McCarthy at The Literary Consultancy for liking the first draft.

Love and thanks to the early draft readers for their thoughtful advice and constructive criticism: Daniel Halpin, Corinna and Peter Hyman, Anna Benbow, Alison Campbell, Helen Bell, Jenny Bullock and Stephen Shieber. And not least to The Fabulous Car Share - Anne Carruthers, Alice de Smith, Trevor Wood (and Pam Briggs).

Oh and a big shout to my magical marvellous mentor Caroline Smailes, who is not only a fantastic writer but understands grammar and everything!

A zillion gratitudes to Zeh Prado for all his Brazilian hospitality over the years. And to The Lovely Ledgers and Delightful Di Lullos. Oh and all my family, most especially my gorgeous selection of nieces and nephews. And love to Paul, and the ever musical Rosh and Mirren.

I wish you were here to Liz Arnold and Chrissie Glazebrook.

And a very special mention to Simone Katzenberg who supported me relentlessly with my writing over the last nine years and without whom I would have given up. I miss you.

A rockin' big slice of gratitude to Alanis Morissette, Fiona Apple, Aimee Mann and Beccy Owen for staying in my headphones the whole way through. Couldn't have done it without you ladies!

Rosalind Wyllie can be found at:
www.rosalindwyllie.com

About the author

Originally from Aldeburgh, Suffolk, Rosalind Wyllie has lived in London and Newcastle. This is her first novel.

READ MORE FROM TONTO BOOKS:

Being Normal
A collection by Stephen Shieber
Paperback, £7.99, 9780955632631, available now

A confident, poignant collection filtered with debauchery, melancholy and black humour, Being Normal is an examination of loneliness, rejection and of living in and against contemporary society.

Stephen Shieber brings together the glory of everyday nothingness and elevates it to great drama; where loveless marriage, teen angst, childhood misadventure, lonely Christmases and family dysfunction are the norm.

Each character in this stunning debut provides a very different slant on the notion of mundane – a book for anyone who has ever found themselves on the outside, dancing to the beat of their own drum.

'There is an incredible freshness and optimism about Shieber's stories that is very rare in writing today. He's like a wonderful new biscuit you've never tried before. Open it up, have a bite, then take the packet home and devour it.'
– Laura Hird

READ MORE FROM TONTO BOOKS:

9987
A novel by Nik Jones
Paperback, £7.99, 9780955632662, available in January 2009

To him, the shop is everything; always neat and tidy, safe and reliable. The rental DVDs carefully categorised, alphabetised and memorised. But when one valued member starts to leave bloodstains on the fresh new carpet, handing back porn still sticky with gore and paying in smeared with rusting red, his careful existence is compromised and uncomfortable.

Then the girl arrives with her pale skin, green eyes and fresh scarlet slashed beneath her thin cotton blouse. He wants to rescue and protect her. He wants to be with her. Forever.

Tragic and dark, *9987* is a story about a wholly jagged and at times disturbing, uncaring world where only three things are constant: fantasy, loneliness and love. A tale about a crime that only one person seems to care about.

READ MORE FROM TONTO BOOKS:

Make It Back
A novel by Sarah Shaw
Paperback, £7.99, 9780955632679, available in January 2009

Why would a loving mother abandon her child? In Make It Back, Muriel leaves her family to nurse sick and injured children in the Spanish Civil War. Forty years later, Muriel's decision leads her granddaughter, Dee, into love, into danger and, finally, into the passion and dust of south-eastern Spain.